TRAPPER'S MOON

TOR BOOKS BY JORY SHERMAN

Grass Kingdom

Horne's Law

The Medicine Horn

Song of the Cheyenne

Winter of the Wolf

TRAPPER'S MOON

BOOK TWO OF

THE BUCKSKINNERS

Jory Sherman

A TOM DOHERTY ASSOCIATES BOOK
New York

TRAPPER'S MOON

Copyright © 1994 by Jory Sherman

This book is printed on acid-free paper.

A Forge Book
Published by Tom Doherty Associates, Inc.
175 Fifth Avenue
New York, N.Y. 10010

Library of Congress Cataloging-in-Publication Data

Sherman, Jory.
    Trapper's moon / Jory Sherman.
        p.   cm. — (Buckskinners trilogy; bk. 2)
    "A Tom Doherty Associates book."
    ISBN 0-312-85773-X
    1. Overland journeys to the Pacific—Fiction.   2. Frontier and pioneer life—West (U.S.)—Fiction.   3. Fathers and sons—West (U.S.)—Fiction.   4. Trappers—West (U.S.)—Fiction.
    I. Title.   II. Series: Sherman, Jory. Buckskinners trilogy; bk. 2.
PS3569.H43T73   1994
813'.54—dc20   94-32371
                                                              CIP

First edition: December 1994

Printed in the United States of America

0   9   8   7   6   5   4   3   2   1

For my son Vic

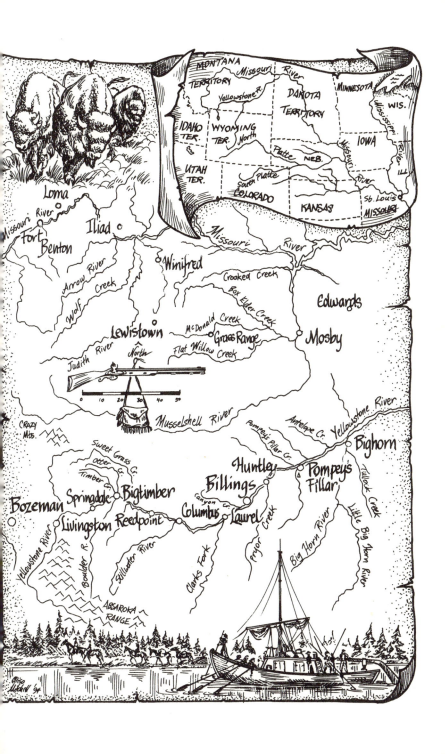

Strange, that people can find so strong and fascinating a charm in this rude, nomadic, and hazardous mode of life, as to be estranged themselves from home, country, friends and all the comforts, elegances, and privileges of civilization; but so it is, the toil, the danger, the loneliness, the deprivation of this condition of being, fraught with all its disadvantages, and replete with peril is, they think, more than compensated by the lawless freedom, and the stirring excitement, incident to their situation and pursuits.

W. A. FERRIS,
Life in the Rocky Mountains

TRAPPER'S MOON

1

Lemuel Hawke and his son, Morgan, were lost.

Morgan had known it for at least the past two hours, ever since they had passed an abandoned hunter's shack after following a trail from the river through thick, tick-infested woods. They were back at the river now, heading west, but Morgan knew they were lost.

Lem didn't believe it yet, but Morgan had a sick feeling in his gut. He was a strapping lad of fifteen, with crystal blue eyes, square shoulders, curly locks burnished golden by the sun. He was already taller than his father, who was thirty-three, lean as a barrel slat, with dark hair and coffee-brown eyes, a thin, ascetic face. Both men wore buckskins, but Morgan's shirt was off and his skin was tanned by the sun. Lem wore a linsey-woolsey shirt, but his arms and face were wind-burned and just as dark as his son's.

"You been follerin' the wrong river," said Morgan.

13

"No, I ain't," argued Lem, reining up Hammerhead, his blunt-nosed horse. The two mules stopped as the lead rope slackened. Morgan brought his horse, Boots, up close, halted him. The horses switched their tails at summer flies. Morgan's dog, Friar Tuck, caught up to them, sat down, his tongue lolling from his beagle mouth. The black-and-tan dog panted noisily, then began to bite at the woodticks on his rump, working his teeth through the fur like pinking shears.

"Let me see that map, I'll show you."

"Morg, I've looked at that map until I'm blue in the face."

"Maybe it's time you let me see it, Pa. You been holdin' onto it like it's a secret. Where'd you get it, anyways?"

"Feller in St. Louis give it to me. Lon Eshelman, the storekeeper. Drew it for me on a piece of paper."

"I bet he's never been out here before in his life."

"He tolt me it was a good map to the fur country."

"Let me see it," Morgan insisted.

"Dang it, Morg, what in Jupiter do you know about readin' maps anyhow?"

"I got eyes," said Morgan. He had caught up to his pa a week ago and had been blindly trusting his father's judgment, until now. But he had been counting miles and by his reckoning, they had come 135 miles from St. Charles. Which was fine, but Morgan was sure that he had started out on the Missouri, while his father was convinced that the Osage River drained into the Mississippi at St. Charles. They had argued about that for two days, but not so seriously as now. Morgan was still walking on eggshells around his pa after running away from Lem in St. Louis, taking up with a tippling house girl that he had thought pure and sweet, but was just a tramp like his father had said.

"What do you mean by that?" asked Lem, fishing the map out of his possibles bag.

"This ain't the same river we started out on."

"It's the Osage. Supposed to lead us right to the Missouri."

"That was the Missouri we were on, Pa. The Osage drains into it, what I heard."

"Where'd you hear that?"

Morgan took the map from his father. He had to pull it out of Lem's hands, so tightly did his pa clutch it.

"In St. Louis. Somewheres. They was talkin' about taking a turn to the north where the Osage comes into the big river. That'd be about thirty mile or so back."

"The hell you say."

Morgan studied the map. Lon Eshelman had drawn the map a little too quickly. There was a line drawn from the Osage River clear to St. Charles, but Morgan knew there had been only one river and it was a sight bigger than this one. There was no fork on the map, which instead showed the Missouri running parallel to the Osage and coming into the Mississippi closer to St. Louis.

"This danged map ain't no good," said Morgan. "You know where we passed that fork last night?"

"I seed it," said Lem, sulking. He picked a crawling tick off his neck, crushed it between the thumbnail and forefinger of his left hand. Each night, he and his son had to strip out of their buckskins and hunt each other's flesh for burrowed-in ticks. There seemed to be no end to the woods that bordered the river and fought the prairie grasses for domain.

"I wanted to take it, but you said that was where the Osage come in."

"That's what the map shows."

"No, it don't," said Morgan. "Somebody got it back'ards."

"I don't believe it."

"This'll lead us to the trail that goes to Santa Fe, but it's a plumb dangerous way to go. Let's go back, before we lose any more time."

"I figger we'll hit the Missouri any hour now."

"Pa, we done hit it and passed it. That was a fork back there some thirty mile ago."

Lem dug out a twist of tobacco from his possibles pouch and cut two inches from it with the blade of his skinning knife. His shirt was soaked through with sweat and his neck hurt from being burnt by the sun. He stuck the chaw in his mouth, worked it around to the side. He shaded his eyes with his hand and looked upriver. It wound through tree-flocked prairie, over rolling land. The grass was high and the trees so thick neither he nor Morgan could see very far ahead. The air was heavy with the promise of rain. They followed a wide game trail laced with old sun-hardened elk tracks that had grown over. They had seen no fresh tracks and that bothered him some.

To the west, the sky was dark, turning darker. The breeze had freshened from the north in the past few minutes, and when Lem looked in that direction, he saw even more clouds lumbering in, closing off the horizon.

Morgan could be right. The map might have been drawn wrong, either deliberately or ignorantly. The country was new to him. He had never seen so much sky all at once as during the past week or so, and not a sign of any other humans in a long while. Yesterday, he had seen faded tracks of an unshod horse, but even these were more than a month old. There were always deer and other game tracks along the river. Morgan was right about one thing. If this was still the Missouri, it threatened to peter out. It was scrawny as a creek and wouldn't float a light raft, much less a bullboat.

They hadn't seen another human since leaving the settlement at St. Charles, and Lem knew there were trappers heading westward. Maybe the Osage Trail wasn't the way to go, after all. Maybe nobody wanted competition in beaver country.

"Looks like we're in for some weather," Lem said, spitting a stream of tobacco juice at the ground. Tuck got up off his haunches and trotted over to inspect the stain in the grass. He sniffed and backed away.

"Tuck, boy," said Morgan. The dog stopped biting ticks and wagged his tail.

"He's plumb wore out," said Lem.

"He's chased ever' rabbit for better'n a hunnert mile," said Morgan.

"And caught nary," said his father.

In the distance, they heard the first rumblings of thunder.

"Looks like we'd best find some shelter," said Lem.

"Way I figger it, Pa, we wouldn't have to go back the way we come. Just head north. Bound to hit the Missouri in a half day, maybe less."

"What if you're wrong, son?" Lem fixed Morgan with a sharp look.

As always, when Morgan was worried, he touched the black buffalo horn hanging at his side. It had been given to him by his namesake, Silas Morgan, the trapper who had first told them about the shining streams and the beaver in the Rocky Mountains. Silas called it a "medicine horn" and Morgan had treasured it as something special ever since he first held it in his hands. There was a comfort in its presence, as if it truly held magical powers, what Silas had called "strong medicine." His fingertips traced the Indian symbols etched into the hard dark shell of the horn.

"We'd know soon enough, I reckon. This ain't the way to go to the mountains. There ain't been a man ride this way for months."

"Eh? That's so. We may have been given a bad way to go. Well, we could head north. It's worth a try. But from the sound of that thunder, I'd say we can't outrun the hard rain in those black clouds. Plenty of trees yonder. We could hole up until the storm passes."

Morgan looked westward, saw jagged lightning slash the clouds. He counted the seconds until he heard the thunder, trying to figure how far away the storm was. It was something his pa had taught him back in Kentucky. Lem told him that it took time for the sound to travel overland and if a man counted off the seconds, he could get a pretty good idea of how soon they'd get rained on.

"Ten miles away," said Morgan.

"More like fifteen," said Lem.

Morgan laughed. He was beginning to like his father again, after the trouble in St. Louis. When the fight broke out over the girl, Willa, at Spanish Jack's, Morgan had thought about killing his father. But, it turned out that the girl was no good and had just made a fool of him. When her father had died in a fire that burned Spanish Jack's tavern to the ground, some blamed Lem for that. Morgan hated St. Louis now. He had thought he'd never see his pa again and it had taken some hard riding to catch up with him. He was glad now he had come. His pa was smart, but he was following a bad map. Morgan was sure of that.

The wind picked up and the horses and mules caught a whiff of the storm. Their ears sharpened to cones and twisted in semicircles to pick up sound. Friar Tuck barked as a dry brittle leaf rattled past him, kicked up by a gust of wind.

The clouds rolled toward them faster and blotted out the sun. The air grew suddenly heavier, and both father and son could taste the tang of dampness on the air. Then, the wind died suddenly, and it grew strangely quiet. The songbirds went silent. Not a breath of air seemed to be stirring.

"We'd better find us some shelter quick," said Lem.

Morgan looked at the strange, low-flying clouds scudding

overhead. They seemed to drip, to hang there like shrouds. There was a strange cast to the light part of the sky, to the north and east of them, a dusky yellowish glow that seemed eerie in the stillness. In the distance, he heard a roar like nothing he had ever heard before.

"Pa, what's that?"

Lem straightened in the saddle. His face drained of color.

"Sounds like a hurricane. I saw one once't in Virginny, 'long the coast. Blew everything to smithereens. Come on, let's get in them trees yonder."

The mules balked when Lem took up the slack in the lead rope. Friar Tuck yipped and Boots bucked, kicking out both hind legs. Morgan hung on, brought the horse under control.

"What's the matter with the mules?" Morgan asked.

"Scared," said Lem, jerking on the rope. He dug his heels into Hammerhead's flanks and the horse pulled the mules into movement. There was a large open sward of prairie to cross on a low hill before they could reach the woods. The noise from the west grew louder. Morgan saw the black clouds swirl and form into a conical shape. It looked like a huge, twisting snake as the cloud mass moved toward them.

Lem saw the funnel too, and just then the winds stiffened and blew hard, rattling the fringes on his buckskins, making his shirt flap.

"Go on, Morg. Hurry!" Lem yelled as the roaring turned him deaf to all but the wind.

"Lordamighty!" cried Morgan, but his utterance was snatched away by the fierce wind. The funnel cloud grew darker, edged still closer, and the roaring in his ears was so loud it terrified him.

Boots galloped ahead. Raindrops began to spatter the river, and then they hit like millions of needles, stinging Morgan's face, blinding him as they raked his eyes. He bent over in the

saddle, felt the wind tugging at him with an almost unbeliev-
able force. It seemed as if he was being held in place by the
wind, but the horse moved forward toward the woods, struggling, too, against the powerful, invisible barrier.

Lem fought to hold the rope as the mules bolted in another
direction. He felt his arm almost pull out of its socket as he
went one way, the mules another. Hammerhead halted and
Lem, blinded by the lancing rain, cursed at horse and mules
until he realized he'd drown if he kept his mouth open. In
seconds, he was soaked to the skin. Hammerhead turned,
started after the mules. Lem tried to turn him back toward the
woods, but the mules headed south, away from the brunt of the
storm.

Morgan reached the edge of the woods, turned to look back.
He saw the dim shape of his father, Hammerhead, and the pair
of mules. They would hit the woods further down. Without
thinking, Morgan turned Boots and chased after his father.
The wind at his back, he rode fast, but the hard rain pelted his
bare skin. The savage roar of the tornado seemed right behind
him.

Lem gave Hammerhead his lead, knowing they'd hit the
woods on their present course. He was glad they hadn't headed
for the river. He didn't see Morgan until the boy rode up
alongside him, shouting something Lem couldn't hear above
the brutal blare of the twister. He looked over his shoulder,
braving the slashing raindrops battering his eyes and saw the
funnel getting even closer to them. It seemed gigantic, towering over the woods like some ominous black dragon.

The twister zig-zagged, struck the river and sucked up
volumes of water in its angry throat. It stuttered at the river,
then gathered momentum and crawled across the open prairie.
It began to jerk trees from the earth, rendering them to

splinters as it roared with violent winds. It smashed trees in its wake, picked up stones and hurled them in all directions as it danced toward the south like some maddened dervish, a slow, mindless beast that flattened everything in its path.

The tornado broadened its path, seemed to grow wider as it carried the river waters in its maw, hurling them with cyclonic force at Lem and Morgan.

The two men rode into the fringe of the woods, the tornado following them with an ear-splitting, terrifying roar.

"Get off your horse and run!" Lem shouted, but he knew that Morgan could not hear him. He managed to ride next to his son and gesture to him. "Get down, find cover!"

Morgan nodded, swung out of the saddle.

He tried to hold onto his reins. A moment later, his father appeared at his side. The sky was now totally dark, almost pitch, and both of them could see the twisting funnel cloud getting wider in girth and closer to them.

"Leave Boots be. Find a hole! Quick!"

Morg released his grip on the reins. He saw, out of the corner of his eye, his pa's horse bolt away, followed a moment later by Boots. The mules were nowhere in sight.

"Where's Tuck?" yelled Morgan into his father's ear.

Lem shook his head, started running, pulling one of Morgan's arms.

Morgan tried to see in the darkness, but the rain burned holes in his eyes and he lowered his head, following blindly in his father's path. Lem headed for a large oak tree, scrambled behind it and fell flat on his stomach. Morgan joined him a second later. There was barely enough room for them.

"Is it safe here?" Morgan said at the top of his voice.

"I don't know!" Lem screamed at his son.

They stopped trying to communicate with each other as the

booming voice of the monstrous storm grew so loud neither could hear. They listened to the sound of trees being uprooted and smashed; the leaves around them rattled with stones that sounded like buckshot.

Morgan felt his stomach muscles tighten. He knew, in his heart, that it was the end of the world. Nothing could live in such a storm, nothing in its path would escape destruction. He had seen trees swirling around on the edge of the twister just before he ran into the woods, and he could hear them now, battering the standing trees, knocking them down as if they were straw.

The darkness enveloped them and they braced themselves for the final smash of the tornado.

Rain poured down on them like water from a millrace. They couldn't hear it above the ghastly thunderous clamor of the twister, but they felt as if they were being washed away by a tidal wave. They dug their fingers into the earth as the winds tore at them. The tree behind them shuddered as if struck by a colossal force. Lem thought the oak would be uprooted, leaving them at the mercy of the tornado. He turned to his son and Morgan put his arms around his father. He knew that this was probably the end for both of them. He, too, heard the big oak shudder and thought he could hear it straining at its roots.

"Pa!" he shouted, but the word tore away with the wind and Morgan felt as if the air had been sucked out of his lungs.

"Hold on, Morg!" screeched Lem, holding his son more tightly. Around them, he heard the thrashing of trees and brush as if a giant was scything down everything around them. The oak still shuddered and its treetop whipped in the winds, snapping limbs, dropping them down on the two men with thumping force.

The tornado swerved toward a different course, wending

southeasterly just as it hit the fringes of the woods. It seemed to be seeking open ground. But its edges were dangerous, and as it turned, it flayed trees to shreds, hurled rocks and debris through the forest.

Morgan heard the terrible howl of the wind, heard the smashing trees, the whistling rocks. He clung to his father, sure that he was going to die. The oak shuddered under a mighty blast of air and strained at its moorings as the tornado made its wide slow turn.

Then, as suddenly as it had touched down, the funnel retreated back up into the clouds. Lightning crackled in its black belly and thunder boomed and cracked. Rain rattled on the leaves, but the roaring sound was gone.

Lem released his hold on Morgan. Morgan reluctantly let loose of his father.

"I-I thought G-God was a-goin' to take us," stammered Morgan. "Did you?"

"God don't take part in such devilment."

"Mother always said He was almighty powerful and could smite us all in a twinklin'."

"Your ma had a lot of queer notions. My pa and ma were God-fearin' folks and I never understood it. One time they'd say he was merciful, next time they'd say he was vengeful. Like the time a flood come through Virginny and kilt folks right and left. The preacher said it was God's will, punishment. But there was babies and good old folks and young 'uns what never did nobody no harm. Didn't make sense to me."

"I never saw no storm like that one," Morgan said, still awestruck. Rain drenched them both, but they were glad to be alive. They stood up and looked around them. Trees lay strewn like jackstraws everywhere, their trunks and limbs split apart, their fibers shattered to bone white pulp. Blown leaves were plastered to tree trunks like flattened green ornaments. Lightning lit the sky with thin silver wires every few seconds and the thunder made them jump.

"Still some buckshy, ain't we?" said Lem.

"I reckon," said Morgan, grinning.

"Welp, best we start huntin' down the stock."

"I wonder if Tuck made it."

"No tellin', son. I'll bet he's one scared hound, though."

Morgan laughed.

The wind still blew hard, dashing freshets of rain against their faces as boy and man stalked through the devastated forest, looking for horses and mules. All around them were signs of the terrible destruction inflicted by the tornado.

"Look, Pa," said Morgan, pointing.

"Sure enough."

A manmade log, hewn from oak, lay against a fallen tree, poking the sky like a ship's mast.

"Must be another hunter's cabin somewheres around here," said Morgan.

Lem traced a path in the direction he had seen the horses and mules run. The ground looked as if something had exploded at its center. Trees were stripped of bark. One tree, exploded by lightning, sent tendrils of soft gray smoke spiralling into the air.

A piece of sodden driftwood, carried from the river, lay atop a pile of broken trees. A stump lay in the center of a clearing, its roots still clogged with fresh dirt.

"Pa, there are folks livin' about. That's a fresh hickory stump yonder."

"Sure enough," said Lem. "But, we got to get them animals back or we'll be walkin' plumb to the mountains."

The rain beat at them, hammered their faces, ragged their eyes. In another part of the woods, they came across the mules, still tied to the lead rope, which was tangled in a briar patch. Lem waded into the briars, hacking at them with his knife. Morgan followed by a different path. The mules began braying, kicking at the brush.

"Hold on, Jack," said Lem, trying to calm them. "Morg, you take holt of that jenny and hold her whilst I pull old Jack out of here. She ought to foller."

They heard a horse whicker. A few moments later, Hammerhead trotted out from between a pair of trees, reins trailing, saddle slick with rain.

"I see he didn't lose my rifles," said Lem.

"Now if we can find Boots and Tuck," said Morgan, as his father led the jack out of the brush. The jenny followed docilely, Morgan patting her neck, talking to her in soothing tones.

"Here, you hold this jack tight while I catch up Hammerhead. Lead 'em out in the open. I'll look for your horse."

"What about Friar Tuck, Pa?"

"Oh, he'll find us, if he's able."

"Danged dog," said Morgan, trying to conceal the worry he felt. He knew Tuck had to be scared. He hoped he had gotten out of the way of the twister. He dreaded to think what would happen to such a small creature in such a fierce wind.

As his father rode deeper into the woods, Morgan led the mules back out into the open. He saw a dead rabbit, then, its eyes popped out of their sockets, staring blindly into the dark sky, the rain pelting them so that they moved, looked alive.

Morgan shuddered. The rain was coming down in ragged sheets now as the wind gusted, sometimes stopping him in his tracks it blew so hard. The mules brayed mournfully and loud, as if they were being beaten mercilessly. That's when he saw the snakes.

Cottonmouths and copperheads, rattlers and king snakes

slithered across the sward, through the grasses, over the downed trees and castaway logs. They came from the direction of the river, gliding faster than Morgan had ever seen a snake move before. The mules made even more racket as snakes squirmed under their legs. None of the snakes struck, but disappeared into the tall grasses, into the woodpile and the woods.

Morgan shivered, turned his face away from the wind and the rain. The rain was cold on his bare flesh and he wished he had his horse back and dry clothes—if any were still dry. He heard a sound, then, a small cry, and lifted his head, trying to peer through the slashing rain.

Out of the corner of his eye he saw movement. Turning, Morgan saw a droopy, sag-tailed Friar Tuck cowering in the rain, but waddling toward him like a whipped pup.

"Here, Tuck, here boy!" Morgan called. Friar Tuck tried to wag his tail, but the effort seemed too much for him. Instead, he gave another little yip and gained speed on tired little legs.

Morgan stooped down, took Tuck into his arms, brought him close. The dog lapped at Morgan's face, squirming, whining pitiably.

"It's all right, Tuck. Good boy."

Morgan embraced his dog, squeezed him, grateful that the beagle was still alive.

Friar Tuck began licking Morgan's ears and neck in gratitude. Morgan set him down and the dog whimpered and cowered as the rain pelted him. Morgan patted the dog's head, spoke to him reassuringly. The mules began to settle down, seemingly reassured by the sight of the little dog.

Morgan had no idea how much time had passed, but it seemed his pa had been gone a long time. The rain battered him as he knelt by the dog. Friar Tuck was still shivering; his tail no longer wagged, but quivered involuntarily with each hard gust of wind.

The wind increased in velocity and Morgan longed for shelter from the spearing lances of rain. If he took to the woods, he was afraid his pa couldn't find him right off. The longer they stayed in the open, the more the animals would suffer. He heard a voice through the raging downpour.

"Help! Help!"

Morgan's blood froze.

"Pa?" he called.

"Godamighty, please help!"

It was not his father's voice. Morgan stood up. Friar Tuck cowered and whimpered as Morg released him.

"Who's there?"

"Over here!" yelled the man.

Morgan turned, saw a strange sight. A man, his clothes soaking wet and in shreds, staggered across the clearing. He was barefoot and bareheaded with a long, full beard. As he drew closer, Morgan saw that he was a white man. He was bleeding from a wound on the head and his face was drenched with blood and rain.

"Oh, God, please help me!" the man pleaded.

Morgan stood transfixed as the man stumbled and fell. When he arose, Morgan saw that he clutched something in his hand. It was then that he noticed it was a hand. The other arm ended at the wrist, white bones, washed by the rain, sticking out of a mass of raw flesh.

Morgan felt his knees go weak. He backed away in horror as the man lurched toward him, holding up that lifeless hand.

Friar Tuck growled and the mules brayed mournfully as the wind blasted their eyes with sharp stinging needles of rain.

"Help me!" the man screamed.

But Morgan couldn't move.

Morgan stepped backward as the screaming man fell to his knees like a beggar.

"Please, for God's sake, help me. I'm plumb bleedin' to death. My hand . . . Jesus, look at my hand."

Morgan stopped his retreat. Something in the man's voice, something in the way he knelt there in the rain touched Morgan, touched him deeply. That tone of utter despair and supplication wrenched at his heart, made him see beyond the horror, made him see the child in pain, the little boy with fingers burned in the fire. A flood of compassion rose up in him and he found his voice, strangled as it was by fear and that loathing reserved for cripples by men whole in mind and body.

"I—I don't know w-what I can do," he said. "What happened? How'd you lose your hand?"

"The storm—that twister, God, can you sew it back on my arm?"

Morgan couldn't answer. He could not look at the man's severed hand without feeling revulsion. Could he sew it back on? He didn't think so. He was about to vomit and his mind raced with images of disfigurement, torn flesh and ruptured blood vessels. Now, as he looked closer, he could see that the man's mutilated arm was bleeding profusely. It was hard to see in the rain, but blood was spurting from the stump so fast that its darker hue made him realize the man was in shock.

"I—I'll see what I can do. Just stay there. I—I'll have to get something to tie off your arm so you won't bleed no more."

"Oh, thank God. I don't want to die. God knows I don't want to die."

"Hold on," said Morgan. Friar Tuck sought shelter in the pile of debris as Morgan started trying to untie the diamond hitch on the jack mule. The wounded man moaned and whined. Morgan tried not to think about that hand, that bloody stump of an arm.

The young man found some strips of leather and a few patches of cloth they had brought along for fixing holes in their shirts. He dug deeper and found an awl and some heavy thread they had carried out from Kentucky. Lem had done a lot of mending after Morgan's ma run off with that Lexington hatter.

The wounded man was mewling pitifully when Morgan knelt down beside him.

"Give me that—that bad arm and let me see can I stop the bleeding."

"You got needle and thread? You take this hand and sew it back on."

"Not yet," said Morgan, steeling himself for what he had to do. He still couldn't look at that bloody, lifeless hand.

Three antlerless deer galloped out of the darkness, eyes fearful and wild as they raced through silver curtains of rain silent as ghosts.

Morgan began wrapping a thong around the man's bleeding arm. The man screamed in Morgan's ear, screamed louder than the wind-blown rain tattering on the leaves.

————.————

Lem heard the horse whinny in terror. He knew it was Boots. He could not see in the driving rain, but he shielded his eyes from the stinging downpour and followed a course toward the sound.

Hammerhead threaded his way through a jumbled pile of hewn logs, overturned trees and broken pieces of furniture. The howling wind lashed Lem mercilessly as he gave the horse its head, guiding him only when he veered too far away from the path to the screaming horse.

On the other side of the rubble, Lem made out the lower part of a log cabin. A crumbled chimney of rock lay strewn about one side of the structure. A few yards away, a man was pulling on the reins of a horse, cursing the animal. The horse was Boots and it was frantically trying to escape.

"Hold on there!" Lem shouted, but the wind snatched his words away.

He dug moccasined heels into Hammerhead's flanks, rode up on the stranger. He grabbed the reins from the man's hands. Boots collapsed on his haunches in mud and water.

"What you doin' with this horse?" shouted Lem.

"Man, I need it. I got to get my woman out of here. She's bad hurt."

"Woman? I don't see no woman."

"In there." The man held up an arm, the shirtsleeve plastered to it. He was young, with long hair, a full beard masking his face. His clothes were sodden; he was barefoot. He pointed toward the smashed log cabin.

"What you doin' livin' way out here?"

"Hunters. Me and my bub. He got his hand sliced off when that twister hit. Axe come off the wall and cut his hand clean off. He run off somewheres."

Lem looked down at the wild-eyed young man. He had never heard such a story before. In the screeching wind, he thought the man must be mad, crazy as a loon.

"Where's your own horse?" Lem yelled.

"Gone. I got to get out of here. My woman."

"You married?"

"No, not exactly."

"What the hell's that mean?"

"I got me a squaw-woman. She's bad hurt, mister. Can you help us out?"

Lem looked nervously toward the shattered cabin. He saw no one.

"I got troubles of my own," Lem said, but the man didn't hear him. Instead, they both heard a loud, animal-like cry from the remnants of the cabin. They turned, saw a young girl standing up. Blood streamed over her face from a cut on her scalp. One of her arms was broken, dangled crookedly at the elbow. She wore a tattered buckskin dress, slick with rain.

"There she is," said the stranger.

"That ain't but a girl."

"She's about twelve, I reckon."

Lem's jaw tightened. He remembered Willa, the young girl at Spanish Jack's in St. Louis who had seduced his son. He remembered his own wife, Roberta, when they were both young and the way she cuckolded him, took up with that hatter, O'Neil, in Lexington. Women were trouble, all of them, and this Indian girl was no different.

"You help her yourself," Lem said tightly, his voice gravelly, husk.

"Goddamn you!" The stranger leaped up, grabbed the fringes

on Lem's buckskin shirt, jerked him out of the saddle. Lem felt the reins flow from his fingers as he lost his balance, tumbled toward the soggy earth. He could smell the foul breath of the stranger as he hit the man midway to the ground.

Hands locked around Lem's throat. Fingers tightened around his neck, blocking off his air. He brought up his own hands, rolled to the side, the stranger gripping him tightly. Lem pulled the man's hands away, gulped in a deep breath. The man clawed at him, reaching for his neck. They wallowed in mud and water, each searching for an advantage.

Lem's fingers slipped as he tried to grab the stranger's hair. He felt something hard smash into his cheek. He shook off the pain, kicked out with both feet, hoping to strike the man's groin. He heard a grunt in his ear as he felt a jarring impact on the soles of his feet.

Lem stiff-armed the man, pushing him away with his left hand. He smashed a fist into his attacker's temple, heard a sodden *smack*. The man went limp for a moment and Lem pressed his advantage. He rolled over atop the man, pinned his arms to the puddled ground. He heard a noise behind him, turned, saw a shadow looming over him. The Indian girl raised a stone war club in the air.

Lem gave a choked cry and released one of the pinned man's arms to ward off the blow. The Indian girl struck. Lem grabbed her wrist, twisted it. She never made a sound as he bent it so far back it snapped at the elbow. Lem heard the loud *pop* and watched her crumple. The man beneath him squirmed and wriggled, trying to get out from under Lem's weight. Lem drove a hard fist into the man's nose, felt it crunch, turn rubbery. Blood streamed from the man's nose. The man gurgled as blood filled his throat. Lem hit him again and again until the man no longer struggled.

The girl tried to rise, but could not with both her arms broken. She scooted around in a circle, kicking up water as the rain hammered down, blown hard by the wind.

Lem lurched to his feet, looked down at the stranger. He was young, not much older than the Indian girl. He wondered what they were doing living way out in the wilderness. Hunters, he supposed, but where was their market?

The girl grabbed his buckskin trousers.

"You take," she said in English.

"No," said Lem.

"Me good girl."

Lem jerked his leg away from her clutching hand.

"You're filth," he spat. His face froze into a mask of hatred. "Nothin' but a goddamned animal."

She shook her head, raised her broken wrist toward him, begging him silently to take her with him.

Lem turned his back on her, caught up Hammerhead and mounted the horse. He rode down Boots, picked up the trailing reins. He rode away from the crumbled cabin without a backward look, the anger in him still seething. The rain seemed to steam as it struck his buckskins, spattered into fine mist.

———.———

Morgan couldn't touch the mangled hand, though the man held it out to him. He gave the tourniquet-thong one last twist and shook his head. The bleeding had stopped for the moment, and he could think no further than that. His hands were shaking so badly he knew he couldn't even sew the wound shut, much less attach the severed hand.

"That's all I can do for you, mister," Morgan said loudly to the other man.

"Please."

"I ain't got nothin' to sew it on with. 'Sides, it ain't agoin' to work."

"I don't want to be a cripple."

"I ain't no barber, neither."

"You sonofabitch," yelled the stranger. He threw his mortified hand in Morgan's face, reached down to his waist and pulled out a skinning knife. He slashed at Morgan, narrowly missing his neck. Morgan rocked back on his feet, the hackles stiffening on the back of his neck. He heard the whisper of the blade as it passed beneath his chin. The man, his face twisted into a hideous glower, came after Morgan, crawling on his knees. The young man slid backward, tried to gain his footing on the slippery, watery ground. His heels could find no footing and slithered out from under him. His rump plopped into a muddy puddle.

The man scrambled forward on his belly toward Morgan. The makeshift tourniquet slipped off his wrist stump, but he seemed not to notice it. Blood gushed from the wound, spurted onto Morgan's buckskin pantsleg.

"D-Don't," said Morgan. "Keep away."

"I'll gut you like a toad," snarled the stranger, his lips wet with rain.

"You're bleeding again," said Morgan, scooting away, trying once again to get his legs underneath him. He felt as if he was in a mud wallow. Everytime he moved, he slid through water and slimy earth.

The stranger got up on one knee, then stood straight up, towering over Morgan, the knife ready to strike. Morgan's fingers sought his own blade. The buckhorn handle was slick and his hand slipped off. He kept scooting backward as the stranger stalked him, eyes glistening with madness and pain.

"You can't get away," the stranger croaked.

Morgan realized that the man was right. He could not get away as long as he was on the ground. He grabbed for his knife again, but he was sitting on the scabbard. The blade wouldn't come loose.

Morgan hurled himself sideways. He crawled quickly toward the pile of rubble, toward the comparative safety of the mules. Behind him, he heard the wet plop of the stranger's feet striking the ground as he broke into a faltering run. Something roiled in Morgan's stomach and fear gripped him like talons at his throat.

Panting, Morgan lashed out, grabbed a chunk of a shattered tree limb. He pulled himself up to one foot, turned. The killer hurtled toward him, holding the knife in his good hand, ready to thrust.

"Stay away," Morgan yelled into the teeth of the wind, into the ferocious gale that whipped rain into his eyes, stung them blind. He jerked his knife free and braced himself.

Then, a strange calmness overcame him. The wind died out in his ears as if he was in the eye of a hurricane. The fear dissipated in a sudden wash, the panic flooded away as newfound sudden strength flooded his veins.

"Come on, then," Morgan said softly and he gripped the handle of his knife, held it close to his belly. "Come on, you crazy bastard."

Lem rode out of the woods, leading Boots, and let out a sharp cry.

Morgan didn't look at his father. Instead, he kept his eyes fixed on the stranger, watching his every move. As the man drew close, drawing his knife back, the young man stepped in under it and shoved his knife straight at the older man's belly. He felt the blade strike the skin, part it and sink into soft flesh.

He heard the man utter a gasp, then a long sigh. The stranger collapsed and the knife fell out of his good hand, glanced off Morgan's shoulder and splashed into a pool of water.

"Morgan, don't!" shrieked Lemuel as he saw his son grapple with the man, saw his son's blade, saw the man crumple—but didn't see the stranger's knife.

Morgan felt the weight of the man, jerked his knife free and stepped back. The stranger pitched forward, fell on his face.

"Godamighty, Morgan, what have you gone and done?" Lem said as he dismounted and dashed toward his son.

Morgan looked up, saw his father's face through the shroud of blowing rain, saw his eyes wide in the hollows of their sockets.

"I reckon I kilt him," he said calmly.

"Christ. Why?"

Lem looked down, saw the man's slashed wrist, saw that the hand was missing.

"Did you cut off his hand? Or kill him?"

"I didn't cut off his hand. I tried to fix it. Then, he come at me, Pa, honest. He come at me with a knife."

"I don't see no knife."

Morgan looked around. He didn't see it either.

"It's down on the ground somewheres."

Lem knelt down, turned the man over. Rain spattered into the open mouth, razed the dead glassy eyes. The look on his face was hideous, the look of a man slain in violence, frozen in a final agony.

Morgan kicked through the puddles until his moccasinned toe struck something.

"This here's his knife," said Morgan, holding it out to his father.

"This must be kin to the one I tangled with back in the woods."

"You run into trouble, too?"

"That storm caused a heap of damage. We better make tracks. No tellin' who these people are. This un's deader'n a doornail."

"He was goin' to kill me, Pa. I sure enough didn't want to hurt him none."

Lem stood up, looked at his sopping wet son, his hair slicked down, blood on his knifeblade, on his wrist. The rain was already washing it away.

"Put your knife away, son. Cotch up Boots and we'll get those mules, get on out of here."

"Shouldn't we—bury him?" Morgan looked down at the dead man.

"Hell, let his own kind bury him. He warn't no good nohow."

"What happened to you?"

"Nothin'," said Lem. "Nothin' as serious as this."

"Pa, I feel funny."

"Killin' a man?"

"Uh-huh."

"Don't feel too good."

"Nope."

"It was you or him, Morg." Lem slapped his son on the back, spraying water droplets in a wide circle.

"I reckon."

Lem took the dead man's knife from Morgan, stuck it inside his belt. Morgan sheathed his own blade. They caught up their horses, untied the mules and rode away from the clearing, back toward the river, both hunched over in their saddles against the brunt of the wind.

Morgan felt a strange tingle course through his veins. For a few moments he felt a kind of exhilaration, then his hands began to tremble slightly. He drew in a deep breath and his hands steadied. His thoughts were all tangled, jumping, skittering, winding around in his mind so that he could make no sense of them. He remembered the terror he felt when the man came after him, and he remembered the blade sinking soft into his gut. He remembered the man letting out the last of his breath in one long final sigh. And, then, he remembered the dead look on his face, the staring eyes, the slack, open mouth, the rain falling into it.

So, that was death, he thought. One minute, someone's alive, the next they're gone.

Then, he felt strange again, and powerful, for some reason. As if he had done something no one had ever done before. But, he knew that was not true. His pa had killed Indians. And some said he killed Spanish Jack, but that was an accident.

Killing wasn't as hard as Morgan thought it would be. But it sure made a man feel powerful strange.

3

All day long, Lemuel looked over his shoulder, stopped to walk around, lay facedown on the prairie, put his ear to the ground. His coffee-brown eyes shimmered with light as they widened, then narrowed again. At times, Lem would pick up a handful of dirt and sniff it, as he once did when they farmed in Kentucky.

Morgan noticed that Friar Tuck was fidgety, too, and the horses and mules seemed just as nervous. He supposed they were still skittery from the storm. At least they had found the right river, finally. They were on the Missouri and heading the right way. His pa had ought to feel pretty good about that.

Maybe his pa was wondering if another twister was sneaking up on them. For most of the morning and half of the afternoon, his pa hadn't said anything. Lem would just look back at the long prairie miles behind them and squint and shade his eyes and wrinkle up his nose like he had got a whiff of pig dung. Friar Tuck hadn't barked once, and he slunk along the river sniffing at every clump of grass, every little bush and bone of root sticking out of the bank of the Missouri.

"Pa, what you lookin' back yonder for?" asked Morgan.

"Shadows, I reckon." He said "shadders," in his soft Virginia accent.

"Shadows? You don't mean black clouds, do you?"

"I seen something back there in those cottonwoods where we fixed up them panniers on the dadblamed mules, and then I seen something out of the corner of my eye out on the prairie."

"I didn't see anything," said Morgan. He had his mother's blue eyes and they crackled in the burning daylight like sharp-cut diamonds.

Lemuel hauled on the reins, pulled Hammerhead to a stop. The old blunt-nosed horse tried to shake out the bit, shivered from forelock to tail as if telling his master he wanted out from under the saddle, too.

Morgan's arms were brown from the sun, his face bronzed from the prairie winds, his hair tawny from the golden light of the long, wending days through high grasses under endless blue skies.

Friar Tuck ranged so far ahead Morgan hadn't seen him for the better part of an hour.

Up ahead, less than another day's journey, was Independence, and beyond that, the Platte. Somewhere along the way Morgan knew Lem hoped to find other trappers heading overland for the Rockies and learn all he could about this new country.

"Well," said Lem, "it worries me some. Man don't want to be seed, he skulks, and that 'un back there is some shy."

"Why don't we wait on him, Pa? Find out who he is."

"Might be more'n one. Might be a Injun."

Morgan felt the hairs on his scalp prickle. Something knotted in his throat. A muscle quivered in his stomach. He wiped a sweaty palm across the front of his buckskin shirt, touched the hammer on the flintlock rifle lying across his calves. He grasped the throat of his medicine horn. Although it held coarse powder for Morgan's flintlock rifle, it was a comfort to him during times of worry.

"We ought to hide someplace," said the young man.

"Hell, I ain't hidin'," said his father.

Morgan kept looking toward their backtrail, but he didn't see anyone. Tuck burst from a clump of bushes, ran toward them, following rabbit trails through the grasses, beagle tail whipping back and forth like a divining rod.

Morgan's horse, Boots, whickered softly and his ears twisted, trapping a faroff sound, the fine hairs glistening in the sun like golden threads.

"Well, we could wait till he cotched up with us," said Morgan.

"He's had plenty of time to ride up," said Lem laconically. He checked the pan on his flintlock, saw that it was black with fine grains of powder. He closed the frizzen, kept the hammer on half-cock. "All I saw was a speck at first, now I make it to be a man a-horseback."

"Likely he don't mean us no harm."

"Likely," said Lem, but he kept looking back more often now, and when he looked ahead, he sought out cover in case they had to make a run for it. Blackbirds took flight as they passed a gravel bar, wheeled in a ragged formation as the flock sought a landing in a different place. They had seen little game along the way, but plenty of sign, both of travelers and critters.

Friar Tuck veered off, gamboled across a stretch of green-sward.

"Tuck, here boy," called Morgan. The dog ignored him. Young Hawke watched as the dog romped out of sight, hot on the trail of whatever had passed through and left scent.

"He's havin' him a time," said Lem.

"I reckon."

They rode another two miles, marveling at the bluffs along the river.

"Sorta spooky, ain't it?" asked Morgan when his father stopped.

"Whatcha mean, son?"

"Looks like Injuns could stay atop them bluffs and see everything comin' upriver."

"Sure could." Lem reached into his possibles pouch, pulled out a twist of tobacco. He cut off a chaw with his skinning knife. He was lean in his buckskins, weathered and tanned. He had four days of beard, giving him the look of an ascetic!

Morgan stood up in his stirrups, looking back over their trail.

"Somebody's comin', Pa."

"I know. Ain't the same one I seed."

"How can you tell?"

"Other feller was big, settin' a pony. This here one's ridin' a big horse and pullin' a mule."

"He sure is," said Morgan.

"We'll wait on him."

Morgan sighed with relief. He hadn't seen another human being in a hundred and fifty miles. Any company was welcome.

"Maybe he knows who was a-follerin' us, Pa."

"Mmm."

A half hour later, they saw the stranger as he drew near. He rode a chestnut sorrel with a buckskin mane and tail, splotches of white on its face and threaded through its coat like gray hairs. The man was dressed in buckskins, had two rifles hanging from elkskin scabbards on either side of his saddle. A full beard hid his face; he wore a beaver hat with a beavertail bill. A beaded possibles pouch hung just below his waist and two powder horns dangled on either side of his chest, a small one for the fine priming powder and a larger one that held a coarser grained powder for the ball propellant. He had a black leather patch over his left eye that bore a colorfully beaded Indian thunderbird symbol.

"Pilgrims," called the stranger, "either of you seen that red nigger of mine?"

"Can't say as I have," said Lem. "You talkin' about a Injun?"

"A damned Delaware buck. Come all the way out to the big mountains with me in ought three from the Ohio Valley. 'Bout as trustworthy as a skinny snake, he be, and damned if he didn't run off a while back."

"Pa, maybe that's who was a-follerin' us," said Morgan.

"Eh, what's that you say, young feller?" asked the mountain man.

"Pa, he seen somebody a-skulkin' on our backtrail."

"That'd be that red heathen, Looking Loon. I calls him Loonie, 'cause he's tetched. He didn't steal nothin' from you, did he?"

"We didn't see him," said Lem. "I saw somebody a-ridin' a pony, but couldn't make it out ner his rider neither."

"Well, likely Loonie's gone on ahead. We got to get to rendezvous at Independence. Makin' camp yonder for t'night. You'uns is welcome to jine us."

"Obliged," said Lem.

"Who ye be, Pilgrim?"

"I'm Lem Hawke. This is my son, Morgan."

"They calls this old coon Patch. Dave Sisco's the name I was borned to, but since I lost this eye to a Pawnee, they just calls this hoss Patch."

"We'll ride along with you," said Lem. Sisco was thirty-seven years old, but looked ten years older than Lem, who was only four years younger. Lem was wiry and lean, with no soft fat on him. Patch had girth to him, but he was what Lem would call "big-boned."

Morgan smiled. It was good to have company and Patch seemed likable enough.

Patch grunted. He clapped moccasined heels to his horse's flanks. The mule he was leading jerked to a start as the tether grew taut.

"Well, now, Lem Hawke, be you the man what burned down Spanish Jack's in St. Louie?"

"It was pure accidental," said Lem.

"Josie Montez, now, he thinks you did it deliberate after rubbing out Jack."

"Who's Josie Montez?"

"Why Spanish Jack's own brother, come up from New Orleans to mourn and pick over the leavings."

"Well, he's damned sure got it wrong," said Lem. "I never meant no harm to Spanish Jack." Lem looked at his son. Morgan was scowling. It was a touchy subject between the two. It had started over a young woman, Jack's daughter, Willa, who worked in the saloon. She seduced Morgan, and Lem had seen red, then gotten into a fight with her and Spanish Jack. A lamp had been knocked over and set fire to Willa's room. Lem had gotten the girl out, and Morgan, but Spanish Jack was unconscious. The flames spread so fast, the tavern had burned to the ground before he could get Spanish Jack out.

"Might be," said Patch. "But Josie's got blood in his eye and you might want to watch your backside ever' now and again."

"I'll do that," said Lem.

Morgan said nothing, but he could see that his pa was worried. Dick Hauser had warned Hawke that Spanish Jack had a brother who might want to take up the fight where it left off. Lem had met Hauser and his partner, Ormly Shields, on the Wilderness Trail when a member of another party had been killed by a band of Tuscaroras. Hauser and Shields had been captured, but managed to escape. Hauser, a trapper, had turned up later in St. Louis, much to Lem's surprise.

Long shreds of clouds floated like an armada of white-sailed galleons across the western sky as the sun lengthened the shadows of men, horses and mules across the afternoon prairie. Three swifts darted downriver, silent as wraiths. A lone hawk screamed like a baby, hovering over a patch of ground with quivering wings until its pinions collapsed and it fell like a stone from the sky.

Morgan looked around for Friar Tuck, but the dog was nowhere to be seen. The old man, Patch, chewed quietly on a chunk of tobacco, his eye taking everything in without seeming to make any effort, as if it was habit.

"You and the boy goin' to the big mountains?" Patch asked as the sun began to level off just above the horizon.

"Yep," said Lem.

"First time?"

Lem nodded.

"Figgered so. Might prove intrestin'."

"Huh?"

"Going by yourselfs, are ye?"

"Just me and Morg there."

Morgan was listening intently.

"Mighty lot of changes since ought three. Them red niggers ain't so hospitable no more. They's some as likes white men's scalps a-danglin' from their lodgepoles and lances. Take the Blackfeet, now. Time was when a man could trade with 'em and get some might fine pelts. But, now, you just don't never know. The Oglallies is the same."

"We aim to stay away from the Injuns," said Lem.

"Haw!" exclaimed Patch. "That ain't likely. They's a sight more of 'em than us. Beggars and thieves both. Might be you ought to learn the trappin' and tradin' from coons that knows them mountains."

"Do you trap with someone?"

"Waugh! Not this coon. But I trapped with some when I come out, first time or two so's I wouldn't lose my hair to the Rees. Once't I larnt to make sets, skin and cure, I trapped free. The companies come in and buys trappers till they own a man, lock, stock and bar'l. Me and Loonie, we stays to ourselfs. We ain't owned by nobody."

"Well, we never done it," said Lem.

"Wal, you got a heap to learn," said Sisco.

"Pa, tell him about Silas," Morgan offered.

Patch looked at the boy more closely.

"You talkin' about Silas Morgan? Why, sure. That's your name, ain't it? Any kin?"

"Nope," said Lem. "Knew him back in Virginny. He's the one what put the idee in my head to come out to the mountains."

"Pa named me after him. Silas, he give me this medicine horn," said Morgan, holding up his powder horn. "He got it from the Injuns."

"Well, if old Silas said he got it from them, I reckon he did. Last I saw of him, he was livin' with the Crow. Had him some Crow woman name of Blue Shell. Right purty woman, she was. You'd be findin' him up on the Yallerstone, I reckon."

"Might be we'll look him up," said Lem.

"Likely," said Patch.

They rode on in silence, watched as the sun went down.

"Pa, I reckon we ought to stop. I'm gettin' hungry."

Patch, who had been studying Morgan, broke in.

"That red nigger'll have some supper for us. He knows where we always camp. I like to ride into Independence fresh.

Be there come mornin'. But Loonie will have somethin' a-roastin' for us—rabbit, sage hen, prairie chicken or goat."

"How do you know?" asked Lem. "Maybe he run off."

"Oh, he does that. But, he knows I'll want vittles when I get to camp."

"How much farther?" asked Morgan.

"Why, I can smell somethin' now." Patch made a show of sniffing the air. Morgan sniffed, too.

"I smell it, too. Makes my stomach plumb jump," he said.

Lem laughed. He, too, could smell something roasting.

They rounded a bend of the river and saw a small fire near the bank. The Delaware's horse was hobbled. He was squatted next to the fire, a small animal spitted just above it.

Morgan stared at the Indian. Looking Loon was tall and lanky, with dark red skin. He wore moccasins, leggings, and a breechclout. His head was shaved except for a roach that split his skull in the middle. He looked fierce until he gave Morgan a lopsided idiotic grin. He touched his hand to the spitted carcass and turned it over the flames.

Patch did not say anything to the Indian when they rode up, but stripped his mule of its packs, unsaddled his horse and hobbled both animals. Lem and Morgan tended to their stock, leaving the horses and mules on long tethers to graze.

"Come on, boys, fill your bellies!" called Patch.

Lem and Morgan walked over to the fire, carrying pewter plates and forks. Patch was tearing off a haunch with his bare hands. Loonie had one side of a ribcage and was gnawing on it, grinning widely.

"Set," said Patch. He handed Lem one of the hindquarters, tore off the other one.

"Smells good," said Morgan.

Lem tore the chunk of meat in half, handed some to his son.

Morgan set his teeth to the flesh, bit off a mouthful. As he chewed, he looked at Loonie, fascinated by the strange-looking Indian, oddly thrilled to be so close to one.

Patch tore at his food savagely, spoke out of the side of his mouth.

"You done good, Loonie," said the old trapper. Looking Loon signed with one hand, then the other.

"Don't he talk?" asked Lem.

"Nope, 'cept with his hands. Jesuits cut out his tongue, he says, when he was just a young buck." Patch made sign with his hands, sticking out his tongue and knifing across it with one finger.

Loonie nodded and grinned, grunted low in his chest. He opened his mouth as if to show Lem and Morgan that there was nothing there but teeth and a gaping hole.

Morgan winced as the image of a knife cutting out a man's tongue became vivid in his mind.

"Lordamighty," he said.

Patch laughed. "You'll pick up sign, too, you talk with Injuns much. They got different tongues, but they can talk with their hands easy as can be."

Morgan watched in fascination as Patch moved his hands, fluttered them like birds. The young man could make no sense of the silent conversation as Looking Loon replied with hand gestures of his own. There was something strange and poetic about such talk, though, and Morgan vowed to learn the language.

"Loonie says he hopes you like the meat," said Patch.

Loonie grinned and patted his belly, moved fingers to his mouth as they were doing with their forks.

"I can understand that sign, Pa," said Morgan. "He wants us to eat, fill our bellies."

"Why, shore," said Patch. "That's what Loonie was a-signin' all right."

The Delaware made some other signs to Patch and the trapper grunted as he tore into a piece of meat, bit off a mouthful.

Morgan was hungry after the long ride and he ate voraciously. Soon, there was nothing left but bones.

"Hey, Pa, I just remembered. Friar Tuck. He'd love to have some of these bones."

Lem looked around.

"I wonder where he went to?"

"You missin' somebody?" asked Patch.

"My dog," said Morgan. "He run off and I ain't seen him in a while."

"He'll be along," said Lem, as he tossed a bone onto the heap.

Loonie belched.

"A little dog?" asked Patch.

"A beagle," said Morgan, standing up. He started to walk away, then turned back to Patch.

"You seen him?" he asked Sisco.

"No, I reckon not. Ain't likely to, neither."

Morgan stiffened.

"What's that supposed to mean."

"Why, Loonie there loves dog," said Patch. "That's why he was so confounded proud of the vittles tonight. Didn't you see what he told me?"

"I don't understand hand talk," said Morgan.

"Well, what you think we et tonight, Pilgrim? Antelope? Jackrabbit?"

Morgan felt sick.

"I don't know," said the young man. "What was it?"

"Loonie there said it was dog. Ain't no finer food, he thinks. Eats 'em all the time. Warn't bad, was it?"

"That was my dog we ate?" asked Morgan.

"Likely," said Patch. "Dogs is scarce as hen's teeth in these parts. Wild Injuns eat 'em, too."

"Pa?" Morgan turned to his father.

Lemuel shrugged.

"I'm a-goin' to kill him," said Morgan, looking at Loonie. But he thought of the meal they had eaten and felt his stomach buck. He doubled over and vomited, tears streaming from his eyes. He staggered away from the campfire, deathly ill.

"Shame to waste a good supper like that," said Patch.

Lem stood there helplessly, watching his son retch.

"I'd be mighty careful of what you say to Morgan about that dog," said Hawke. "He could be a mite touchy about what he et."

Looking Loon laughed soundlessly, his hands weaving curious images in the air as the sun died in cold flames over the horizon.

4

Morgan stopped vomiting, finally. His face flushed and the veins stood out like ruddy ropes on his neck. He balled up his fists, wiped his mouth with his sleeve. He glared at Looking Loon, a rage flaring in his eyes.

"Morg," warned Lemuel.

"You sonofabitch," said Morgan, breaking into a run toward the Delaware.

"Whoa there," said Patch, sticking out a buckskinned leg. Morgan didn't see the barrier in time. He pitched forward, fell straight into the fire, skidded through it in a boil of sparks, scattered chunks of flaming wood and cherry-red coals.

"Yow!" exclaimed Morgan as a hot coal burned his stomach.

The Delaware rose to his feet, put a hand on the buckhorn handle of his skinning knife.

Lem reached for his own knife, but did not draw it.

Morgan turned over on his back, flailed at the sparkling coals on his belly.

"Simmer down, boy," said Patch, still sitting by the fire. "Loonie there'll slit your gullet and think no more of it than squashing a bug."

"He kilt my dog," said Morgan, struggling to his feet. He brushed soot and ashes from his buckskin shirt.

"He didn't know it was your dog," said Patch. "And he didn't mean no harm. Fact is, he was a-tryin' to do some good, give us all some vittles to fill our empty bellies."

"It ain't right," said Morgan, still glowering.

"Sonny, you got some lessons to learn," said Patch softly.

Lem said nothing, but he kept his eyes on the Delaware, who still gripped the antler handle of his knife.

"Whatcha mean by that?" asked Morgan.

Patch stood up slowly, careful to make no sudden move. He stood where he could watch Lem as well as Looking Loon and Morgan. Sparks still glittered in the dry grasses around the fire and tendrils of smoke rose from some that had caught fire briefly, died out.

"Well, now, that little dog of yours, he was a civilized dog, warn't he?"

"I reckon," said Morgan sullenly.

"My guess is he never would have made it to the mountains, nohow. They ain't no laws out here and there's lots of Injuns what love dogmeat. And, if Loonie there hadn't of et him, then somethin' else would have made a meal of him. Might of been a griz or a timber wolf or a painter, but sooner or later that dog would have wound up in one belly or another."

"I could of took care of him," argued Morgan.

"I can see that," said Patch, smiling.

"Ain't no need to rag the boy," said Lemuel, his voice stony hard.

"Didn't mean no harm," said Patch. "A dog ain't worth a man's life, nor a boy's either."

"I ain't no boy," said Morgan.

"No, I reckon you ain't, but you ain't all haired over yet neither. Ain't no rules out here, Morgan Hawke, 'ceptin' those you make as you go along gettin' snakebit and ball froze and clawed and chased and shot at. Them's the rules you live by or you don't live long."

"Well, dammitall," said Morgan, "he ought to pay me for my dog."

"Morgan," said Lemuel.

"Pay you?" asked Patch. "For what? For fixin' your supper? Fillin' your belly?"

"I lost my supper," said Morgan.

"Ain't Loonie's fault. He did what he thought was right. Now you back off and do some thinkin' on this. That Injun might not talk, but he sleeps with one eye open and he's meaner'n a cornered painter when his back's up."

Patch made a sign to Looking Loon. The Delaware laughed soundlessly and took his hand away from his knife. He held up his hand, palm out flat, in the sign of peace.

"He wants to make friends with you, Morgan," said Patch. "All you have to do is hold up your right hand to show him you ain't got no weapon."

"I ain't a-gonna do it."

"Morgan," said Lem again.

"All right." Morgan held up his empty right hand. The Delaware grinned. He made signs with both hands, but neither Lem nor his son understood.

"Loonie thinks you got sick on the meat. He still doesn't know that was your dog. He's sorry if his cookin' don't agree with you."

"What?" asked Morgan.

Lem started to laugh. Patch joined in. The Delaware bounced up and down, shoulders shaking in silent laughter. Morgan saw the idiocy of it and began to laugh, too. He pointed to Loonie, then rubbed his belly. Loonie rubbed his own belly, then acted out the vomiting sickness. He danced around, showing them all what had happened to Morgan. Patch howled with glee. Lemuel doubled up, gasped for breath. Morgan laughed until tears came to his eyes.

Later, as he lay in his blankets, Morgan looked up at the stars. He could hear Patch snoring softly. His father was asleep beside him in his own bedroll. The Indian lay in a sitting position with his back against his saddle. Morgan didn't know if Looking Loon was asleep or not.

He thought about Friar Tuck and the things that Patch had said. Perhaps the dog would not have survived the journey to the mountains in any case. But, it was sad to think of the dog in his last moments, probably wagging his tail and trying to make friends with the Indian. He hoped Loonie killed him quick, but he didn't want to think about that. He would miss the dog, but he'd get over it, just like he got over his mother. Almost.

———.———

Lem, Morgan, Patch and Looking Loon rode into Independence the next morning. Camped just outside the settlement were several groups of men, some of them drunk, most of them noisy and full of ginger. Some shot off their fusils and shouted a greeting to the newcomers. But others stood around in morose groups, strangely silent, smoking their pipes like mourners at a funeral.

"Somethin's up says this chile," said Patch.

The Missouri was over its banks, its waters raging, tossing chunks of driftwood and trunks of trees in its turbulent maelstrom. A keelboat lay on its side, well off the bank, its hull caved in, a large gaping hole below the waterline. Several men encircled a man lying on his back. Two men were pushing on his chest and belly, slapping his face. The man on the ground was soaking wet. He appeared to have drowned.

"Pa, is that man dead?" asked Morgan.

"I dunno," said Lem. "He don't look alive."

"Deader'n a stump," said Patch. He and Looking Loon spoke in quick sign.

"There's Jocko DeSam," said Morgan, pointing to a buckskinned trapper at the edge of one group.

"I thought he was long gone up that river," said Lem.

"Ain't nobody goin' up that there Missoura," said Patch. "Look at that keelboat stove in."

A tall man walked away from the group surrounding the dead man. He was smartly dressed in fringed buckskins, a brace of pistols tucked in his sash. The shoulders of his shirt were gaudily decorated with quillwork and his moccasins were colorfully beaded. He carried a large, knife, possibles bag, powder horns. The man looked at the newcomers and frowned.

"Who's that?" asked Lem.

"That tall feller? Major Angus Llewellyn MacDougal is what he calls hisself. Slick as a buckhorn blade, wily as a timber wolf. That's one of his boats a-lyin' there. He had him three last I knew."

"There's the other two," said Morgan, pointing upstream. "They're busted up, too."

Lem saw the boats. They were even more badly battered than the one close by. One of them had a tree driven through its hull. The other didn't look like a boat so much as a pile of broken lumber.

As they rode closer, the noise of the river increased, roaring in their ears like a flood. Men were climbing over the broken hulks of the keelboats, salvaging their packs, food, weapons, traps, odds and ends. Several of the men onshore were clad in sodden buckskins, hatless, their hair flattened with dampness. The waters of the Missouri boiled with angry gray and black water. A man looking through the debris cursed in several tongues, angrily threw his tomahawk against the hull of a keelboat, where it stuck.

A man spread out his blankets to dry in the sun, shook his head as he looked at the destruction around him.

Morgan and Lem saw DeSam arguing with a taller man, shaking his fist.

"Same old Jocko," said Lem.

Lem and Morgan could not hear the voices above the roar of the river, but Jocko DeSam stopped shaking his fist at the taller man and turned toward them.

Morgan lifted his hand in a tentative wave.

Jocko turned from the man, waved back. In a few moments he called out to them.

"Bienvenue, mes amis," called Jocko DeSam, walking toward them. "You have come, at last. There has been much rain up on the river, look what she do to our boats. We have lost several horses and mules. Some men have gone to look for them upstream. But I saw a dead mule float by a few minutes ago, *sacré bleu!"*

"It's a mess," said Lem. "What will you do now, Jocko?"

"Ah, some will fix the boats, but I am going to walk, no? It will not be so fast, but *c'est la vie, non?"*

"We been lost," said Morgan.

"Maybe that is good, *non?* The wind she blow and the twister, she tear everything up."

Several of the villagers stood next to trader's tents, jabbering in low tones.

"Light down," said Patch. "Looks like there's goin' to be a pow-wow."

"What's that?" asked Morgan.

"Talkin'" said Patch. "Them as figger to use the river are going to have to go overland, either up it or straight acrost to the Platte."

"What about you?" asked Lem.

"All the same to me. I didn't figger to find room on a keelboat nohow."

Lem and Morgan dismounted. Jocko DeSam, whose real name was Jacques Decembre, shook Lem's hand. The Hawkes had first met the French trapper in Kentucky. All three had shared a jail cell together after a brawl in a hatter's establishment.

"Where can we ford?" asked Lem.

"Where did you come cross the river?" asked DeSam. He showed no trace of the anger he had shown the tall man, who now seemed to be barking orders at some of the other trappers.

"Way down yonder where the Osage feeds in. We just hopped from gravel bar to gravel bar."

"Ah, the gravel bar. She is always big trouble for the boats. But, I think we go up the river, *non?*"

Lem and Morgan exchanged looks.

"Ain't that where you broke up?" asked Lem.

"But the storm she has passed, *non?* The river she will calm down like a woman when she is petted and we will find a place to cross. Even if we do not, we can always climb the hills like goats, eh?" Jocko laughed. The Hawkes failed to see the humor. They were going into a great unknown, and so far, they had seen that unknown turn savage.

Jocko beckoned to them. He walked back to the rubble and picked out his horse and pack animals. Dick Hauser emerged from behind a broken keelboat and waved to them. Men looked at Jocko as if he had gone insane.

"Wait'll I get my horse," said Dick. "I'll ride with you."

"Ha, you are one crazy man, Dick," said Jocko. "We go without the boat."

"I ain't stayin' around here," said Hauser. "That goddamned Scotsman's plumb crazy." He jabbed a thumb toward the man the Hawkes had seen arguing with Jocko. Hauser was a lean, scraggle-bearded man, five foot nine or so, with a chaw of tobacco bulging one cheek. His buckskins were worn smooth, black from charred wood and streaked with grease from past meals on the frontier. "He thinks he's God almighty."

Lem smiled wanly. He felt nervous around Dick Hauser. He was a man he had thought dead, killed by Tuscarora Indians back in the Cumberlands, only to turn up alive and seasoned in St. Louis. His partner, Ormly Shields, hadn't been seen, but Dick said that he had survived the war party as well.

A tall man, dressed in a light capote, buckskin trousers and leggings, separated himself from a party of men working on one of the damaged keelboats. He walked towards Jocko and the Hawkes as Dick caught up his horse and pack mules.

"Uh-oh," said Jocko, "we are going to get the argument. Do you have your licenses?"

"Who's that?" asked Morgan, staring at the broad-shouldered man DeSam had been shaking a fist at moments before. The stranger carried a big knife thrust in a studded leather scabbard in his sash. The man wore a wide-brimmed hat with a large eagle feather jutting from its beaded band. He carried a long flintlock rifle. It looked like a toy in his oversized hand. The man wore a neatly trimmed beard, large sideburns. His hair was thick and shorn just above the shoulders. A large birthmark colored his forehead like a swatch of rust or faded vermillion.

"That is the Major," said Jocko, sotto voce. "Old Angus himself."

Jocko had mentioned the Major before, back in Kentucky when they had first met.

"Do you work for him?" asked Lem.

"Not anymore," said the Frenchman bitterly. "Shusss! Be careful. He's now the booshway."

Before Lem could ask Jocko what he meant, Major Angus Llewellyn MacDougal was upon them, taller than the horses.

"Och, Jocko, do you leave us with the boats to go on ahead?"

"Mais oui," said Jocko DeSam. "We ride the river."

"Who is this boy?" demanded MacDougal. "I hope he's here to see one of you off, because he's much too young to go to the mountains. And you," he said to Lem, "if you're going past this point, I'll need to see your license."

Lem took papers wrapped in oilcloth out of his possibles pouch.

He had obtained his trapper's license from the French bourgeois, the "booshway," just before leaving St. Louis. But Morgan had not been with him, and Lem had not gotten a license for his son. Usually, the brigade leader saw to it that all his men were licensed, but Lem had spoken to Pierre Choteau, Sr., and gotten a license through the St. Louis Missouri Fur Company.

Lem handed the license papers to the Major. MacDougal looked at them, frowned, then handed them back.

"Those are just for you. The boy cannot go."

"He's my boy," said Lem. "And he's a-goin'."

Angus scoured Lem with a raking look, cocking one eyebrow so that it arched up into his scarlet birthmark.

"Aye, and you'll bury the lad somewhere between here and the land of the Crow. How old are ye, laddie?"

"I'm fifteen," said Morgan, bristling as he thrust out his chest. "We come all the way from Kentucky, my pa and me."

"Then you must be the scalawags who burnt down Spanish Jack's and raised such a ruckus in St. Louis. Aye, I've been hearin' tales of you Hawkes all the way from Nashville from Jocko here and Nat Sullard and a dozen other flapmouths."

"Warn't my fault," said Lem, taking an instant dislike to the Major.

"But it shows a bungling that will give ye a grave marker in a land that tolerates no mistakes, am I right, Jocko?"

"He will make his way," said Jocko quietly. "He can trap on his father's license—or I have an extra one."

"Then, you've decided not to come with my brigade, is it, Jocko? Well, you still owe me beaver from last year."

"I will pay you, Major. I do not wish to have you cheat me with the furs."

The Major's eyes flickered dangerously.

"Aye, laddie, be careful what you say now. I expect an honest day's work and a fair tally. I take what's me due, no more, no less. And, you are making a big mistake not coming with my brigade. I can make trouble for you."

Jocko said nothing, but the battle lines were drawn.

"Come," said DeSam. "We go."

"I'll not have you talkin' to my men," said MacDougal. "Stay to your own grounds. If I catch you with furs taken from my creeks, I'll tack your French hide to a willow hoop."

"I trap where I please," said Jocko, kicking his heels into his horse.

"Mind it's not where I please, then, Jocko laddie."

The Major's voice was pleasant enough, but there was an undercurrent of threat in his tone. He doffed his hat to Lem, scowled at Morgan.

"Mind I warned you, Hawke," said Angus. "That lad's not dry behind the ears yet and there's perils ahead, perils enough for a man grown and seasoned. And, if he takes fur, he'd better have a license. I ought to throw you both in irons as it is."

"I can take care of myself," said Morgan defiantly, but he urged Boots to a trot just to get away from the man.

"I don't like that Scotsman," Lem told Jocko. "He pure puts a burr under my blanket."

"He's a hard chunk of rock," said DeSam. "I see how he cheat me, so I do not trap with him this year. And, now he is the booshway for the dam' government. Well, maybe he is not so smart. But, he knows the beaver, eh? He is one hell of a fighter, *non?* He speak with Indian in Indian talk, and they think he plenty brave."

"I ain't afraid of him," said Morgan, looking back over his shoulder.

Angus MacDougal was still standing there, staring at Morgan, shaking his head.

5

Calvin "Pappy" Roth and Nat Sullard joined DeSam's bunch. Major MacDougal watched the men go, the only sign of his anger a clenched fist that he quickly flexed back to normal once everyone had seen it. He smiled to himself with the secretive smile of a man who has just set a concealed trap.

As the small band of men and Hawke's boy, Morgan, rode from sight, Angus walked over to a man working on one of the keelboats. Fletcher Bancroft was a short, muscular man with sloping shoulders, a heavy beetled brow, hair matted and tangled to his shoulders. He was bare to the waist and carried a ten-pound maul in his gnarled left hand. He had been knocking at the pins of a deck cannon.

"We lost the bow gun, Major," said the man.

"Never mind that. How long before we're in the water?"

"Two days, three maybe."

"I want one boat loaded and ready to sail on the morrow."

"Too damned soon, Major."

"Not soon enough, Fletch. Tomorrow. Put all available men on a single craft. You pass the word, then there's something I want you to do."

"What might that be, Major?"

"I want you to get three men and go after Jocko. Bring him back to me."

"He won't like it none."

"He knows too much to go on ahead. I don't want him as competition."

"You want me to kill him, Major?"

"That would be an acceptable alternative."

"How's that?"

"Yes, if you can't get him back here without trouble, put his lamp out. Oh, and bring the lad back here, too. I'll not have a young 'un muckin' up the year's work. We'll put him in irons and send him back to St. Louis."

Fletcher grinned. He threw down his maul and started calling out to the men working on the keelboats.

"Hear ye, hear ye!" he yelled. "Gather 'round and listen up, you mangy bunch of gap-toothed louts. We got work to do!"

Angus smiled that strange slow smile of his. There was no warmth in it. It was the smile of a mourner at a funeral where his worst enemy was going six feet underground.

A few yards away, Patch Sisco slunk back behind a stack of barrels. He had gone there to piss and had heard every word between Major MacDougal and that worthless scoundrel, Fletcher. But something about the Major's behavior made him wonder if Angus wasn't up to something. He had the odd feeling that he had just seen a man step out onto a stage, give a speech and then go off the boards to laugh at everyone in the audience.

———.———

Dick Hauser joined Jocko, Lem and Morgan as they rode away from Independence.

"Feller tolt me they was some pirogues cached up yonder and some feller put a bullboat in the bushes thirty mile upriver."

"That is good," said Jocko. "I will bet the prime beaver plew we can find a keelboat with some room if they put the boat to shore when the storm she hit."

"We might get lucky," said Hauser.

"We couldn't fit all these goods in a pirogue," said Lem.

"No, but the river could carry some of us until we find a big keelboat. There were three or four boats ahead of us."

"Seems like a lot of fuss. Horse can take a man anywhere."

"Ah, but not like the boats, eh? In the boats, a man can look for Indians and sleep at night with both of the eyes closed, *non?*"

Lem laughed wryly.

"I think I'd rather be on dry land," said Morgan.

"We will see," said Jocko cryptically.

Morgan rode away from the others, swelling up inside with the immensity of the country, feeling dwarfed by the sky. Cottonwood trees marked the serpentine course of the river, green beacons cutting a swath through wild prairie. Morgan glutted himself on it, watching every waterbird take flight, gazing in awe at the bluffs that seemed like monuments built by some ancient giant. He saw eagles and hawks, the lazy carousels of turkey buzzards, floating in circles on invisible currents of air. He heard the *yawp* of a blue heron and watched its ungainly stride as it flapped across a sandbar, disturbed from its fishing by the passing horsemen and pack animals. Morgan felt his own muscles strain until it finally gained flight and soared above the trees, majestic at last.

That night, they camped below some bluffs some fifteen miles upriver from Independence. Jocko explained that they'd have to take turns standing guard.

"With the rocks behind us, we do not have so much to watch, eh?"

"You think Indians will attack us?" asked Morgan.

"I do not think so, but sometimes they are very quiet and when they do not want to trade, they like to take the hair and the goods for free." Jocko laughed at his joke. Morgan looked at his father. Lem only shrugged and began to strip the mules of their cargo.

Morgan thought it would have been better to have ridden to the top of the limestone bluffs where they would be able to see and hear anyone approach, but he said nothing. There were signs that others had been to this place before. There were burned rocks and flattened grasses, remains of firewood. For such a big country, it seemed to attract a lot of travelers. However, he knew that once someone left the river, or rode away from a creek, such country would swallow them up. Anyone who rode into the country had to stay close to water, or die.

The dank smell of the river wafted on the close summer air as dusk drew the shadows long and thickened in the grasses and on the ground. The littoral cacophony of insects shattered the silence and a great horned owl hooted like a rooster with laryngitis, its bass notes quavering in the distance.

"No fires," whispered Pappy Roth, as he strode up to the Hawkes. "Jocko says to stay quiet."

Pappy turned on his heel and went back to where the others were making camp for the night.

"Pa, do you think we'll see Indians?"

"No. Jocko probably knows what to do. Just keep your eyes open and don't make no noise."

Morgan finished stripping Boots and helped his father unload the panniers from the pack saddles. He and Lem hobbled their horses and put all the stock on a single tether line, anchored it to a cottonwood in sight of their camp. They broke out their bedrolls, set them head-to-head as they had done each night along their journey.

"Let's us find us a spot to ourselves, Morg," said Lem, taking one of the wooden canteens and a leather pouch that they carried their "day grub" in. "Get some food in us and talk, just you and me."

Morgan grinned. Sometimes his pa made him feel full growed.

They walked to a spot down the bluff where there was a slight depression, almost a cave. Lem hunkered down and searched through the "day grub" pouch for some dried elk and fried dough.

"Set," he told Morgan.

"What you wanta talk about, Pa?"

Lem handed his son a chunk of brisket and an oblong piece of fried dough. He held an index finger to his lips.

"Well, we done started," said Lem, biting into another quarter pound of dried brisket, "and so far not much has gone right. I got me a bad feeling 'bout this bunch."

"You don't like 'em, Pa?"

"Didn't say that, son. It's just that it seems that Major feller back downriver didn't like us all goin' none. And, they's got to be some reason these mountain trappers go in such big bunches."

"Indians, likely," said Morgan, chewing a morsel of sun-toughened meat.

"Likely. So, I think we better watch ourselves, ever' step of the way. DeSam has got him a grudge with that MacDougal, and if you notice, he keeps watchin' over his shoulder."

"I noticed."

Lem swallowed a half-chewed wad of elk meat. His Adam's apple bobbed and rippled like a snake swallowing a field mouse.

"We stay together all the time, you and me, Morg. Don't trust nobody too much."

"Aw, Pa. . . ."

"You just mind your P's and Q's, like I say."

"I will, Pa."

"I got me some funny feelin's," said Lem.

"Like what, Pa?"

"I can't rightly say. But, I got me somethin' pricklin' at me like a itch."

"Maybe it's because we don't know where we're goin'," said Morgan.

Lem nodded. They spoke no more until they had finished washing down the last of their supper with the warm water from the canteen.

———.———

DeSam called all of them together just before dark.

"We all have the fatigue, no?" he said. "But, we do not all sleep at once, eh? Maybeso, we draw the grasses to see who take the turns standing guard. I will take the watch nobody else wants. We do the four watches. Dark to the tenth hour, the tenth hour to the midnight, the midnight to the third hour and the third hour until the light she break. We start with the longest blade of grass. Does it not make the sense?"

All of the men nodded. Pappy Roth cut several blades of

grass with his knife, handed them to Jocko. Jocko turned his back on the assemblage and bit the grass stalks to various lengths, counted out four blades.

He fisted his hand, held the jutting grasses to each man. He skipped Morgan.

"We got us an extry two men," said Dick Hauser.

"We will have the two men on the last of the watch," said DeSam.

"I want to draw one," said Morg.

"*Non,*" said Jocko softly.

Morgan's face reddened and he started to rise. Lem put a hand on his shoulder, pressing him back down.

"But, Pa . . ."

"When you get a little more experience," said Lem.

"Aw, but . . ."

Lem silenced him with a narrowing of his eyes, a slight shake of his head.

Dick won the eight to ten watch, Pappy the ten to midnight, Nat Sullard had the next shortest. Lem got the morning watch.

"Is there anybody who wants to make the change?" asked Jocko.

They all shook their heads.

"I will take the last watch with Lem Hawke," said DeSam.

"I could do it with you, Pa," said Morgan as the two walked toward their bedrolls.

"I know, son. Let Jocko run it his way until he gets to know you better."

"But, I want to watch, too."

"Why don't you ask Dick if he needs some he'p?" said Lem.

Morgan's eyes flashed with light. He ran off to talk to Hauser while Lem laid out his rifle and pistols, checking pans and flints.

Dusk crept over the camp, shawling out the last of the

western light. Frogs croaked in the river bottoms, and insects sawed a cacophony of sound. Lem sat there on his bedroll, listening to a whippoorwill yammering from a nearby tree.

Morgan came back, a hangdog expression on his face.

"Dick didn't want no help," he told his father.

"Set, then. If you're a-itchin', best you start lookin'. I done kilt four ticks and swatted two of the biggest 'skeeters I ever saw."

Lem scratched his leg, probed inside the tops of his moccasins. He dug a tick out of his flesh and put a thumbnail to it. Morgan reached back over his shoulder, put a hand inside his shirt. He, too, found a tick and sliced it in two with his fingernails.

"Likely, there's more," said Lem.

"I can feel the little boogers," said Morgan, searching in earnest now, under his armpits, around his back, in his crotch. Lem slapped at a mosquito. His palm smacked against his cheek.

"Critters'll eat a man alive," he said.

"They don't bother me," said Morgan proudly.

"They just ain't seen you yet," said his father.

A few moments later, Morgan heard a buzzing in his ears. He slapped his face, but missed. A second later, a mosquito was drawing blood from the welt.

Later, the two stopped their bug hunt, having scratched themselves raw and slapped their faces long enough.

"I don't like it here, none," said Lem softly.

"Why, Pa?"

"Dunno. Just a feelin'."

"Feels kinda closed in," said Morgan.

"This close to the river ain't good."

He was remembering the storm, thought Morgan. He could hear the river now, almost like a whisper underneath the other sounds. It sounded far away, but he could imagine it in his mind, see its forbidding muddy waters swirling past the cottonwoods, nibbling at the banks, moving earth, turning it to silt and sand. It was a powerful feeling he had about that river. It meant a journey to him, but it also meant adventure and danger. The river was everything and it was not tame. He had already seen its power, what it had done to the keelboats.

"Best turn in," said Lem, sighing.

"I reckon," said Morgan, but he sat there for several moments until he heard his father's soft snores. Then, he lay on his bedroll, found the right position, closed his eyes.

The night sounds soothed Morgan to sleep.

Later, he was awakened roughly, and he thought he was dying.

Morgan felt a hand over his mouth, smothering him. He struggled to rise, but powerful hands pinned him down. He smelled the foul breath of a man as he leaned down in the darkness.

"Don't make a sound, son. I come as friend."

Morgan whipsawed furiously, trying to break free.

"Be quiet or you might be dead," said the voice. He recognized it as belonging to the trapper they had met downriver: Patch. "Here's your sack of possibles. I've got your rifle."

Morgan stopped struggling.

"We got to get you out of here quick. Just foller me," said Patch, taking his hand away from Morgan's mouth.

"Where's my pa?" whispered the young man.

"With Loonie. Come on, follow me."

"I don't—"

"Shh!" said Patch.

"Where's my horse?" Morgan whispered as Patch guided him through the darkness.

"Taken care of. Don't talk no more."

Puzzled, Morgan allowed himself to be pushed along blind. His mind was still foggy from sleep and he wondered where Patch was taking him.

Morgan stumbled and Patch had to pull on the youth's arm to keep him from falling. Morgan knew they were climbing up the bluff.

Patch shoved Morgan down behind an outcropping of rock and handed him his rifle.

"You set real still, young 'un. If your teeth get to chatterin', you bite down on a stick. No noise."

Morgan nodded. He shivered, but he knew it was not from the chill. He heard the soft pad of Patch's moccasins and then it was still. He knew the trapper had gone back down the spine of the bluff. But why?

It was quiet for a few moments. Then, Morgan heard a moccasin scrape on stone. Something rustled in the brush down below, where the trappers were camped.

Gradually, Morgan's eyes adjusted to the darkness. Clouds hid the moon and stars, but there was enough light that he could distinguish shapes. He could not tell what the shapes were; he could only guess. The night changed everything, and he was always fascinated by it. At times, back in Kentucky, when he was in the woods late, he would watch the shadows take shape and try to guess what they were. Or, when he went into the woods early in the morning, when it was still dark, he would mark each shape. Often, they resembled the heads or bodies of animals. Then, in the light, he would see that they were only trees and bushes, leaves and stumps, or rocks.

He made no sound as he looked around. He thought he might be alone, but he heard someone breathing a few feet away. The silence took on an eerie aspect. He wished whoever was there would say something. Anything. He felt as if he was being watched. But he couldn't see anyone's eyes. He couldn't even see a face in the pitch-black hood of night that pressed on him now with a slow, suffocating terror.

Morgan slid his right hand down his side, searching for his knife. He touched the handle, then something moved close to him and he felt iron-hard fingers close around his wrist. His heart bumped as it skipped beats and his throat froze with a terrible lump that had not been there before.

He felt a man's hot breath on his face and then a hand clamped over his mouth. He felt himself being pushed backward, toward the edge of the bluff. He wanted to fight back, to kick his attacker, but the man straddled him, pinning his legs to the ground.

He wriggled to free himself from the grasp of whoever had hold of him, but the man only increased the pressure.

Morgan couldn't see who it was, but he knew that in another few seconds he would be shoved over the bluff to fall to his death far below in the empty, mindless dark.

6

Morgan heard footsteps crunching softly on the loose stones atop the bluff. He heard a branch brush against a deerskin legging.

"Leave him be, Loonie," said Patch softly.

Suddenly, Morgan felt a release of pressure over his mouth as the Indian took his hand away. He felt himself being pulled roughly away from the edge of the precipice back to a sitting position.

"I told you not to move, kid."

"Damn you, Patch," growled Morgan. "If your nigger ever touches me again, I'll gut him."

He knew Patch was laughing because there was a change in the man's breathing, but the laugh wasn't out loud. He saw two shapes dimly silhouetted against the black sky. He felt that both of them were probably laughing at him.

Patch knelt down next to the boy.

"Looky yonder," he whispered into Morgan's ear.

He felt a hand at the back of his head. Patch turned the boy's head to the east.

"What is it?" Morgan asked, his voice barely audible. He saw flames dancing in the darkness. On the river, or near it.

"Torches," said Patch in his ear. "Them coons was comin' to grab you up and take you back to MacDougal."

"How come?"

"'Cause the Major's got forty kinds of bat in his belfry, that's how come. He wanted them niggers to cotch Jocko, too, and drag him back."

"I don't understand."

"MacDougal don't have all his hinges in place, son. Now, you just set and keep your flap shut."

Morgan watched the torches disappear and reappear through the trees. There were three of them. If he had felt odd before, he was deeply bewildered now. It was as if he was not really there, sort of dreaming. He felt as if he was watching something strange and evil and was powerless to do anything about it.

"Where's my pa?" he asked.

"I got him in a tree. Jocko's in another. You just sit tight, son. You be quiet as a dead beaver or I'll put the butt of my rifle to your skull and put you to sleep."

It was quiet for a long time after that, except for the incessant sawing of mosquitoes. Morgan watched the torches until his eyes burned in their sockets. Then, they winked out. He thought the men might have dowsed them in the river, but he heard no hissing sound. The only sound was in his mind, and it wouldn't go away.

———·———

Lem listened harder than he had ever listened before, trying to shut out the whine of a mosquito in his ear. He, too, had seen the torchlights, knew what they meant. Patch hadn't told him much, only that some men from the Major's brigade were coming to do them harm. He sat in the crotch of a cottonwood tree, a portion of his butt dead and bloodless. He didn't dare move, though he felt the sting of a mosquito's needle on his cheek. He could not see Jocko DeSam, but he knew that he was sitting up in another tree like a raccoon, not twenty yards away.

It was so quiet for such a long time that Lem thought he was no longer breathing. That everything in the world had disappeared or come to a halt.

Then, he heard it. The soft rustle of moccasins on the grasses, the quiet rasp of 'skins brushing against bushes, the faint tink of rustled leaves.

The noises stopped. Then, he heard a low whisper. He scanned the ground below, thought he saw someone skulking toward his bedroll. A second later, he saw shadowy movement, then heard a loud crunch.

Lem brought his rifle to his shoulder, careful to make no sound. As the shadow bent down, he drew a bead from memory, for he could not see his sights in the darkness.

Suddenly, without warning, Lem got the shakes. He hadn't had those since he was a boy, the first time he saw a buck in his iron sights. And he hadn't had them since. But he had them now. He couldn't find a target, didn't know whether he was shooting a bear or a man.

Sweat beaded up in his brows, dripped downward, stinging his eyes.

Then, the night exploded with bright orange blossoms and the thunder of big bore rifles. Lem heard the deadly whisper of flints striking steel, the low *whoosh* of powder igniting in the pan. The camp lit up with dark shapes as men scurried out of the crossfire. The leaves rattled in the trees, lead balls thunked into limestone and burnt bark from cottonwood trunks. Lem tried to find a target, but the light faded, leaving his retinas glowing with fiery sparks.

Lem heard men shouting, running.

"Goddamnit," he muttered. Stuck in the tree. Helpless as a pig on an iced pond.

"Get the hell down out of that tree, Hawke," yelled Dick Hauser.

"By gar, they get away." Jocko's voice.

Lem listened to the crash of men running through brush, the crackle of small limbs, the thrash of leaves. Rocks rattled down from the bluff and the dank breath of limestone assailed his nostrils, mixing with the heady scent of the mud and sand-laden river swirling past banks thick with vegetation clinging to fragile moorings.

Hawke dropped from the tree, bent his knees to absorb the shock. He gripped his rifle tightly, rocked back on his heels until he regained his balance.

On the ground, he could see even less. The noises were drifting away. He stood there, not knowing what to do, wondering if he'd knocked all the powder out of his pan when he jumped down from the tree.

"Hawke, come on," said a voice.

"Who's that?"

"Hauser."

Lem felt a hand touch his elbow.

"Dick? Where we goin'?"

"After them bushwhackers."

"Hell, I can't see a thing."

"Foller me."

Dick stepped into the darkness and Lem had to jump after

him to keep up. He followed Hauser more by sound than sight, but knew they were heading toward the river. Ahead, they heard shouts and the sharp crack of a rifle.

Blindly, Lem raced after Dick Hauser. Sapling limbs slashed at his face, brush tugged at his leggings. He tripped, cursed silently. His breath burned hot in his chest and he gulped in air as the pace quickened.

He wondered how Dick knew where to go in the darkness. Then, he saw dark sky, the silhouettes of trees growing along the river. A few moments later, Hauser stopped at the bank of the Missouri. They heard men talking in low, gruff tones. Then there was another rifle shot, followed, in quick succession, by two more. Bright flashes of orange light sprouted from barrels downriver.

"Hoooowaaay!" shouted Jocko DeSam.

"Come on," said Hauser. "It looks like they got 'em."

"Who in hell are they?"

"Damned if I know. Thieves. Scundrels."

Dick walked downriver, Lem right behind him, holding his rifle at the ready.

Nat Sullard and Pappy Roth stood looking down at the ground. Jocko was on his knees, turning over one of the men he had shot. There were three men stretched out, their chests soaked with blood. One had been shot in the groin as well.

Lem's breathing settled down and the fire in his chest subsided. His nostrils filled with the smell of dank river water and death.

"One got away," said Jocko, standing up. He stood his rifle on its butt. His powder horn rattled as he brought it to the muzzle. "Goddamn dark. Can't see no goddamn thing."

He poured powder down his muzzle, going by instinct and feel. Then, he pulled a strip of patching from his possibles pouch. He stretched the cloth across the muzzle, fished a ball from his pouch and centered it, thumbed it down the barrel until it was flush. Grabbing his patch knife, he cut the excess patch away. With his wiping stick, he eased the ball six inches down the barrel, then rammed it home atop the ninety or one hundred grains of powder he figured he'd poured. He seated the ball, then primed his pan, blowing away the excess powder, shoved down the frizzen plate over the pan.

"Dick, strike us some light," said Nat Sullard. "Let's see who we got here."

Hauser stepped away from the bunch and knelt down. Lem heard the clatter of a tin box, the rattle of flint and steel. Dick scratched sparks from the steel, set the tinder afire. A few moments later, he had a small fire. Jocko tore cattails from the river, set them afire. He swung the torches over the faces of the dead men.

"Know 'em?" asked Lem.

"That one, he's Lucien LeBoef," said Jocko with solemnity. He kicked the corpse in the side, muttering *"Merde."*

"This 'uns Dave Trask," said Nat, pointing to the middle man.

"And that other'n, he be Ernie Parsons," said Dick Hauser. "Warn't none of 'em no account."

Lem sucked in a breath. The men looked like lifeless husks, their faces gaunt in the fireglow, the eyes vacant, the skin pallid as if the blood had drained out of their heads. He felt queasy.

Jocko DeSam looked over at Hawke, muttered something to Nat Sullard. Nat spoke to the others. Lem heard them stripping the dead men of their possibles pouches, moccasins, knives, stacking their rifles. A moment later, he heard a splash and turned around. He started toward the men coming after the second body, when Jocko stopped him and braced him by the shoulders.

"What in hell are you doin'?" asked Lem.

"That be as good a-buryin' as they deserve, eh, *mon ami?*"

"Goddamnit, Jocko, you just killed three men. Why?"

"Ah, it is a long, long story, eh?"

"Well, maybe you better start explainin'."

"Ah, *oui*, maybe so, it is a good time to talk of this and of other things. Come, we find Patch and Loonie and your boy. We hold the pow-wow, *non?*"

There were two more splashes and Lem shook his head.

"There was another man, Jocko. I seen him," said Sullard.

"Yes, he is not here. Patch told me it was Fletch."

"Who's Fletch?" asked Lem.

"Fletcher Bancroft," said Dick Hauser. "A damned snake, that one. I shoulda figgered this was his handiwork, skulkin' up to our camp in the dark, sneakin' up on us."

"I just don't know if I want anymore of this," said Lem. "All this killin', this treachery."

"Ah, *mon ami*, this is nothing," said Jocko. "These men were the vermin, eh? They kill plenty men before they get the number come up, *non?* This MacDougal, he give Jocko the double cross and now he want to rub me out, put the grass in my mouth."

Lem didn't understand what Jocko was saying, but it was something to hold on to while he tried to settle his senses. He could not get the images of the dead men's faces out of his mind, and he thought of the man Morgan had killed and wondered if he was not bringing his boy into a worse world than they left back in Kentucky.

"Bring the torch," said Jocko to Hauser. "We will light the fire and make the big pow-wow. We will smoke the pipe and make the talk, eh? Maybe we burn the woodtick, is it not? Come, Hawke, you listen to Jocko DeSam, eh? He tell you plenty." Jocko scraped a tick from the back of his hand, pinched it deftly between thumb and forefinger until blood oozed from its flattened body.

Jocko tugged on Lem's sleeve. They followed the torch back to the disrupted camp through the eerie shadows it cast, single-file, like men going to the gallows, silently, each with his own thoughts about the night's foul work.

————·————

Morgan followed Patch and the Delaware down the bluff. His brain was teeming with questions, but he was having too much trouble with his footing. The Indian and the trapper made no sounds with their moccasins, but Morgan kicked stones loose and he felt as if the bluff might slide out from under him and pitch him into the blackness below.

At the bottom, clouds of mosquitoes rose up and enveloped Morgan's face. He swatted blindly in front of his face to keep from breathing them in.

He heard the other men coming back to the camp, their voices low-pitched, throaty with manly rumbles.

Patch and Loonie disappeared in the shadows of the bluff, leaving Morgan alone by his bedroll.

"Hallo the camp," called Hauser.

"We'uns be here," answered Patch. Moments later, the band of men stalked into view, single-file shadows carrying rifles.

"Dick, make us the little fire, eh?" said Jocko. "The smoke she will make the mosquitoes go back to the river. Nat, you keep the eye out, *non?*"

"I reckon I kin," said Sullard.

Morgan slunk over to his father, whispered a question into his ear.

"What happened, Pa?"

"I'll tell you later," Lem said quickly.

Hauser soon had a small fire ablaze. The light flickered on the men's faces. Sullard stood a few yards away, behind an Osage orange tree, his rifle nestled between a fork in the limbs, pointed toward the river.

"Why would that damned Scotsman send those killers after us?" asked Lem, looking directly at DeSam.

"Ah, it is the politics," said Jocko. "It is the goddamn fur, *non*? Eh, these company, they kill for what they want."

"We don't work for no company," said Morgan, feeling his father's anger, sensing that his pa was all by himself, that something had changed between him and the other men. "We ain't done nothin' to them."

"That's right," said Lem. "Was it you they was after, Jocko?"

"Eh, mebbe so," said DeSam, shrugging. He waved a hand through an antic scrim of mosquitoes. The other men slapped their faces at random, scratched at woodticks crawling into their moccasins. "Maybe he also want the boy." He pointed to Morgan. Young Hawke's expression of consternation showed his puzzlement. His eyebrows knitted in a sudden scowl and he blinked like a barn owl.

"Me?" Morgan asked.

"You tell him, Patch, eh?" said Jocko.

Patch walked over to the fringe of the glow thrown by the fire, hunkered down on his haunches. His hand slid down his rifle barrel and stopped at the brass trigger guard.

"The Major, he's got him some conscripts," said the grizzled old trapper. "Young 'uns he totes up to the mountains. He buys 'em, trades for 'em, don't pay 'em much er nothin' 'tall. I reckon he had his eye on your boy all right."

"You mean he wanted to steal Morgan?" asked Lemuel.

"Likely he wouldn't call it stealin', more like teachin'. Slavery's what I calls it. Cheap labor. He's cheated more'n one lad and a few growed ones, too, I reckon."

Morgan swallowed an imaginary lump in his throat. He looked at his father.

"Well, he better stay away from my boy," said Lem. "He even looks at Morg cross-eyed, I'll lay him out cold."

"I think we meet the Major again," said Jocko. "I think he work for that bastard Astor."

"Time was you was askin' me to hook up with him," said Lem.

"I did not know him so well, eh?" replied DeSam. "I worked for him, I see him cheat the trappers. So, I cheat him."

"He don't like Frenchy none," said Patch, referring to Jocko.

"The Major don't like nobody much," said Hauser. "I worked for him a season, too."

"What is this about Astor?" asked Lem. "Who's Astor?"

"Ah, he plenty rich man," said Jocko. "He owns American Fur Company. I think this Major he work for American Fur."

"And who do you work for?" asked Lem.

Jocko did not answer right away. Sullard and Hauser looked at Lem, shook their heads, as if telling Hawke that he had gone too far.

Patch stared at Jocko as if demanding an answer.

DeSam heaved a sigh, shrugged.

"It is late," said the Frenchman. "I will take the first watch." To Lem Hawke, he said privately, "Do not worry yourself over these little politics, eh? You trap the beaver and let Jocko take care of the business, my friend. You and your son will make fine trappers, eh?"

"Are you asking me to work for you?"

"Well, do you have the license?"

"Yes. I got a license from Missouri Fur."

"Ah, then, do not worry. You trap, you work. Jocko will see that you get the fair deal."

Jocko slapped Lem on the back, winked at Morgan. He walked over to the fire and kicked dirt and rocks on it to put it out. The men wandered off to their bedrolls. Patch and Loonie disappeared into the darkness.

"Pa?" Morgan called from his bedroll.

"What?"

"Do you like Jocko?"

"I dunno," said Lem. "Makes no nevermind."

"How come?"

"We mean to go trappin' anyways we can. Jocko knows the way. He can learn us how to do it."

"He might cheat you."

"He might," admitted Lem. "But he'd only do it once."

"Then what?"

"He wouldn't do it no more."

"How come?"

"He'd be dead or cripped up so bad he wouldn't want to do it no more."

"Maybe we should go back home," said Morgan, his voice lazy with sleepiness.

"We don't have no home no more, son. This is home. Wherever we be is home."

"It don't feel much like home."

"I know," said Lem. "Get some sleep, son. Hard as this day was, tomorrow's bound to be harder."

"Good night, Pa."

"Good night, Morg."

Morgan looked up at the pulsing silver stars. Mosquitoes buzzed around his head. He felt a tick burrowing in his leg. He was too tired to scratch it. The buzzing lulled him to sleep as soundly as if he had been drugged. He saw dead men in his dreams. One had the face of the man he had killed during the storm. Then the face changed and became the Major's. And the face was laughing.

7

The Missouri River still boiled, its writhing waters a yellowish brown, contrasting sharply with the slate-gray seethe of the Mississippi. Fletcher Bancroft and another trapper tugged on the boat hook. The body of Dave Trask slithered over the rail. His sodden pantleg caught on a davit. Fletcher jerked the pole attached to the hook and Trask's remains landed on deck with a thud.

The river rats had gotten to Trask's face, had dug out the eyes and eaten into the sockets. Part of his nose was chewed away. Major MacDougal joined the group of men looking at the waterlogged body of the dead trapper.

"I told you to take care of this yourself, Fletch," said McDougal, stepping close to whisper in the trapper's ear.

"They had us outnumbered, Major."

Fletch dragged the body away from the gunwale and spread the linsey-woolsey shirt.

"Square in the breadbasket," he said, pointing to the hole in the dead man's stomach.

A man stepped up close to the Major. He had swarthy skin, eyes black as raw coffee beans and a thin scar bleeding away from one eye as if a large tear had left a track. His lips had been mashed by countless fists and heavy objects. Some of his teeth were missing, the others carious.

José Montez was dressed more like a sailor than a trapper, but he had been both.

MacDougal nodded to the Spaniard, his eyes as cold as cave rocks.

"That one of 'em you sent after Jocko?" asked Montez.

The Major nodded.

"You sure that Hawke sumbitch was with DeSam?"

"And his whelp," said the Major. "I swear I'll have all their hides stretched on willow withes before I'm finished with this expedition."

"Them Hawkes is mine," said the Spaniard.

"Montez, you have all the hair you want of the pap, but that boy looked to be prime goods. He didn't have a hand in killing your brother, anyway."

"He's a nit from a louse," said Montez. He looked at the bank as the keelboat slipped past, guided by men poling the boat, two on the rudder. Ahead, other men kept the horse herd moving overland. The square sail on the forward mast snapped in the breeze, its long cordelle dangling like a tree snake from the masthead to the deck.

Another boat followed, its goods stacked amidships in a long boxlike structure, lashed down tight, forty-odd men aboard. Montez had ridden up the evening before, just as the men in the Major's brigade were loading the two keelboats.

The men had pulled into the landing stages that same morning, early, cursing in the dark, shadowy figures in the swirling fog. Montez had gotten aboard the lead boat in time to help cast off the lines and set his shoulder to a pole. Then, one of the trappers had spotted the body of Trask, bobbing next to the bank, a leg caught by an exposed cottonwood root.

Montez puffed on a thin cheroot, his eyes glittering with the feral brilliance of a man who started every day with a shot of gut-wrenching whiskey. His small-billed seaman's cap sat atop a shock of thick, black curly hair. His loose homespun shirt was unbuttoned at the neck, revealing more curls on his chest, coiled tangles that looked like wire springs. His hands were rough, the joints knotty, the fingers gnarled as twisted manzanita roots. Buckskin trousers, smoked over greasy campfires, snugged tight against his lean hips. He carried a Spanish flintlock tucked in his bright red sash; a large knife hung from a wide belt with an ornate brass buckle.

By then, everyone aboard the keelboats knew that Montez was the brother of Spanish Jack and that Lem Hawke had been responsible for burning down the tavern in St. Louis. Spanish Jack hadn't made it out and had ended up ash and bone. His daughter, Willa, had told her uncle the whole story when Montez arrived from New Orleans. Now, Montez wanted revenge for his brother's murder, for that's how he figured it. He meant to rub out Lem Hawke at first sight.

The Major had known both Montez and Spanish Jack. Like everyone else, he knew the story of the fire at Spanish Jack's tavern. Lem Hawke, angry at Jack's daughter for seducing Morgan, had started a fight in Willa's bedroom. During the brawl, Lem had either knocked over or thrown a lamp. The fire had spread quickly. Jack's daughter, Morgan and Lem had gotten out, along with all the patrons downstairs in the saloon, but Spanish Jack had perished in the flames. Willa told the story that Lem had knocked her father out cold and had deliberately set fire to Spanish Jack's.

"Fletch, throw that corpse back in the river," ordered MacDougal. "Big 'Un, get 'em movin'."

Big Mike Finnegan, patroon of the two keelboats, stood atop a large cargo box and yelled lustily: "You thar. Set poles for the mountains." His clean-shaven head, his enormous girth and thick neck gave him the look of a hydrocephalic mushroom. Josie tossed his cheroot over the side just as Trask's body splashed back into the river. He grabbed an oar and joined Fletch and four other oarsmen forward of the cabin. They swung their oars over the side, braced for the first thrust. Forward, twenty polemen poised to port, preparing to shove off with their long, iron-clad poles.

Mike swung the helm with one mighty arm, lifted the hunting horn hanging from a thong lacing his chest and put the mouthpiece to his lips. He blew the signal to start, a throaty mellifluous moan that increased in pitch and ended up in a vibrant tremolo that hung in the air like thick fog.

The six oarsmen dipped their oars in unison. The polemen, facing the stern of the keelboat, slid their poles into the murky water, set them against the river bottom, threw the muscle and sinew of their shoulders against the curved sockets at the tip of the poles. They heaved, shoving the boat away from shore and upstream against the current. They slogged their way, in single file, toward the stern.

Mike began singing a sea chanty and the polesmen picked up the melody. When they reached the stern, the patroon yelled "Ho!" and the men all turned quickly, raced back to the bow, rammed their poles back to the bottom again and once more braced themselves against the sockets and pushed. The boats slid upstream, lumbering against the tug of the current.

Major MacDougal stood by the cabin watching the men strain against the Missouri. His face bore no expression, but he looked at the eyes of the young men with the poles as they lunged aft and his eyes glittered like coals fanned by a whispering wind. They were strong young men, most coming back for their second season of trapping.

On the western shore, the men with the horses and mules paced themselves, letting the animals graze and drink along the shore. Some of the men looked at the sky, dreading the next spring storm. Others rode off, singly and in pairs, to seek game for the brigade.

MacDougal nodded silently in satisfaction as the keelboats gained headway. They were headed for the mountains, and among the men in his brigade, with its many internal factions, there were some he trusted, some who served as his eyes and ears. None but he knew who they were. He suspected that Jocko DeSam would prove a problem later on. Those who had gone with him were of the same ilk, not to be trusted. In the fur trade, the Major knew, beaver were not the only animals that must be skinned; competitors, be they few or several, were fair game. He now considered Jocko, Patch and his crazy Indian, the Hawkes, and the others who had ridden off with the Frenchmen to be competitors, possibly spies for a rival fur company.

He looked down at Josie Montez, now just another oarsman earning his keep. That one could prove useful, MacDougal thought. Montez wanted to kill Lemuel Hawke. Perhaps he would consider killing the others who followed Jocko DeSam.

As the work got harder, the men stopped singing, but Big 'Un kept up a steady chant as he steered the keelboat upriver, guiding the helm with one hand, swatting at mosquitoes with the other.

"Put your muscle into it, boys," sang Mike. "Bear a hand there, Paddy. Let's see your neck bow, Harold me boy."

The unwieldy keelboat, a hundred feet long and twenty feet wide, gained headway mainly through the efforts of the *voyageurs*. With their necks bowed, their heads nearly touching the track of the running board, they pushed with all their might to the stern. They followed the patroon's commands to return to the bow for each new "set." With its shallow draft, the keelboat did well on such a river as the Missouri. When the boat gained deeper water, the oarsmen took over the work of propelling the boat upriver and the sweat-soaked *voyageurs* could relax for awhile as they watched for treacherous snags, sandbars, floating trees.

When they were well underway, Big 'Un ordered Fletch to set sail and they caught the wind and the men rested as the boat cleaved through rushing muddy waters, listening as the occasional thud of a log or tree branch turned to flotsam by a storm struck the hull. The mast stood a third of the way down from the bow and the sail was a tall square piece of heavy cloth. There were not many stretches on the Missouri where the sail could be used, since the river writhed like a giant snake through bluff-dominated prairie and there was often a terrible surprise waiting at each dramatic bend.

And MacDougal, setting the glass to his eye, scanned the horizon beyond both banks and looked ahead for any sign of Jocko DeSam's renegade party. He wondered if they would try to go to the Rockies by river or travel overland, out of sight, but not out of his raging, vindictive mind.

———·———

Morgan Hawke was glad that they had left the river and were riding well away from the clouds of mosquitoes that had plagued them ever since breaking camp that morning. Morgan could see the trees that marked the river's banks, the way they twisted through the stark, beautiful land, with its high bluffs like castle fortresses. Beyond the river, the land rolled gently, high grasses waving gently in the morning breeze that was fanned by the heat from the rising sun. Jocko had decided, for all of them, that it would be better if they did not try and find a keelboat ahead to take them on. Instead, he said they would follow the river at a distance until they reached one he called the Platte.

"There's a man keeps lookin' over his shoulder," Lem told his son later that day.

"I noticed it," said Morgan softly. He and his father rode alone, following well behind Jocko, Loonie and Hauser. They had been delegated to handle the spare horses and pack mules. Jocko had said they would all take turns. Patch was well ahead of the party, followed by Nat Sullard. Pappy Roth had gone off hunting.

"Seems like he done changed his mind oftener'n his shirt."

"You mean about the Major?"

"Him and a lot of things."

Morgan wondered what his father was driving at. His pa was a hard thinker sometimes; slow to speak, but when he did say something it was more like a riddle than fact.

"Where are we going, Pa? I mean did Jocko say?"

"Some river."

"He knows this country then."

"I reckon."

"How come Patch is ridin' so far ahead?"

"Figgers to see we don't get no big surprises."

"Indians?"

"Maybe. Nat tolt me this was all Injun country, but big enough so's you might never see 'em."

"I hope we see some."

"Son, you don't want to flap your mouth like that. Injuns, from all I hear, is trouble. All of 'em's pure mean, 'cordin' to Hauser and Sullard."

"You talked to them 'bout it?"

"This mornin' whilst you was packin' up."

They heard the sharp crack of a rifle far off and then the quiet rushed in giving the day a special silence for a few moments. The wide game trail they followed was trackless after the rains. To the north, the sky was more black than gray and the air seemed laden with moisture. The sun, wherever it was, sent a heavy sweaty heat down on them.

"I'll go see if he needs help," said Lem. "You stay put."

Lem rode off, leaving Morgan to follow Jocko and the others on a march that roughly followed the river. Boots kept nipping at the rump of one of the mules. Morgan finally got tired of it and slapped his horse's neck. Boots' ears went flat for a moment and he shook his head. The mule brayed as if he was the one who had taken the blow.

The country was strange to Morgan, so unlike any he had ever seen. Missing were the vast forests of Kentucky and Tennessee, replaced by tall trees wrapped in wild grapevines. When he glimpsed the banks of the river, he saw the trees rose out of tangled brush that was too thick to walk or ride through, and he avoided those places, swinging wide with the pack animals to avoid the fallen trees, huge giants that blocked his path. He looked in amazement at a place where several trees had fallen on top of one another. They were overgrown with shoulder-high nettles. He rode too close, once, and the nettles struck at him, stinging his wrists, burning into his skin like the sharp cuts of a whip. He got tangled in the climbing roses and buckthorn, and vowed never again to ride or walk anywhere near such dangerous plant life. Boots began to buck with the gouge of thorns before horse and rider were free of it. Morgan was covered with ticks, and though he brushed off those he could see, others burrowed into his flesh. Mosquitoes, swarming from fetid ponds created by the flood waters, found him, covered him with burning welts.

A buck deer, flashing a white tail like a flag, burst from a thicket and Morgan stifled the urge to cry out to those ahead. Instead, he was caught up with the beauty and grace of the buck as it bounded through places too thick for a rabbit to hop and disappeared into a swallowing darkness of thicket and vine.

He heard the faroff crack of a rifle and wondered if his father had found game. Perhaps his pa had seen the big buck with its fourteen-point rack, but the buck had not gone that way. Morgan found the image of the deer lingering in his mind and he wondered then why he heard no birds calling. Suddenly, a wave of lonesomeness swept over him like a silent tide and he felt alone and friendless, fatherless as well.

Then, Morgan heard the distant hammering of a woodpecker and thought of the forests of his boyhood in Kentucky.

Sometime during the afternoon, when still he had heard no birdsong, Morgan was surprised by a loud screeching. Ahead, he saw hundreds of what he took to be flying leaves, all flittering from branches like butterflies. As he drew closer, he saw the birds, wild parakeets startled by the riders ahead, dozens of them, flying erratically through the tall trees like leaves before the wind.

As he watched the green birds dart from tree to tree, creating the worst racket he'd ever heard, Morgan lost sight of the horses and mules. Moments later, he realized the animals had gotten ahead of him. He put moccasin heels to Boots' flanks, rode two hundred yards around a bend in the treeline. The herd was not there.

The other riders were nowhere in sight, either.

Panic rose in Morgan's throat, squeezed it tight. He felt a sense of suffocation. He stood up in the stirrups, trying to see far enough ahead to spot the others, or the animals in his care. It seemed suddenly quiet, with only the sound of his heartbeat thrumming in his ears.

Dark clouds were moving in and Morgan felt a soft spray of rain against his face. The parakeets stopped their raucous screaming now that he was away from their habitat. The wind lisped in his ear, a whisper from the northwest, not yet heavy but freshening, cooling.

Morgan wanted to call out, but the stillness, the emptiness of the land seemed too forbidding. He saw the swath through the grasses where the horses and mules had gone and kicked Boots again to hurry him along. He felt a pang of embarrassment that he had let the herd get away from him. He did not want the others to know that he had neglected his duty.

On he rode, the anxiety in him increasing with each moment. He looked at the darkening sky, watched the clouds float like silent barges until they shrouded the sun. The trail petered out, as if the herd had scattered. There was no single swath any longer, but tendrils of paths recently trod, fanning out in bewildering directions as if someone had scattered the animals.

The panic in him changed to fear. He clutched his flintlock, realized he had unconsciously folded his hand over the pan after the first kiss of rain. Now, he fumbled in his pouch for a blackbird's wing quill that fit the touchhole. He stuck it in the hole, kept his hand over the pan. He looked down, saw the fine patina of powder lining the tiny bowl and felt its dryness. He looked toward the hidden river, the tall trees. If the horses or mules got into that, well, he wouldn't know how to get them out.

Morgan followed a single trail and then he lost it. He stopped Boots and drew in the first deep breath he'd taken since losing sight of the pack animals.

His throat went dry. He heard the rain begin to spatter and Boots began to sway his head in annoyance as heavy drops stung his eyes. Morgan felt the darkness closing in on him. Ahead, he saw the distant horizon flash with lightning and seconds later heard the thundercrack booming like a cannon shot.

The wind stiffened, but it was a warm wind and heavy now with moisture. Morgan went on, but he saw no track, no sign that anything had passed his way. Another staggered flash of light in the sky and the thunder boomed closer, warning of danger.

Five minutes later, the rain burst over him like a waterfall and he could no longer see the trees. It was a steady, soaking rain, blinding, wind-driven, blotting out the land, driving it away from his eyes until he knew he was all alone, lost and caught in the open where the lightning could fry him like a moth caught in flame.

Morgan felt suddenly, strangely, calm.

He turned Boots to the right, toward the river, seeking shelter from the storm that broke over him with a vengeance.

The fear was gone, but the loneliness, like a smothering blanket, left an ache in his chest as if his lungs had been singed.

He wondered if his pa even knew that he was lost.

Morgan slackened the reins, gave Boots his head.

"Find us a place, Boots," he said, patting the horse's neck. The rain soaked the powder in his pan, wilted the blackbird's quill in his touchhole until it drooped limp as a rag.

But Boots turned away from the river and Morgan heard it roar like a maddened beast as the raging water collapsed banks and snatched trees from the shore, snapped them like string beans and gobbled them into its maw.

There seemed, just then, no safe place to go as lightning streaked the sky with silver lace and thunder cracked so close Morgan jumped inside his sodden buckskins.

And the horse stopped dead in its tracks, lost and blinded by the surging, pelting rain.

8

Morgan realized why Boots had balked at going on. The horse had probably saved his life.

Flooding waters roared through a deep gash in the land a few yards ahead. It seemed as if the river had changed course, gone wild, lashing angrily at everything in its path along an old dry wash.

The flash flood cut a swath twenty feet wide, four or five feet deep, tearing chunks out of the bank as it streamed past, widening the ancient streambed. He heard, above the din, the scream of horses, the hysterical braying of mules, the shouts of men like ragged pennants of sound flapping and fading in the angry lash of the rain. The sounds were eerie, almost unearthly. So, too, the din of the boiling torrent that devoured the land as it rushed toward the big river.

Morgan rocked backward in the saddle, the fear in him suddenly palpable, an iron thing so cold he could taste it in his mouth, so hard he could feel it pressing against his senses, numbing them like whiskey hot in the veins.

He knew that if he stayed there, the flood waters would take the ground from beneath him, snatch him up like a rag doll and hurl him to a watery death, bury him in a grave no one would ever find.

Turning Boots, Morgan felt the ground pull away from the horse's hooves. Currents he could not see, burrowing under the earth, were nibbling a new course for the sudden stream. He dashed toward Boots; The horse moved as Morgan tugged on the reins. His eyes swept the terrain, squinted against the pelt of rain. He reined the horse in a tight circle, clapped moccasined heels to the animal's flanks.

With the roaring of the floodwaters in his ears, Morgan sought high ground, knowing there was little likelihood he'd find any the horse could climb. The only high ground he'd seen had been steep bluffs bordering the river. Beyond those, the land was as flat as a pine board.

As he rode away from the flooded creek, Morgan saw someone waving to him. Just a shadow with the shape of a man, but enough to catch his attention. Turning Boots, Morgan guided the horse to the solitary figure. The man was afoot, stranded on a tiny island amid raging waters.

"Ho, boy. Help!"

The man calling to Morgan was Nat Sullard. His face was streaked with mud, his buckskins torn and sodden. Something seeped from under his hairline, something that looked like blood.

Morgan felt Boots fighting the bit as he drew closer.

Then, the horse stopped.

Another outlaw creek had formed, bursting through a new channel, slashing a separate course from the other, winding toward lower ground. Nat Sullard stood alone between two floods, horseless. All around him water surged, ravishing deep passages in the plain.

"I—I can't get no closer," shouted Morgan. "Look at it. It's ever'where."

"You got a rope?"

"Nope."

"Come on, Morg. We didn't mean nothin'. We was just jokin'."

"Huh? What're you talkin' about, Mister Sullard?"

"Just funnin' ye. Now, come on now. It's real important." Nat's voice quavered with fear. Morgan could sense the man trembling, shaking inside. Nat seemed to have lost his reason.

"I don't have no rope. This horse won't come no closer."

"You got to help me, Morgan. Your pa would want you to."

"Where *is* my pa?"

"I don't know. That water come down on us 'thout no warnin', God. Drownded, maybe. Morgan, you got to get me outta here."

"If you can get acrost that one stretch," said Morgan, "I can help you. Give you a ride out of here."

"Hell, I can't swim, Morgan."

"Me neither."

"Dammit, boy, this ain't no time to be holdin' grudges."

"I don't know what you mean, Mister Sullard."

"Oh, shit," said Nat.

"Where's your horse? Maybe I could go and fetch it."

"Swept off when it hit. Damn, boy, you goin' to come get me?" Nat's voice rose to a hysterical pitch.

As Morgan watched helplessly, Nat Sullard looked all around him. Water lapped at his moccasins. The island began to shrink. The lone trapper began to blur before Morgan's eyes as the rain fell harder than before. Wind-driven, the downpour lashed at Morgan's face, stung his eyes.

"Jesus," said Sullard.

"Maybe it ain't as deep as it looks," said Morgan, but he knew that was a lie. The water was deep and getting deeper. In another minute or two, he would have to ride away or the flash flood would sweep him up in its grasp. "You want to try and jump it, maybe grasp the stock of my rifle."

"Too danged fur," said Sullard.

"Where's everybody else did you say?"

"Scattered ever' whichaway," said Nat. "Hell, boy, we didn't mean nothin'. We was just a-pullin' yore leg."

Morgan had no idea what Sullard was jabbering about. He wondered if Nat blamed him for his predicament. The man sounded plumb addled. Morgan started to say something, when he heard a sound that sent spiders scurrying down the nape of his neck.

Just then, the waters surged and widened. A sudden rolling tide rushed toward the hapless Sullard. Like a battering wall, a two-foot-high wave careened from a point behind him, seeming to come from nowhere as if a giant had thrown out a bucket of water.

"Look out!" called Morgan.

Sullard yelled something, but Morgan couldn't hear him above the roar of water. He held on to the saddle horn as Boots turned, began to gallop away through the sheeting rain.

"Whoa boy," said Morgan, hauling in hard on the reins.

Morgan saw the wall of water hit Nat in the back of his knees, pitch him forward into the swirling maelstrom. There was a terrible force in the water, an energy that belied its small size. The way it hit Sullard, cut him off at the knees, told young Hawke that. That small wave was more powerful than a span of horses. Morgan's stomach knotted as he saw Nat flailing his arms, helpless against the surge of the flood. He wondered if Boots would be able to swim the swollen, surging wild creek. He slapped the horse's rump and withers with the reins, dug his heels into its flanks. Boots kicked and sidled, but he would not go near the flooding waters. Morgan knew that if he threw himself into the rampaging waters, both he and Nat would go under. Helplessly, Morgan stopped beating the reluctant horse. He turned in the saddle, saw Nat swept away, farther and farther from where the island had been until he disappeared where the twin creeks converged once again.

Morgan's senses were jumbled, spun with fragments of distorted sensation, as if something was snatching at his mind, clawing all his thoughts to shreds. Seeing a man go like that, down and under and away . . . a terrible thing. Morgan felt helpless, small, powerless, as if he was anchored in stone.

And, he felt something else, too, the odd feeling that someone was watching him. Maybe God. God or someone was watching him. He looked around, tried to look up into the rain, but the water blinded him.

He tried to shake off the spooky feeling, tried to erase the image of Nat Sullard's arms flailing against the force that plunged him to his death. It was hard to breathe as he thought about Nat trying to suck in air and getting only lungfuls of water.

"I—I'm sorry, Nat," he whispered, and then felt ashamed that he had said such a thing. To no one.

No, he had the curious feeling that *someone* had heard him.

Boots galloped to the west, away from the boiling, rampaging waters. Morgan gave him his head. Maybe the horse knew a safe place to go.

Morgan let the rain wash away his tears, slumped in the

saddle, broken by the death he had witnessed, beaten down by the maddening drum of the rain, scourged by the hard wind that drove needles into his back, flayed his face, stung his eyes.

He hated the country at that moment. Hated it as if it were a living thing.

But what about his pa? He could see his father swept away like Nat, helplessly trying to swim, going under, drowning. But, he had heard voices, hadn't he? Maybe his pa and the others were still alive. Maybe they were stranded, too, cut off from high ground by the flash flood.

He tried to remember from which direction the shouting voices had come when he had first heard them.

He knew he couldn't go back to the creek. Boots wouldn't go anyway.

Still, he had to do something.

Angrily, Morgan turned the horse, headed him on an angle that would take him toward the flooding creek higher up. He had no real sense of direction, could only bore into the rain using dead reckoning, hoping he would find a place above the wash where he could cross to the other side.

He had heard of flash floods before. His pa had told him about one he'd seen coming over the Cumberland Gap from Virginia when Morgan was growing in his mother's belly. Pa said it was mighty powerful and they were lucky he and his ma were on a hill when it swept through a big gully, washing away trees, wagons, everything in its path. His pa had told him about a family that had got caught in it.

"You ever see one, get to high ground fast," his pa had told him.

But where was high ground? The earth smelled dank, stank of dead animals and rotted vegetation. The land seemed flat, but from the saddle, he knew that there were small undulations in the surface.

Boots did not fight him, so Morgan knew he must be headed in a safe direction.

Then, he heard the voices again. Men shouting. Their voices sounded muffled in the incessant splash of rain. They faded and resurfaced on the wind currents. Boots jumped ahead at Morgan's prodding.

"Hold on to 'em!" someone shouted.

"Damn you, Hauser, grab that rope!"

"Hawke, come quick!"

At first Morgan thought they were shouting at him, but as he rode closer, he heard the horses and mules clamoring with frenzied voices. The mules brayed in terror and the high-pitched whinnies of the horses screeched on the wind like a thousand hawks in full cry.

The men floundered in mud, their horses caught in the quagmire. Some of the pack animals were belly deep in the sinkhole. Patch and Loonie were trying to pull their mule out of the bog. Jocko was whipping his horse to no avail, trying to pull a pack mule onto dry ground.

Dick Hauser, more muddy than the others, was twisted up in three ropes, horses pulling in opposite directions, panniers and packs askew, mud up to his knees.

Morgan's pa was trying to find a dry patch so that he could help Hauser, but he kept slipping on slick, boggy soil. Lem was covered with mud from head to toe, literally, and Morgan scarcely recognized him through the gauze of rain.

"Turn loose of 'em!" yelled Lem. "Dick, dammit, cut 'em loose."

Hauser, bewildered, tried to move, but the animals hemmed him in. They were terrified at being caught in the muck. Dick fell and got up again, even more encumbered than before.

Finally, Lem clambered over to Hauser, grabbed one of his arms and jerked him free of the bog and the tangled reins. He dragged Dick up to high ground as the stock clambered to gain footing in the mire.

Jocko DeSam floundered in mud up to his thighs. He cursed in French as he tried to catch up his horse. Packs were scattered on the edge of the quagmire, panniers rode cockeyed on the backs of the mules trying to find shelter in a grove of cottonwoods.

Looking Loon and Patch Sisco dragged a foundering mule from the edge of the swampy bottom onto higher ground, both pulling on a thick rope wrapped around a water oak's trunk. Morgan rode over to them and dismounted. He helped pull the jenny out, then shouted through the rain.

"Gimme the rope, Patch. I'll help Jocko."

"Take it, son," said Sisco.

Morgan loosened the loop around the mule's neck, gathered up all the slack. He ran to the other side of the slough and threw the looped end to Jocko.

"Grab a holt!" shouted Morgan.

Jocko, sinking even deeper into the swamp, reached out for the rope. His hand failed to grasp it. Morgan retrieved it quickly, stepped closer to the edge of the bog. He swung the loop over his head and hurled it toward DeSam. Jocko lunged forward, grabbed one side of the loop.

"Slip it around your chest," said Morgan, as Patch and Loonie joined him.

Jocko struggled, settling even deeper into the mire, until he was up to his waist.

"Quick!" yelled Morgan.

"He's got hisself in a sinkhole," observed Dave Sisco. "Damnfool pork eater."

Jocko rammed one arm through the loop. Morgan stood there helplessly as the Frenchman tried to get the other side around his shoulder. He seemed to be disappearing slowly into the sinkhole. The mud was almost up to his chest on his right side.

"Get your other arm through," Morgan pleaded.

DeSam twisted, shrugged the loop over his other shoulder, then sank against the rope, exhausted from his struggles.

"Hold on!" Morgan bent his knees, pulled up the slack. The loop tightened around Jocko's chest. Morgan crabbed backward, pulling hard. Loonie and Sisco stepped up and wrapped their hands around the bitter end of the rope. Their feet skidded on the gut-slick ground, but they managed to pull the Frenchman a few inches.

Jocko's hands kept slipping down the rope. The strands dug into his armpits, the loop squeezed his chest. He struggled to draw air into lungs that would not expand.

Morgan grunted and turned around, leaning forward until he faced Patch and Loonie. He strained against the tug of the rope, feeling his slick-soled moccasins slipping on the rain-soaked soil. But, he felt a give and moved forward a few more inches.

There was neither tree nor bush to wrap the rope around. The three men slithered to an angle, all tugging in unison. Jocko made no sound, except for the wheezing in his strangled chest.

On the other side, Lem and Dick saw the struggle taking place, but had their hands full trying to rescue the panicky horses and mules still stuck in the swamp.

"Let 'em go, Dick," said Lem. "We're only makin' it worse."

Hauser, exhausted, sank to his knees, releasing the single rein in his hand. The horse backed up, tried to buck its way free of the mud's suction. Lem grabbed him by one arm, dragged him away from the horses. The horses settled down, then, calmed by the men's retreat. They began to move their legs up and down, heading toward firmer ground.

"Maybe they'll get out by themselves," muttered Lem.

Hauser couldn't utter a word. When Lem released him, he sank to the ground, cold, wet and thoroughly discouraged.

The rain made the rope hard to hold. Morgan's hands kept sliding on the soaked strands.

Patch didn't have much energy left. Loonie was conserving his; wasn't much help.

Morgan turned around to see if Jocko was making any progress. It didn't seem as if the rope had moved for the past two or three minutes. In fact, it seemed as if DeSam had slipped back an inch or two.

The mud still gripped Jocko's hips, but his waist was out of the sucking clutch of the quagmire. He looked like a dead man, though. Morgan sighed, tried for a better grip on the rope.

"Jocko?" he called.

Jocko didn't answer.

"He looks daid," said Patch.

"Shut up," said Morgan. "Pull, damn you, pull."

"Testy, ain't ye?"

Morgan shook his head to shed rain from his eyebrows and bent forward, girdling his waist with the rope for more leverage. He felt the rope move and his chest swelled as he took in an exultant gulp of air.

Patch bore down, then, encouraged by the movement. Loonie, too, seemed to apply more effort to his piece of the rope.

"We got him goin', don't let up," panted Morgan. "He's a-comin', he's a-comin'."

It was true. Jocko slithered out of the tugging muck, his legs numb, useless. He twisted until he was on his back; his feet broke free of the sludge, his moccasins buried somewhere in the bog.

He looked like a corpse as he slid toward the bank on his back, his eyes closed, his chest barely moving.

Morgan and his helpers dragged Jocko out of the swamp. Patch loosened the noose around DeSam's chest.

"He ain't hardly breathin' much," said Sisco.

Morgan looked at the Frenchman. He looked blue in the wash of rain on his frozen face.

"Jocko? You alive?" asked the young man.

Jocko didn't answer.

Across the bog, Lem and Hauser watched as the three men bent over the body of Jocko DeSam. Hauser rose to his feet.

"He alive?" called out Lem.

Patch stood up, shrugged. He held the looped end of the rope in his hands.

Morgan knelt down and began slapping DeSam's face. He hammered a fist into Jocko's chest.

"Come on, Jocko, breathe, damn you."

Patch hunkered down, leaned his ear toward Jocko's mouth. He listened for a few seconds, shook his head.

"I don't think he's got no air in him," said Sisco. "Deader'n a willer stump."

"No!" shouted Morgan, and he grabbed the collar of Jocko's buckskins, began shaking him. "Don't you die, Jocko, God damn you, don't you dare die!"

Morgan's high-pitched plea seemed torn out of his throat. Loonie's eyes narrowed as he watched the boy shake the Frenchman as if trying to jar life back into his lifeless body.

When Lem heard his son's anguished cry, he started to trot around the bog.

"Hell, son," said Patch quietly, "what you gonna do if he don't come to—kill him?"

9

Jocko's chest heaved. He drew in a breath and his eyelids fluttered.

"Damned if Frenchie ain't come back to life," said Patch, wryly. "I done seen a miracle."

Morgan stopped beating on DeSam's chest and rocked back on his legs, suddenly ashamed of himself.

Lem and Dick arrived just as Jocko took his second deep breath and opened his eyes.

"Yore boy done pounded the breath right smack back in that Frenchman," Patch said to Lem.

"Jocko?" said Dick.

Lem glared at the man on the ground, then he looked up at Morgan. Morgan stared back at his father, a blank expression on his face. A feeling of lassitude surged through him.

Jocko sat up, gulping air into his lungs. He rubbed his chest where the rope had left its marks in the flesh.

"Ah," he breathed. "It is good to be alive."

The men around him, all except for Looking Loon and Lem, laughed.

DeSam wiped rain from his face, squinted up at the sky.

"Pretty soon, she stop, no?"

Morgan looked at the sky. The rain was slowing down, thinning out.

"You sonofabitch," said Lem. "You almost got us all kilt. Now we got to chase down stock. I got goods, goods bought and paid for, lost. I got to track it all down."

"Wonder where Sullard went to?" asked Hauser, trying to change the subject. Morgan saw that he was squirming over something. He wondered what his pa was so mad about. At the mention of Sullard's name, Morgan squirmed some himself.

Morgan cleared his throat. Everyone there, including Jocko, looked at him.

"You seen Nat?" asked Dick.

"He—he," stammered Morgan. "He got carried off."

"Carried off?" asked his father.

"Flood," squeaked Morgan. "I couldn't do nothin' to help him."

"Jesus," said Hauser. Patch looked away, but Morgan saw the look in his eyes. Jocko DeSam paled visibly.

"Having some goddamned fun were you, Jocko?" taunted Lemuel Hawke. "That's what your funnin' done, you bastard."

"I did not know she was coming a storm," said Jocko lamely.

"Maybe we better straighten this out right now," said Lem. "You want to lead us to the mountains, but you've done a piss poor job so fur. You give me one good reason why we should pack with you."

Jocko lay there, panting. He seemed unable to get to his feet.

"Yair, Jocko," drawled Patch, "why don't you tell Hawke there what you got up that sleeve of your'n. 'Pears to this old coon you been playin' high and loose with what you been doin' on this frontier. You bucked the major and he's one blood-thirsty company bastard, but you did it sneaky and I don't cotton to a man who runs out on a fair debt."

"Eh, Jocko, he pay what he owe, Patch." DeSam glared at Sisco.

"I been tryin' to figger how you come to owe the Major any coin as it is," said Patch, scrinching up his face. "You and him now used ter be close. You was his shadder, prac'ly; his right hand. Now, all of a sudden-like you and him is fallin' out. Don't make much sense."

Jocko heaved his shoulders in a Gallic shrug.

"What are you drivin' at, Patch?" asked Lem.

"Somethin' mighty peculiar 'bout Jocko here cuttin' out on his own, when he did. Either him or the Major's up to something. I got sour poke in my belly 'bout it."

"Hell, the Major sent men to bring Jocko back and kill us."

"I reckon he did," said Patch, but the look of puzzlement on his face stuck there like flies in spilt honey.

Jocko looked up at Lemuel.

"If I get up, you do not hit me, no?"

Lem clenched and unclenched his fists.

"I'm studying on it," Hawke said.

Hauser helped Jocko stand. DeSam's sodden leathers creaked and rustled. Mud dripped down his leggings onto his bare feet. He swayed there, unsteadily, for a few seconds. Lemuel glared at him, but made no move to strike him.

The rain became just a pattering, like light hail tapping on a sod roof, as scudding gray clouds thinned, blew eastward toward the Missouri at a fair clip. The wind flapped mildly at the men at the edge of the bog. Horses and mules still foundered, struggling to break free of the muck.

"Major says you're a spy for another fur outfit," said Patch, skewering his quarry on words it seemed to Morgan he'd held in his craw for a long time. Funny thing was, Jocko always swore by the Major, asked him and Pa to jine up with him back in Tennessee. Seemed Jocko was singing a different ditty now.

"The chest, she hurts," said DeSam. "I am trying to get the breath."

"You're breathin' same as me," said Lem. "Spit out what you got to say. You workin' for a company. Hell, it don't make no difference to me, I just want to know who I'm dealin' with is all. I heard tell of free trappers and company men and you been jumpin' twixt and tween ever since I met up with you."

Jocko heaved a draught of air and sighed deeply.

"Ah, what we must do, eh? We have to play the games with the companies. We have to follow the rules or the booshway, he throw us in irons. My friends, you know what we must do to take the fur, eh?

"I don't ken any of this stuff," said Lem. "All I know is that you played hob with the stock and damned near got us all kilt, not to mention what you done to Morgan there."

"It is to test the boy's mettle, no? I play the little trick. I see what he do."

Smouldering sparks of anger flared through Morgan's senses.

"You done got Nat Sullard kilt is what you did," said Morgan. He stepped toward Jocko, the anger in him raging to the surface.

"Hold on now, Morg," said Lem. "This is my fight." He turned to DeSam. "That boy's been tested a'ready," he said. "Maybe I ought to give you some testin', Jocko."

Jocko shrugged, lifted his arms, turned the palms of his hands upward, as if in surrender.

Lem relaxed his guard for a moment, indecisive.

Jocko swung around, hauled back his right fist and drove it

square into Lem's belly. The air rushed from Hawke's lungs as he doubled over in agony. His face purpled, swelled from the rush of blood to his brain. Jocko waded into him, swinging his left hand, which hooked into Lem's right temple. Lem staggered to one side. Jocko cracked his other temple with a right cross. Lem jolted sideways.

Morgan cried out, but was frozen in place, rooted to the ground in surprise.

DeSam kicked Lem in the groin. Lem rocked backward on his heels as Jocko charged in, pressing his advantage. The two fell to the muddy ground as the force of Jocko's lunge drove Lem off his feet.

Jocko grabbed Lem's hair and jerked him forward. The Frenchman lifted his leg. Lem screamed as Jocko's knee rammed suddenly into his genitals. He doubled up and Jocko kicked Hawke in the side, spinning him around. As Lem tried to gain his footing, DeSam threw Lem to the ground, pounced on him. He bit Lem's ear, gouged at his eyes.

Lem fought back, then, groggy from pain. He grabbed Jocko by the throat and pressed thumbs into the Frenchman's windpipe. He drew his legs back and kicked at Jocko's stomach.

Morgan started to rush forward, but Patch grabbed his arm, held him back.

"Let 'em fight it out, son," he said softly.

"Turn me loose, Sisco. I—I got to help my pa."

"You'll only get hurt yourself," said Patch firmly, increasing his grip on Morgan's arm.

Morgan wrenched loose from Patch's grip and shoved the older man in the chest.

"Leave me be, Patch!" Morgan yelled.

Loonie made a move to stop the boy. Morgan saw him coming and grabbed the handle of his knife. The Indian stopped. Patch nodded to Loonie, made a sign with his hands. Looking Loon held up both hands to show that they were empty.

Morgan started across the mud-sogged ground, his moccasin soles slipping. He saw his father roll on top of Jocko, then go underneath the more experienced fighter again.

Lem lost his grip on Jocko's throat, stabbed frantically with rain-slick fingers to get a purchase on DeSam's beard. Jocko grunted and plowed his right fist into Lem's nose. Blood squirted from both nostrils. Pain brought tears to the elder Hawke's eyes.

Morgan reached Jocko just as the burly Frenchman was about to slam his fist into Lem's face again.

Hauser stepped up but Morgan batted Dick's arms aside and bowled him over with the force of his rush. He ringed Jocko's neck with slender, deceptively strong arms, jerked him backward, wrenching hard to the left.

Hauser rolled out of the way as Morgan and DeSam tumbled backward.

Jocko flailed his arms, trying to get Morgan off his back. But young Hawke held on, squeezing DeSam's neck as he twisted it sharply.

"Aagh," grunted Jocko, finally grabbing Morgan's wrists, digging his mud-clogged nails into the flesh. He pulled mightily and loosened Morgan's throttling hold.

Lem scrambled to his feet, glared at DeSam as the Frenchman crabbed in a circle, regained his footing with a powerful thrust of his legs. Morgan, panting, pushed up to a squat, then stood up, fists clenched.

"You want to see what I'm made of, Jocko, you come on," said Morgan, his voice a wheezy whisper.

"Ah, the pup thinks he is a wolf, eh?"

"Morg, this is my fight," said Lem.

"Then you gang up on Jocko," said DeSam. "Two against the one, eh?"

Morgan stood there, breathing deeply now, flexing his muscles as if to summon strength enough to overpower the burly Frenchman.

"You come on, little boy. Jocko, he teach you how to make the fur fly, eh?"

The Frenchman, a grin on his face like a hideous stain, beckoned Morgan to engage him.

Morgan gulped in a deep breath, lowered his head and charged. The trapper sidestepped like a dancer and slammed a knot-hard fist into Morgan's left ear.

Morgan's head exploded with shattered fragments of bobbing lights. A dark blinding hole filled in the empty spaces. Tears stung his eyes and he choked on the sudden pain that flooded him like a grease fire.

Jocko stuck out his leg. Morgan stumbled headlong but stayed afoot, the pain jabbing through his ear. He whirled, the rage in him a towering black funnel, fuming with heat.

DeSam, surprised that the boy didn't go down, was caught off guard as Morgan charged again.

Morgan barreled into Jocko, his head like a battering ram slamming into Jocko's chest, knocking him backward toward the mudhole.

Jocko tried to grab Morgan's head, but the young man twisted free of the trapper's grasp and grabbed Jocko's leg at the calf. Morgan tugged the leg out from under Jocko and stalked in a short circle. Jocko fell, his leg seeming to twist out of its socket at the hip.

Morgan pounced on his back, rode him into the ground.

Jocko cursed in French just as Morgan grabbed the Frenchman's neck and squeezed it with both hands. But the burly DeSam rolled underneath Morgan and broke the hold, leaving Hawke with two handsful of air.

Lem, Dick, and Patch crowded closer, watching the young man and the Frenchman battle for position on the slick, muddy ground. Lem lunged everytime his son did, pantomiming his movements, growling instructions low in his throat.

"Grab him, Morg."

"Come on, Jocko," yelled Hauser.

Patch said nothing, but watched as Morgan slid away from Jocko's grasping hand.

"Damn little pup," said Jocko, as he got to his feet and hurled himself in a low crouch after his young assailant.

Morgan started to stand up, then hunkered back down to take the brunt of Jocko's charge. Just as DeSam struck his knees, Morgan dove over Jocko's back, but he was caught up short as Jocko grabbed an ankle with both hands. Morgan kicked free, but his forward motion was halted and he fell to the ground, knocking the wind from his chest. His ear throbbed as if a stake had been driven through it, clear to the brain.

Jocko held on, twisted Morgan's ankle. Morgan cried out in pain, kicked three times to free himself from the man's iron grip.

"Move, son, quick," ordered Lem, crouching in a pugilist's stance. "Get away from the bastard."

Morgan shook free of Jocko's hand and crawled out of reach.

Jocko stood up, breathed in air like a blacksmith's bellows.

"Keep your hands off him, Jocko," said Lem.

"He start the fire," said DeSam. "He can put it out if he want."

"Morgan," said Lem to his son.

"Leave me be, Pa."

Morgan's eyes slitted. He wondered if he could whip Jocko. The man outweighed him. He was stronger. He seemed unbeatable. But, he didn't like being treated like a boy anymore. Maybe if he beat Jocko, the other men would look at him differently. Even his pa. It would be something to do, all right.

Suddenly, Morgan felt strong. He felt a surge of strength through his muscles. He saw that he was as tall as Jocko. Yes, he was leaner, but a lot of the weight DeSam carried was fat. If he could just stay out of his way and pound at him, maybe Jocko would get tired and go down. Morgan would give him a sound drubbing then, beat him into the muck until he begged for mercy.

"I'm ready, Jocko," breathed Morgan, a sense of lightness in his head, in his body.

"Eh, Jocko he is ready, too."

Morgan filled his lungs. Then, he charged toward Jocko. But just as Jocko reared back a cocked fist to throw at him, Morgan glided out of reach. He jabbed a left to Jocko's head, caught him on the jaw. It was a glancing blow, but it gave him satisfaction.

Jocko spun around to catch Morgan, but the boy made an even wider circle.

Morgan darted in and out, jabbing, ducking, swinging his head from side to side.

He lashed at Jocko with light blows that seemed to cause no harm. But it was evident to the others that Jocko was irritated. They watched as Jocko grabbed for Morgan and came back with empty hands.

Morgan gained confidence each time he struck Jocko and came away untouched. He began to take more chances. He darted in closer and used his feet. He kicked Jocko in the leg when Jocko was looking for a fist. He socked him in the chin when Jocko was bent over holding his knee.

"You stop running, you little whelp cub. Jocko show you how to fight."

Morgan said nothing. Jocko stalked after him now and Morgan stayed out of his way. He kicked backward, once, when it seemed he was running away, and then he came up on Jocko's side and rammed two hard punches into the back of Jocko's neck.

Jocko staggered under the blows and Morgan kicked him behind the knee. Jocko went down on one leg, seemed to struggle to get back up.

Young Hawke followed up on his advantage. He kicked Jocko in the side, then kicked him hard in the face, landing the heel square on DeSam's mouth. Blood oozed through the cracks in Jocko's lips. Morgan stepped in close and hammered rapid blows to Jocko's cheeks, each blow landing harder than the one before.

Jocko held up his arms to escape the punishment, but Morgan, the fury in him hardened now to a cold metallic purpose, struck again and again until Jocko's beard was running with blood, until his cheeks were mushy as apple pulp.

"*Assez,*" yelled Jocko. "*Suffisante. Arrête.*"

"He wants you to stop, Morgan," said Patch.

Morgan grabbed Jocko by the hair, held his head up and delivered one last smashing blow to his nose. There was a *crack* and blood gushed from DeSam's nostrils like a crimson fountain.

"That's enough, son," said Lem. "You've done beat him. Beat him fair."

Lem looked around at the others to see if anyone challenged his assessment.

Jocko slumped to the ground as soon as Morgan released his grip on the man's hair. They all listened to the ugly sound of Jocko's wheezy breathing. Blood sprayed from his nose in a rosy cloud, peppered the wet ground with tiny red spots.

"What are you going to teach me now, Jocko?" Morgan mocked as he stepped away, panting for breath.

Jocko waved a solitary hand in surrender.

Lem walked over to his son, patted him gently on the back of his shoulders.

"You done mighty fine, Morg."

Morgan nodded, too weak to say anything. He started to shake then and hoped his father couldn't see it. It wasn't fear, but more like the excitement that came when he had big game in his gunsights, something he couldn't control.

"You'll be all right," said the elder Hawke. "It's like buck fever. Sometimes you get it when it's all over."

Morgan looked at his father gratefully, nodded again.

"Let's get shut of this bunch," said Lem. "Ain't a damn one of 'em a bit of good."

"You mean go to the mountains by ourselfs?" Morgan asked.

"We can do it. With a sight less trouble, too."

"What happened, Pa? Why did you get so mad?"

"They played a joke on you, son. It was Jocko's idee. They snuck up on you and stole the horses and mules. I didn't find out about it until it was too damned late."

"I thought they run off," said Morgan, shaking his head.

At that moment they all heard a rumbling, then the ghastly sound of splintering wood and men screaming.

"The river!" yelled Hauser. "There's trouble on the river."

Morgan looked off to the right. It sounded so close. He hadn't realized how near they were to the Missouri.

All heads turned as the first cries for help wafted their way.

And, above it all, the horrible sounds of men in agony, men screaming with their last breaths above the roar and tumult, the crunching sound of a keelboat being crushed by something big and heavy.

10

Major Angus MacDougal saw the downed tree jutting out from the bank at a bend in the river. Too late to warn the helmsman, he knew. Instead, he cursed at the snag that caught the prow of the keelboat. The curse died on his lips, however, as the craft spun wildly in the current and slammed against the bank beneath the bluffs.

One of the men yelled a warning and Angus looked up at the bluff. The rain had stopped, but there was a fine mist hanging in the air like shreds of gauze. Atop the cliff, a chunk of limestone slid down a crevice, then stopped. The chunk teetered, then continued its slide, dislodging other formations in its path.

"Look out!" yelled Fletcher Bancroft. "She's gonna come right down on us!"

Josie Montez, manning one of the poles amidships, measured the angle of the boat, its position in the river and the course of the small avalanche in a single instant. His brows furrowed and his face blanched to a sickly pallor. He threw down his pole, backed away, headed toward the stern. If the rocks all came down and struck a ledge, they could strike aft of the bow. Men would be hurt, possibly killed.

"Major," said Montez.

MacDougal looked at Josie, saw where he was going and moved in that direction.

A huge section of limestone broke off the cliff and tumbled straight down, struck an outcropping and caromed out over the boat, landing on the foredeck of the keelboat. The craft shuddered like a wounded beast under the impact; timbers shivered the length of the vessel. Wood cracked and splintered as the shower of rock smashed the cargo box, fractured deck planks and surged deep into the hull. Men at the bow scattered as they frantically tried to escape the destruction, but two of them were pinned by a large slab of rock that had sheared off another when it struck. The boat tipped queasily, throwing men against the gunwales, slamming them against iron davits, knocking them to the still quivering, shattered deck.

Loosened by the miniature avalanche, the whole side of the bluff seemed to teeter for a moment, then come apart as pieces of rock broke off, knocked other pieces loose and dislodged still others in random downward flight. Tons of soft limestone roared downward, smashing trees and rocks, exploding into fragments that flew off and struck the boat all along its length. The men on the second craft, behind the lead boat, tried to swing clear, but rammed into the stern of the Major's vessel. The prow impaled itself in the lead boat's scuppers, stuck there like a giant wedge, stuck fast as if it had been bonded there by nails and iron straps.

Several men on the Major's boat were struck by flying rock and shattered wood slivers. Some went down, bleeding profusely from head and facial wounds. Men screamed and cried out in terror and pain as the keelboat broke up and began to founder. A man grabbed the side of his head and came away with half of his ear in his hand, scalloped neatly by a razor-sharp fragment of stone. Those on the second boat scrambled over the sides and some leaped up on the railings and jumped into the swirling waters of the Missouri, following the men escaping from the lead boat. Those who could not swim sank like stones and drowned in a strangling silence deep under the current.

"Men, don't panic," shouted the Major as he fought off choking clouds of dust. "Fletch, get some men and start throwing our supplies toward the bank. Get as much as you can off this boat and then get the hell off yourself."

"There's no time for that," said Montez. "This boat is going down."

"Montez, shut your mouth," said MacDougal. "Men, get the traps off or you won't earn a penny this year."

Although MacDougal appeared outwardly calm, there was a shrill edge to his voice. The deck tilted under his feet and the boat seemed to sink deeper at the bow.

"Men, save what you can," said MacDougal. "Save yourselves."

Bewildered trappers stared blankly at MacDougal as he stumbled through the debris and climbed over the side of the boat, rifle in hand. In a moment, he was wading toward shore, fighting the pull of the current, leaning hard to port, straining to keep from being sucked under. He kept his eyes on the bluff above, as if ready to duck another shower of rocks. Other men began to crawl over the sides of the boat, following him. A few grabbed their rifles, others abandoned ship with celerity, forsaking their belongings as well as their injured companions.

Fletcher led the pack.

Josie Montez started to follow the panicky men, but the keelboat began to break up, the hull cracking in two amidships. The halves of the boat tilted and he was hurled to the port side, slammed hard against the gunwales. He fought for breath as the craft wallowed in its death throes, water filling its ballast compartments, tearing at its bowels like a feeding whale.

On the opposite bank, Dick Hauser clambered up out of the thick brush, halted. A floundering man, weighted down by wet buckskins, reached the bank and held up a hand. Dick stooped down, grabbed the man's wrist and hauled him ashore.

The man lay there for several moments, spitting water, gasping and choking. Dick knelt down beside him.

"You gonna live, child?"

The man looked up at Hauser.

"Who might you be?"

"Why, Dick Hauser. And you?"

The man sat up, wiped water from his face with a swipe of a swarthy paw.

"Josie. Josie Montez."

"Then you'd be Spanish Jack's brother."

"You knew Jack?"

"I did. Drunk his grog enough."

"Were you there when he was murdered?"

Montez's tone gave Hauser pause. He scratched his head.

"Why, I don't rightly recollect. I 'member the tavern a-burnin' down."

"I am looking for the man who knocked my brother cold, set the fire and left him to die," said Montez.

At that moment, Patch and Looking Loon appeared out of the willows and brush where they had stopped and waited for Hauser to look around first, staring at the sinking lead boat, then at the stricken second vessel. They stopped when they saw Hauser talking to Josie Montez.

"Well, I couldn't help you there," Hauser said warily. He got back to his feet and looked out at the river.

———.———

Most of the surviving men on the lead boat waded ashore and gathered around the Major, who had walked well clear of the unstable bluff. Men from the second boat began to abandon ship in a more orderly fashion, making for the eastern shore, small clots of survivors sticking together like bewildered rabble. It was clear to them that their boat would be useless unless it could free itself of the sinking lead vessel. A few men foundered in deep water and were helped ashore by their companions.

Farther upstream, Morgan and Lem emerged from the underbrush. They saw the men on the opposite shore and the bodies on the deck of the lead keelboat.

"Pa, lookit," said Morgan.

"'Pears that bluff done toppled down and broke that boat up, kilt some men."

"What can we do?"

"Don't look like we can do much. I'm thinkin' it's a damned good thing we wasn't on that boat. Looks like the Major's done got hisself some troubles that ain't gonna go away right quick."

Morgan felt a surge of elation, despite the soreness in his legs and fists. He could see men on the deck of the lead keelboat who appeared dead or sorely wounded. There was an arm sticking out of the rubble next to the cargo box. The arm did not move; the hand attached to it hung limply like some grave marker made of human flesh. The side of the bluff where the massive face had sheared off was dry, like an old dark scar. Dust still hung in the air and Morgan heard a series of low, pathetic moans coming from somewhere inside the boat. Men still scrambled over the side of the stricken vessel, some limping, holding onto their legs, others staggering like drunks, grasping bloodied heads, capless, their buckskins dark with sanguinous stains.

There was a stench in the air that reminded Morgan of hog butchering, right after their bellies were slit and coils of intestines spilled out onto the ground like newborn snakes, all a-glistening, slick with an oily slime.

Beyond, he saw men gathered around MacDougal. The Major looked up, seemed to catch Morgan's eye. MacDougal scanned the bank where Morgan stood, as if looking for someone. Morgan's gaze shifted upstream where Hauser stood with another man, a swarthy Spaniard who looked somewhat familiar.

"What're you lookin' at, Morgan?" asked his father.

"That man with Dick. He look like someone we know?"

Lem saw the man. He studied him carefully.

"I can't put him in no place."

The Spaniard looked downstream.

"He's lookin' at us, Pa."

"I see it."

The Spaniard looked away, began speaking to Hauser.

"He's askin' Dick about us, Pa."

"Aw, Morgan, you don't know what he's a-sayin'."

"He's pointin' at us," said Morgan.

"Probably askin' who we are."

It struck Morgan then who the man was. It was just a feeling, an odd feeling, like he had seen him before, but he knew he never had. His thoughts went back to that last night in St. Louis, when his pa had come up to Willa's room and caught him naked with Spanish Jack's daughter. He remembered Jack coming into the room, the fight, the broken lamp scattering fire and oil all over the bed, the walls. Spanish Jack was knocked cold and his pa couldn't get him out. The tavern owner had died in the blaze that burned the building to the ground.

"I'll bet that's Spanish Jack's brother," said Morgan softly.

He heard his father draw in a quick breath, saw him look upriver at the Spaniard.

"Damn. Might could be. Looks to be a Spanisher."

"Pa, let's go. I don't like it here. Ain't nothin' we can do."

"Yep, we best get on," said Lem.

Josie Montez called to them.

"You there."

"Don't answer him, Pa," said Morgan.

"He's a-comin' this way."

Morgan grabbed his father's hand and pulled on it. Lem followed reluctantly.

"Come on, Pa."

"I'm a-comin'."

Montez started toward them, then thought better of it when he realized he had no firearm. The Major started barking orders at the trappers on the opposite bank, urging them to unload the boats. Some of the men began to venture back to the boats, sheepish expressions on their faces. Some clambered aboard the second vessel and began throwing lines to those on shore. Others began rigging a line to the first boat, which was sinking badly, breaking up in the surging current. Pieces of sundered trees and other flotsam floated past, testifying to the power of the current with freshly fallen rain propelling it with enormous force. It wound past the banks, shouldering the boats up against the bank, surged on like an angry serpent mining a new path through the earth.

"You there! Hawke!"

Lem and Morgan halted, turned toward Josie Montez.

"I will catch you!" yelled Montez, holding up a clenched fist. "You will pay! Goddamn you!"

"Let's go, Pa," said Morgan.

"I ought to settle this now," said Lem.

"How?"

Lem patted the handle of the knife hanging on his belt.

"No, Pa." Morgan spoke softly, a chill inside his belly like a cold fog.

Montez drew his own knife, held it up. He beckoned to Lem with his free hand. There was a grin on his face, visible even at that distance.

"Some other time!" Lem yelled.

"You bet, *cabrón!*" Montez slashed the air with the blade of his knife. "I will kill you like you killed my brother!"

A muscle quivered along Lem's jawline. His eyes narrowed for a brief moment. Then he followed Morgan into the underbrush.

When they returned to the muddy buffalo wallow, there was no sign of Jocko DeSam.

Some of the horses were missing, others stood disconsolately under still dripping trees, their heads hanging in weariness. After they caught up their own stock and mounted Boots and Hammerhead, Lem pulled the mules to the north.

"We goin' to the mountains by ourselfs, Pa?"

"I reckon. We got all what we need."

"But we don't know where to go."

"I expect we can find what these fellers found, all right."

"How?"

"We'll just foller the river until we come to the mountains. Then we'll go up 'em and find the beaver, the mink and marten."

"Do you know how to cotch 'em?" asked Morgan.

"I can figger it out, son. Silas, he tolt me how to set the traps, bait 'em. I got me some castoreum in Saint Louie for bait."

Morgan remembered Silas coming to their farm, showing them a beaver pelt with its thick shiny fur. That was when Silas gave him the medicine horn, told them about the riches in the mountain streams.

"What's 'castoreum'?"

"It's beaver piss, I reckon. Silas says it plumb draws them to the traps set in the water."

"Must have a smell to it."

"It's 'bout as powerful as skunk, I reckon."

Lem made a clicking sound in his mouth. Hammerhead began to move around the perimeter of the mudhole. Morgan, on Boots, followed, checking the pan on his .64 caliber Kentucky-made rifle to see if the powder was dry. There was only a small amount and it was damp. He spent the next several moments wiping the pan dry, repouring fine powder in the pan, blowing away the excess. He checked the striking flint, adjusted it slightly so that it sat just right in the leather, not so firm that the flint would break when it struck sparks off the frizzen. Satisfied, he began to take notice of the country again.

Later, Morgan's thoughts drifted back to other times.

"Pa, I got a question."

"You go right ahead, son."

"Are most people bad like Josie Montez? Always wantin' to fight or kill somebody for no good reason?"

"I reckon some of 'em is."

"Seems like we keep runnin' into trouble ever'where we go. Meetin' up with bad men."

"Women, too," said Lem wryly.

"You mean Willa Montez?"

"And your ma."

"Ma? Ma bad?"

"She wasn't bad exactly, son. She just did some bad things. Run out on us. Made some mistakes, maybe."

"I wish I could have got to know her better," said Morgan.

"Might have helped if she had stayed home more, not had all them fancy idees."

"I guess she didn't like us much."

Lem laughed harshly, but he knew his son was not trying to be funny. Morgan was so serious the way he said it and it was really wasn't anything to laugh at.

"I reckon there are some good people, Morg. They all probably start out good enough, but they's hard lessons in this world and maybe some folks don't take kindly to teachin'. I figger a man goes bad because of what other men do to him, maybe when he's just a boy, or a-growin'. Seems like it just keeps gettin' passed along, the bad, until it's real hard for a man to be good anymore."

"You mean it ain't no use bein' good, then?"

"You can be as good as the next man will let you, Morg."

"It don't seem like nobody cares much. I mean, what's inside a man, how a man feels about things. I seen more bad men than good since we left the farm."

"I reckon you have at that."

The sun showed for a moment, then clouds slid into the hole above the two riders to darken the sky once again.

"Sometimes I wish we could just be all by ourselfs."

"Well, that ain't growin' none, Morg. It ain't natural. You don't learn no lessons. You get hard inside after seein' enough meanness in the world. You get to knowin' ain't nobody goin' to help you except your own self. You don't lean on nobody and you don't let nobody lean on you. That's what you learn if you're payin' attention."

Morgan chewed on what his father had said, but he was still trying to make sense of what had happened to them. Going down the Natchez Trace they worried about robbers and Indians, but the only trouble they'd ever had was when they were in a town or around other men. And they had had nothing but trouble ever since leaving St. Louis. He wondered if going to the mountains was such a good idea after all. And he wondered, if they'd ever make it out there alive, if they'd get back to civilization alive.

There were times, like now, when living seemed such a hopeless chore. A damned chore, like chopping wood and then seeing it all go up a chimney in smoke. And then have to do it all over again. The thought of it made him feel tired. It just didn't look like there was much to look forward to, even if they did make it to the mountains and got rich trapping beaver and such.

They skirted a marshy spot full of cattails and blackbirds, a low place where the river made another bend. Scudding gray clouds still hid the sun, draping the country in gloom.

"What about Silas, Pa?"

"Huh?"

"Is Silas Morgan a good man?"

"Good as any, I reckon. Why?"

"Oh, nothing. I was just figgerin' if we ever saw him again how it would be."

"Why, it'd be just fine, Morgan. I named you after him. He was always right with me. Your ma didn't like him much."

Morgan said nothing, but his thoughts scrambled wildly to find some meaning, something he could rest easy on, like a pillow, where it was all safe and quiet and there were no bad men in the world.

They followed the river as it meandered south, then north again, stretching westward toward the falling sun.

"I reckon we can find our way, long as we foller this here

river," his Pa said late that afternoon. It had been so quiet, his voice startled Morgan.

"I reckon, Pa."

The sun was out again. Morgan's buckskins and moccasins were dry. He was hungry and his belly growled at the emptiness. He kept thinking of the fight with Jocko, wondered where the Frenchman had gone. A few moments later, when the sun was an hour above the western horizon, he had part of his answer.

They heard voices. Many voices.

His father reined up, put a finger to his lips.

Morgan rode up alongside his father, a puzzled look on his face.

Lem slid out of the saddle. Morgan did the same. They tied up the animals to sturdy trees and took their rifles with them as they sneaked toward a hillock, crouching low.

The voices grew louder.

Lem lowered himself to the ground, crawled the last few feet to the top of the mound. Morgan slithered up beside his father. They looked down on a strange sight.

There, where the river took one of its innumerable bends, a horde of men were breaking camp, tearing down hide and canvas shelters, packing up goods, loading them on horses and mules, storing them in pirogues and canoes that bobbed on tethers along the bank. Others were digging in the side of the hill that sheltered them from the view of anyone on the river.

Overseeing all the bustle stood Jocko DeSam, atop the bank, pointing to caches yet undug. He barked orders in French and English.

"Pa . . ." Morgan whispered.

"I know. Jocko knew what he was a-doin' all the time. Likely those men been a-waitin' on him."

"What's that those men are diggin' outen that hill?"

"Looks to be trade goods or such."

One of the men dropped a box and several kegs rolled out onto the ground.

"Nails?" Morgan asked.

Behind them, they heard a soft, rustling sound. Turning, they saw Patch and Looking Loon walking up. They were carrying rifles, their stock tied near where the Hawkes had left their horses and mules.

Patch crawled up beside them. Looking Loon stayed behind, crouched low.

"Whiskey, most likely," said Patch.

"Whiskey?" said Lem. "I thought . . ."

"Illegal as hell," said Patch. "That damned Jocko. I knowed he was up to no good."

"What's he do with it?" whispered Morgan.

"Swaps it to the Injuns for furs. Likely he's got trade guns in those blankets, too. Injuns'll pay dearly for such."

"Guns illegal, too?" asked Lem.

"Mebbe not, but you give a Injun a thunder stick and you're jest askin' him to use it on you."

Looking Loon slid up to them, silent as smoke.

As the four men watched, some of the trappers began pushing off in pirogues and canoes, cargo piled high between two paddlers in each small boat.

"We best get along," said Patch. "Jocko won't like it none, us knowin's he's smuggling whiskey upriver past the booshway."

"I reckon," said Lem.

"You want company?" Patch asked. "Just me and Loonie there."

Lem looked at his son. Morgan shrugged.

"We'll see how it works out," said Lemuel.

"This chile knows you been burnt by folks," said Patch.

"We mind our own business, me and Loonie. Don't look in another coon's poke. They's some trails you might not know about yonder." Patch nodded toward the west where the light was strongest in the sky now that the sun had disappeared behind a cloud bank.

"Where you headed, exactly?" asked Morgan.

"Have to see when we get to the mountains. They's plenty of places a man can trap and trade if he knows what he's a doin'."

"I just don't want to run into Jocko again," said Morgan.

Patch looked at the boy.

"Why, I don't reckon he much wants to run into you, neither," said Patch, a wry smile playing on his lips. "But you never know for sure what's around the next bend of the river, son. You know that Josie Montez will be on your trail?"

"Yeah, I know," said Lem.

"He'd be a bigger worry than Jocko, I'm thinkin'."

Lem looked away.

"Best we keep movin'," said Patch. "Montez got him a horse from the Major's herd on shore, swam him to the boat for his rifle and possibles. Me'n Loonie'll keep a eye or two on our backtrail."

Lem nodded but said nothing.

The four men slid back off the hillock, walked to their horses, the sounds of the men on the river fading away.

Just before he mounted up, Morgan looked at Patch and Looking Loon as they rode off ahead.

Maybe, he thought, Sisco wasn't a bad man, like the others. The only thing he knew about the silent Delaware was that Loonie had eaten his dog.

Morgan got sick to his stomach every time he thought about it.

As if reading his thoughts, Looking Loon turned around and looked at Morgan, doubled up a fist, feinted with it, then ducked as if avoiding a blow. He then made the sign of approval with the same hand. And grinned wide.

11

Patch pointed across the river.

"See that lake yonder?" he asked Morgan and Lem.

Father and son nodded.

"Lewis and Clark called it Sugar Lake. River takes a long northern swing here. If'n we cut across due west, we'll meet up with it again. Take us less'n a week and we'll gain some ground on Jocko and the Major."

"Be fine," said Lem tightly.

"Fill your canteens. Ain't much good water 'twixt here and there."

Morgan watched as Patch unslung a large furry pouch and walked to the river.

"What's that water jug made out of?" asked young Hawke.

"Buffler balls."

"Huh?"

"Shot me a buffler, made a canteen out of its ball sack, glued hide to it. Keeps the water wet and cool."

Morgan didn't know whether to believe Sisco or not.

They filled their canteens at the river and rode on across the prairie. Patch led them with an unerring eye, always looking back to see if anyone was following them. Lem and Morgan did the same. Looking Loon ranged far ahead, scouting and hunting. The men fed on his kills of rabbit, squirrel, prairie chicken, quail and fawn at night under clear, star-flocked skies in sheltered depressions while the Delaware sat away from them, watching, listening.

The silence was eerie at times, and Morgan felt it like a cloak on his shoulders. When the coyotes howled, he crouched closer to the fire until he got used to their plaintive singing, but the sound always startled him when he first heard it.

"What made that bog you got caught in?" Morgan asked Patch one night.

"Old buffler waller, son. Used to be a passel of 'em along the river, but the Injuns and trappers comin' up the Missoura run 'em off."

"Are the buffler big?" asked Morgan.

"Why, I reckon some of 'em get bigger'n a horse," said Patch. He made sign with his hands and Loonie grinned.

"Will we see any?"

"Shore, son. And a mite more, too. If you see buffler, you'll likely see Injuns."

"Are the buffler good to eat?"

"Best vittles on God's green earth," replied Patch. "Onliest thing is, the Injuns figger they own 'em. And one tribe owns 'em someplace and another tribe in another place, so you always got to watch out where you are when you shoot a buffler."

"You think we'll run into Injuns?" asked Lem, scooting

closer to the fire. There was a chill blowing off the river and this was the first fire they'd had that was big enough to warm a man.

"Biggest trouble we're likely to have is with them scurrilous Blackfoot," said Patch. "Andy Henry come back to St. Louie last year with some ha'r-raisin' tales. Near ever'body thought he was dead."

"Where are these scurry Blackfoot?" asked Morgan. Patch didn't laugh.

"Mostly where the fur be, but they's places we can go, I'm thinkin', and if we keep a sharp lookout, we can keep our hair."

"How'd you find these places?" asked Lem, backing off from the small fire. He no longer looked into it because it blinded him to the night. The fire was dying anyway.

"I want to hear more about the Blackfoot," said Morgan.

"You ever heard of Colter?" asked Patch. "Drouillard?"

"I reckon not," said Lem. Morgan shook his head.

"John Colter now. There be a mountain man. Ever hear tell of Manuel Lisa?"

"We've heard about *him*," said Morgan.

"Back in ought seven, Lisa and a bunch traveled up this very river, built a fort at the mouth of the Big Horn, that's a river what runs into the Missoura. He come back in ought eight with beaver a-plenty, and marten, mink, lynx, muskrat, too, got ever'body fired up in St. Louis, by gum, and General Clark hisself got George Drouillard, Tom James, me, and about three hunnert or more men to go up there and trap those beaver ponds. We got up to Fort Manuel, that's what Lisa called it, went on up to Three Forks Basin to set our traps. We was lookin' all over creation for the place, when them Blackfoot jumped us. Kilt three men who was scattered out scoutin' trails. They robbed them, they kilt them and then come on the rest of us a few days later. Kilt a whole bunch, including Drouillard. Some of the brigade pulled out, but some of us stuck with Andy Henry.

"But them damned Blackfoot swarmed down on us again and took the heart out of all of us, scattered us all over them mountains like wild partridge. Henry, he set out for the Snake and I come back to St. Louis with nothin' to show for it. Last year, I went back up the Missouri with the Major and we done pretty good. We thought Henry might have lost his hair, but he showed up last summer lookin' like a hard winter, which he done had. He come in with forty packs of beaver. That gave us all heart and here I am again, ready to find me some plews."

"What about the Blackfoot?" asked Lem.

"Oh, they'll be lookin' after their huntin' grounds, but I learnt somethin' last winter. They don't much like them high places when the snows come in thick, but the beaver, why, they do just fine in their mud-and-stick lodges. I got me the idee to go some deeper into those mountains. I stuck it through last winter, and Lisa said it was the worst he'd ever seed. So, we might stay out of the way of the Blackfoot, least until spring."

"I hope so," said Morgan dreamily.

Lem looked at the silent Delaware, wondering if he understood what Patch had been saying. Looking Loon didn't appear to show any interest in the conversation. He just sat there, grinning idiotically.

"How come you got an Injun partner after all that trouble with the Blackfoot?" Lem asked.

"Oh, Loonie, he ain't like them other Injuns. He's right tame, compared. He don't have much use for the Blackfoot, neither. His brother was one of them kilt with Henry's bunch. Loonie would as soon kill a Blackfoot as a snake."

———·———

Morgan did not count the days, but marked their passage westward by the rivers Patch Sisco pointed out to them. They passed the Platte, the Nodaway, the Tarkio, rode north and camped one night at the confluence of the East and West Nishnaboina rivers, just to avoid running into other trappers. They rode south again, following the Missouri. Patch pointed out Council Bluffs to them, rode around a hunting party of Otos, always staying well away from the Missouri until nightfall, when they filled their canteens.

Everyday they saw deer and the wide paths of buffalo herds. Morgan wondered when they would see buffalo, but he kept silent. He began to get a feeling for the land that was strange to him. He had never before seen so much space all at once—the land, the sky, the distant horizon, all seemed new to him, as if he was walking on ground no one had ever trod before. Every sunrise was startling to him, each sunset more spectacular than the one before.

It was sometime in June when they camped on Soldier River, and a few days later, they saw Blue Lake, and beyond, Blackbird's grave. It was early July, the days having passed in a haze of sun and rain and always the land stretching out before them and receding behind them. Morgan's pulse beat faster and he began to feel a part of the country as if it was where he was supposed to have been all his life. He played cruel tricks on Looking Loon, hiding one of his moccasins while Loonie bathed, putting bugs in his possibles pouch when the Delaware wasn't looking, sticking a live blacksnake in his saddlebag where he kept his dried food. Loonie acted surprised each time he discovered something alien among his belongings and yet he never did more than flash Morgan an idiotic grin.

"You ought not to tease that Injun, Morg," said his father.

"I don't mean no harm."

"One of these days you'll go too fur, and he'll get his dander up."

"I don't think he's got no dander to get up," Morgan cracked.

———.———

Morgan shook Patch's shoulder gently. This was the morning the old trapper had promised to take the boy hunting. Loonie had told Patch of a water hole laced with deer tracks, some two miles from camp. Morgan and Patch had scouted the hole the night before, selected spots where they might sneak in and wait for game should the wind be right.

Fog hung in the tall grasses, motionless in the still dawn. Patch stepped softly, following a swath that only he could remember from the night before. Morgan stepped in his tracks, careful to make no sound. His ears seemed tuned to the slightest sound. The silence was acute.

They came to the edge of the water hole. The cream light in the eastern sky barely made the water visible. There were two knolls some seventy-five yards from the pond, each separated from the other by a distance of fifty yards.

Patch grabbed Morgan's shoulder, turned him toward the knoll on the right. Morgan nodded and set off for his spot. Patch disappeared in the high grass. When Morgan sat down in the grasses, he could not be seen. The wind was at his face. He looked off to the left and could not see Patch, but knew he was sitting there, hidden in the swale.

The land lit up gradually, the shadows pulling across the water hole, gold touching the tips of the grasses, turning them tawny, the pond taking on a pink glaze. Morgan listened intently, heard the distant piping of a bird he could not identify. Then, he heard the rustle of grasses and his senses tautened like rawhide drying in the sun. A mosquito sang in his ear, but he sat stockstill, peering toward the sound of the whispering grasses.

The pond lay in a shallow depression, a high bank on three sides. The deer would have to come down into it. The walls would slow them down if they tried to get out in a hurry. Morgan studied the pond carefully, figuring all the ways a deer might run if he and Patch missed their shots, or if something spooked the animals before they could touch off shots.

Minutes snailed by in an agony of waiting. Finally, the grasses parted and a deer stepped out of the swale. It stood there, stiffly, sniffing the windless air, its ears flicking as they moved in half-circles. Morgan's heart froze as the deer, anterless so that he could not tell if it was a buck or a doe, looked straight at him. Then it lowered its head and moved toward the water hole. A moment later, another deer came out of the same swath, not so warily as the first, but moving slowly, its slender legs jerking with each step.

When the second deer got to the water and bent its head to drink, Morgan took a bead on the first animal, which stood to the right. It had already slaked its thirst and stood rigidly still, its head facing off to the east. Morgan figured Patch would take the one closest to him.

Slowly, he brought up his rifle, careful not to slide the barrel against the grass. He stopped his motion as the second deer lifted its head, water dripping from its chin and muzzle.

Morgan held his breath, listened to his pulse tap out the seconds as time crawled by slower than a snail through thick grass. It seemed to him that the deer could hear his heart pounding, that they could see him holding the rifle he had not yet aimed.

Finally, the second deer dropped its head down to the water and began to drink.

Morgan eased the muzzle of the rifle downward, fixing his right eye on the blade front sight. He held steady on the deer's flank where its heart should be, just behind the shoulder. He let his breath out in a silent whisper. He took another breath, held it. His finger curled around the trigger, squeezed.

The flint struck the frizzen, showered sparks into the pan. There was a *poof* as the fine powder ignited, shot flame through the touchhole to the main charge. The rifle roared and bucked against Morgan's shoulder. White smoke and orange flame belched from the muzzle. The smoke obscured the two deer and everything between Morgan and the water hole.

Morgan heard another explosion to his left a split-second after he fired and knew that Patch had taken his shot, as well. Morgan listened for the sounds of hoofbeats, but heard nothing. He rose up, grasping his medicine horn. He stuck the plug in his teeth, pulled it free. He poured fresh powder into the palm of his left hand, mounded it up over an imaginary ball. Quickly, he drew his fingers into a cone, poured the powder down the barrel. He shook the loose grains from his palm, brought the rifle up, tamped the stock to knock the powder to the bottom.

He dug patch and ball from his possibles pouch, placed them over the muzzle. He started the ball with his thumb, took his wiping stick and rammed the load home, tamped it down tight. He shook fine powder from the smaller horn into the pan, blew the excess away.

The smoke cleared as he walked toward the water hole, reloaded, the frizzen knocked down over the pan. He checked the leather scrap and flint to see that they were tight and straight. Patch met him where the two deer lay, their hearts smashed, their eyes glazed with the frost of death.

"You shoot true, son," said Patch.

"So do you," replied Morgan, looking at Patch's deer. Its

tongue was caught between its teeth. It had dropped in its tracks, a .62-caliber ball through its heart.

"With a little seasonin', you'd do to ride the river with."

"What's that mean?" asked Morgan.

"Means a man can count on you. When his hair's standin' on end or his belly's full of wooly worms."

"I hope so, Patch."

The two men gutted out their deer, skinned them and used the hides to carry the choice chunks of meat back to camp. Along the way, they stopped to rest on a knoll. It was still early and the earth smelled sweet and summery. Bees plumbed the wildflowers and prairie birds chortled in the greening grass.

"Let's take a look at that powder horn you got there."

"That's my medicine horn," said Morgan, making no move to hand it over.

"Set store by it, do you?"

"I do."

"How'd you come by it?"

"A friend of Pa's give it to me."

"Looks like a buffler horn, all right. Kin I look at it, son?"

"Sure," said Morgan. He slipped the medicine horn from his shoulder, handed the carrying thong to the old trapper.

Patch took the horn, held it to the light.

"Mighty fine work," he said. "Good polish to it."

Morgan said nothing, but beamed inwardly at the compliment.

Patch studied the symbols, cocked his good eye, brought it close to the horn.

"These be Absaroky markin's," he said. "Crow. You got yourself a Crow powder horn, son."

"I know. Silas told me."

"Silas Morgan. He might of got it off one he kilt, or he could've traded for it, I reckon. He say which?"

"No, I reckon not," said Morgan.

Patch handed the powder horn back to Morgan.

"Do you know what those markings mean, Patch?"

"Big medicine, fur as I know. Maybe you might need it."

"What do you mean?"

"Nothin'."

But, there was something in Patch's craw. Morgan noticed lately that Sisco watched Lem a lot, as if trying to figure him out. It wasn't spying, exactly, but Patch showed an uncommon interest in Lem Hawke.

"Is it somethin' about my pa?"

Patch jumped as if startled. An expression fled across his face too fast for him to hide it.

"He's packin' him a load is all."

"What do you mean?"

"The man keeps lookin' over his shoulder and at night he don't sleep good."

"I seen you lookin' over your shoulder, too."

"Ain't the same. He's lookin' for something what ain't there."

"Ain't nothin' there when you look, neither," said Morgan.

"I know what I'm lookin' for," said Patch. "And, he still don't sleep real good. Like he's fightin' someone in his dreams."

"He's always done that."

"Always?"

"Since—since Ma left us."

"He ought to get him another woman right quick."

"He don't like 'em much, I reckon."

"Welp, he'll find him one, maybe. I think he's got Josie Montez on his mind some, too."

"Pa ain't afraid of nobody," said Morgan.

"Might be he ought to be a peck afraid of Josie Montez. That 'uns got a scalp or two on his belt."

"He better not try to stick Pa. I'd shoot him dead."

"Montez ain't the kind to walk up to a man and say what for. He works best at night behind a man's back."

"You don't worry about us none, Patch, hear?"

"I hear you, Morgan." Patch opened his mouth as if to say something else, but he closed it quickly. He got up, then, hefted his meat and set off for their camp.

He noticed that they took a different way back and Patch stopped every so often to listen. Once or twice, he lay flat on the ground and put his ear to the earth.

Everytime he did that, the hairs on the back of Morgan's head bristled and he shivered with the odd chill of it.

Josie Montez waited until after Jocko DeSam had beached his
dugout on the sandy bank. He had been riding along the river's
course watching the Frenchman and his companion, staying
just out of sight until the two decided to come to shore. He had
long since lost the trail of the Hawkes, Sisco and the Delaware.
But, he knew that DeSam's bunch were strung out for miles on
the Missouri, way ahead of the Major's brigade.

DeSam climbed out of the boat, lashed its prow to a tree near
the shore. Dick Hauser, in the stern, grabbed his and DeSam's
rifles and stepped over the gunwale onto the bank. He handed
DeSam's rifle to him and looked downriver. Another craft
rounded the bend: a canoe carrying three men and goods.

Montez rode up and dismounted a few paces from DeSam.

"Ah, you leave the Major's brigade," said DeSam in English.
"I thought you would come by boat."

146

"Let us speak the tongue," said Montez in fluent French. He looked at Hauser, cocked his head.

The other boat, a canoe, shot onto the shore a few yards from where DeSam's dugout lay tethered. The three men spoke in rapid French, secured their craft and began unloading their cargo, carrying it to a stand of cottonwoods.

The river rose and fell with its own surging pulse. This was a wide point and the water flowed gently, calmly. The sky was cloudless, blue as periwinkle, the air, warm and summery, seethed with insects, mayflies and yellow-winged butterflies. Two more canoes carved a path to the shore and beached upstream. The babble of voices speaking in French drifted through the willows and cottonwoods, strangely disembodied.

"But, yes. Jean Lafitte taught you well our language."

"Jean taught me a lot of things," said Montez. "Did you get the goods I had brought up for you?"

"They are in the boats. We found the cache, as you said we would. We went by the forts at night. It is good."

"Smuggling is my trade," said Montez.

"And Lafitte? What has become of that pirate?"

"He prefers to be called a privateer. He did not fight for the British at New Orleans. He helped the Americans."

"Andy Jackson? I heard in St. Louis that the American soldier won."

"They made him a major-general. He won the battle with ease, but the war was already over. There was a treaty, but the American government did not sign the papers. Many British died."

"And which side did you fight on?"

"I fought with Jean. He is going to ask for a pardon."

"Ah, fat chance."

"He will get something," said Montez.

Dick Hauser grumbled under his breath. Another pair of canoes rounded the bend, skidded across the flattened waters, twisted toward shore. Upstream, a plover piped a plaintive curlicued trill at the presence of intruders as men stalked the shore for firewood.

"You want me to go away, Jocko? You and him don't want me to know what you're sayin', I know."

"We are old friends, Dick," said DeSam. "It is easier for us to talk in French, *non?*"

"It don't make me no never-the-mind," grumphed Hauser. "If you and him want to talk that gibberish, it's right fine with this old coon."

DeSam ignored Hauser, who began unloading the dugout.

"This whiskey you sent me will buy many furs," said DeSam.

"I don't give a Spanish curse about furs," said Montez. "I am after bigger game."

"Ah, Lemuel Hawke, the greenhorn. You have been tracking him?"

"I lost his trail."

"So it is in this country. The trails criss and they cross and they lead into bad places. It is not a place for trackers. You follow the river, she takes you where they must go. Everybody, he follows the river. You want this man, eh?"

"He murdered my brother. His life must pay for Jack's."

"That is one way to look at it, my friend."

"There is another?"

"You do not care about the furs, but the beaver skin is money. This Hawke, he has no money. Let him get the furs. When he comes to trade or sell to the *bourgeois*, you kill him and take what he has. Then you have the revenge and you have the money."

"Killing the two pigeons with one stone, eh, Jocko?"

"Revenge lasts but a moment, no? The money lasts a little longer."

Montez laughed drily.

"Besides, you may get three pigeons with the one stone," said DeSam.

"What you say?"

"The boy, Morgan. I do not think he will be a camp-keeper, that one. He will trap. He will get the furs, too. You take them."

"Jocko, Lafitte could learn something from you."

"Ah, that is so," said DeSam, his chest swelling.

"Maybe you are right," said Montez. "Maybe I will catch this Hawke when he has something to give me."

"You will probably have to kill the boy, too."

"I have already thought to do this. One, two, it makes no difference."

"As long as they are not together when you do it," DeSam said.

"What is this you say?"

"I think they will both fight hard if they are together. It would be two against the one, *non?* You shoot them like the turkey. First one, then the other."

"Like the turkey," Montez repeated. "Yes, that is good, I think."

Jocko made a gobbling sound. Both men laughed.

——.——

Nearby, where the Nemeha River flowed into the Missouri, men dipped buffalo-hide pouches into the lesser river's depths, bringing forth water for the cooking fires. Clouds in the western skies glowed with an apricot tinge. A prairie wind blew warm and sweet from the west, redolent of tall grasses and sugar in the stems, tasting of summer flowers.

———.———

The days were sweet except when it rained or the squalls rose up on the Missouri, driving the men to shelter. The nights, most of them, were just as sweet under fair skies strewn with stars, a gibbous moon gliding like a silent wraith's eye across silver-shadowed velvet. Morgan wondered at the change in the country, the sights of strange birds and the tracks of unknown animals—the badger, the prairie chicken, the coyote.

Morgan hated unpacking the mules every night, packing them back up the next morning when it was still dark. He hated tending to their sores, thumbing grease on raw patches worn by rope and leather, on wounds caused by the constant rubbing of the panniers against their hides. Bone-weary, his head still spinning images of the sights he had seen that day, he crawled into his blankets and let the tiredness seep out while he watched the stars, trying to detect their faint movement. He smelled the buffalo chips, the reek of a skunk, the fetid stench of beasts he had never seen. When at last he slept, he dreamed of beaver and elk, of mountain goats and furry things shining on a rainbow-colored hill deep in the Rockies.

———.———

Another night he dreamed of the buffalo bones they had seen that day, still a-wonder at their size and multitude. At one place, he suddenly noticed that the skulls were all facing toward the east.

"Injuns hold that the buffler is some kind of special animal, made just for them. They thank 'em when they kill 'em and promise to feed their kin when they die and sleep under the grass," Patch told Morgan. "They turn them skulls so the spirits can see how they treated 'em after they kilt 'em."

It was very spooky for Morgan to hear this from Sisco. He felt as if he was riding through a graveyard and could almost feel the spirits of the buffalo in the air. The Indians were strange people; they knew things that nobody else did.

Morgan noticed that the bluffs along the river had changed, lost their trees. Now, they were grassy and stark against the skyline. The air had a dryness to it, beating warmly against his face. The land was an ocean of grass as far as he could see and sometimes the silences filled his ears like whispers of far-off waves seething on a seashore.

There were times when he felt swallowed up by the country, lost in it. He knew they had come a long way, would go a lot further before they came to the beaver ponds in the mountains. He felt hopeless some days and overwhelmed with the size of the sky and the land. He wished, at odd moments, in the silence of his mind, that they would see a road, or a house, a person waving to them. When these wavery, half-formed images appeared, he felt smothered by a powerful homesickness, a deep sense of loss and a fear of never returning to civilization. He wanted a girl to talk to, someone to touch, to hold him, to say hello or ask him how he was feeling. He had to take deep breaths and put such thoughts from his mind, for they were fearsome thoughts, dark and foreboding, as if something terrible would happen to him and no one would ever know that he had left the earth. No one would ever find his grave or his bones, and if they did, it would not matter, for no one would know that he had wandered into the wilderness and died. Worse, no one would care.

Patch and Looking Loon led them over old game trails,

mysterious highways trampled by countless legions of animals in migration along the course of the big river. Morgan derived some comfort in knowing that living creatures had passed by and that, probably, other men had hunted the creatures and eaten them and then gone on living.

They swam in blue lakes, rode past a few silent graves of unknown men that pulsed with meaning for young Hawke. The graves had no markers and Patch did not know their names. Morgan felt himself being drawn deeper and deeper into a strange land with loud eerie silences, endless skies and deep nights when the sky was black and sparkling with winking stars, cold and distant, mockingly quiet in a hushed ocean of space.

"That be the Big Sioux River," said Patch, one day. "We've been makin' good time. Likely see buffler any day now."

Morgan looked around for any signs of buffalo. He saw only a young killdeer trying to take flight, the last of its baby-down clinging to its wings, the orange fuzz glowing with sunlight. It wasn't until the next day that they saw sign of buffalo, piles of dung, some fresh, that littered the trail for miles.

"Might be we'd better bunch up some," Patch told Lem and his son. "Where they's buffler, they's Injuns."

"Where are the buffalo?" asked Morgan.

Patch shrugged. "They's liable to be anywheres. This is fresh sign. They been here. They come and go. And, if they're in a hurry, they don't care what's in their way."

That night, they made no fire and camped well away from the junction of the James and the Missouri rivers. Patch explained that they were deep in Indian country and needed to stay quiet and listen to every sound.

"You might hear a bird what ain't no bird," he told the Hawkes.

Morgan stayed awake a long time, listening to every night

sound. He finally closed his eyes, fell asleep in the soft wash of silence.

Toward morning, young Hawke was jolted out of sleep, rolled out of his blankets, grabbed his rifle from force of habit. He groped blindly in the dark for his possibles pouch and powder horns.

The ground shook and there was a distant rumbling, like muffled salvos of thunder. Morgan's throat tightened in fear and his stomach quivered with a sudden spasm.

"Pa," he shouted, breaking the constriction in his throat, "earthquake!"

"Be quiet," said Lem, a disembodied voice in the thick pitchblende of night.

Morgan's senses clamored to make sense of the sounds and the tremors in the earth. He strained his eyes trying to see in the darkness. He saw only dark shapes, drew in dust through his nostrils, tasted grit in his mouth. He breathed in the thick aroma, tried to isolate it. It was like nothing he had ever smelled before, an invisible steam, thick and gamey.

"Steady, son," whispered Patch, so close to Morgan that when the youth turned, he brushed against the old trapper's shoulder.

"What is it?" asked Morgan.

"Buffler," grunted Patch. "Listen."

The rumbling sound grew louder until it was a thunder in Morgan's ears. The dust in the air thickened.

The dawn sky paled as a milky light bleached the eastern horizon and the streak along the skyline spread. Morgan saw the dust hanging in the air like a smoky cloud.

"Get your mules packed, your horses saddled," Patch said to the Hawkes. "We don't want them buffler to trample us."

Morgan's blood surged at his temples. He heard the pounding of his heart beneath the low rumbling of the distant herd.

Lem stepped to his son's side. "Stay close," he said. "Let's catch up those mules."

"Feels like that earthquake back in Kentucky," said Morgan, as they headed for the feeding mules. The animals were dim shapes in the pale dawn light. "But Patch says it's buffalo."

"Likely," said Lem, bending down to untie a hobble.

"Where we goin', Pa?" Morgan found the other mule and grabbed its trailing halter rein.

"Either away from 'em or right close, I reckon," said his father.

As the sky lightened, father and son worked faster, loading the panniers onto the pack mounts, stringing rope through the O-rings. Within fifteen minutes, they had their horses saddled.

"Check your priming pan," Lem said to Morgan.

"Already did, Pa."

Lem grabbed the lead rope from his son. "I'll pull the mules, son. You stay right close."

The two climbed into their saddles. A moment later, Patch rode up, his flintlock laid across his pommel. Morgan thought he looked different, and as the trapper turned toward the east, Morgan saw that Sisco had smeared his face with dirt. Looking Loon loped up, his rifle hanging from a thong looped around one of two saddle horns.

"Like to get us a buffler," said Patch. "But this be Pawnee country. That herd might be chased or it might be running towards somethin'. No way to tell, rightly. But, we got to be mighty careful. If you shoot a shaggy, stay with it until we can skin it out." Patch paused. "I declare, this coon's mouth is plumb waterin'."

Morgan laughed nervously. "Where are they?" he asked.

"Off yonder, five miles or so, I calcalate."

"They sound close."

"If they was real close, you couldn't hear me a-talkin', son. You'll know when we get onto them."

They rode through dust thick as rain, toward the sound of the running herd. Morgan didn't see how there could be that many animals in the whole world. Patch didn't hurry, but followed behind Looking Loon, who kept his horse at an easy walk, as if he had time to spare. The thunder grew louder in Morgan's ears and he fingered the trigger guard of his flintlock, eager to see a buffalo through the veil of dust and bring it down with a lead ball. He wondered if they would see Indians, Pawnee or Sioux, maybe Blackfoot.

He lost sight of Looking Loon, then Patch disappeared, too. It was then that Morgan realized that he was deaf to all but the sound of the huge surging herd. It was like standing under a pounding waterfall, like being in a cave high on a hill where the thunder boomed and echoed until you were inside the thunder and the thunder was inside your head.

"Pa," he croaked, trying to keep his voice from shrilling to a high pitch. "Pa," he called again, more loudly.

But Lem had disappeared into the dust and Morgan had no bearings.

It was as Patch had said: nobody could hear him now, even if he shouted. He could feel the herd's hoofbeats through the ground and through his horse, through his bones and flesh, until he could feel the earth shaking under him, making his hair stand on end.

Morgan's horse balked, tried to turn away from the herd.

"Boots, dang you."

The horse danced in place for a moment, then stepped forward in a slow, sidling gait. Boots turned his head and shook it vigorously. The horse's eyes were wide, the whites as bright as boiled hen's eggs.

Morgan felt a rush of air against his face. At first, he thought it was from the unseen buffalo, but the breeze freshened and he knew it was the morning wind, rising off the earth. He saw his father's back, then, dimly beyond, the shapes of Patch and Looking Loon. The dust wavered, then wafted to the southwest and lifted so that he could see a long way. The sun's rim slid above the eastern horizon.

Then Morgan saw a sight he would never forget. A dark wave undulated like a shaken blanket, rolling with the thunder, moving northwestward. He did not know what it was, for he had never seen anything like it. He realized, a moment later, that he was looking at a vast migration of buffalo and when he took his eyes off the main body of the herd, he saw individual animals, with their shaggy humps, their oversized heads, horns sprouting from curly tangles of wooly hair.

Then they swung toward him.

Boots tried to back away, but Morgan dug his heels in the horse's flanks and yanked down on the reins. Ahead, Lem and Patch were halted, his father leaning over, listening to something the trapper was saying. A few yards from the two men, Looking Loon waited in silence, watching the herd stream by like a river gone mad.

Suddenly, Boots swung around, fighting the bit.

"You ornery cuss," said Morgan.

Then, his face went white and he froze, letting the horse have his head.

Several buffalo sheered off from the main herd and, led by a monstrous bull, charged straight for Morgan. He heard his father shout something, but he couldn't hear the words over the clamor of the herd. Boots bucked and fishtailed, jerking Morgan out of the saddle. Morgan's hand gripped his rifle. He landed with a thud square on his butt as the horse galloped away in panic.

The giant bull, followed by dozens of bellowing buffalo, changed course and headed straight for the downed youth. For a frozen second, Morgan thought he must have landed in hell and the devil was bearing down on him, steam jetting from his nostrils, eyes black as anthracite.

13

More and more of the shaggy beasts left the main body of the herd, following the lead of the huge errant bull. From their vantage point, Lem and Patch could see the stream of bison clearly, dozens of others following blindly after its maverick leader.

"What in hell is that out front?" asked Lem.

"That's the biggest bull buffler I ever seed," breathed Patch with a reverence that made his statement sound like a prayer.

Morgan, scrambling to his feet, saw that there was no place to run. He glanced down at his lock, saw that his fall had jolted the flint loose; it had slipped sideways inside the leather and hung crooked in the gooseneck cock. He jammed the flint back in the jaw as he rose to his feet, but he knew it was still not square. He thought it would probably shatter when he pulled the trigger.

The buffalo bull was no more than fifty or sixty yards from

him, shrinking the distance at a nerve-grating pace. There was no time to bring the rifle to his shoulder and take aim. Morgan gritted his teeth, swung the rifle to bear on the bull and cocked the hammer. He prayed silently that the powder in the pan was still dry as he slapped the frizzen in place with his thumb. He thought of the sight on the end of the barrel, saw it lined up at the bull's chest.

When the charging animal was ten yards away, Morgan squeezed the trigger.

Sparks flew from the pan, peppering Morgan's face. He didn't even feel the heat. White smoke and flame belched from the muzzle, obscuring the charging bull and the other buffalo from his view. He turned and began to run, bore to his right, in the opposite direction the herd was running.

Patch and Lem both raised their rifles at the same time when they saw Morgan fall.

"I'll take the big bull," said Patch. "You try and drop the cow directly behind it."

They each took aim. Just as Morgan fired his rifle, Lem squeezed off a shot. He did not hear the report from Patch's rifle, and a cloud of flour-white smoke mingled with his own, so he knew the old trapper must have fired at the same time.

"Got him," said Patch, triumphantly.

"I can't see a thing," said Lem.

"Me, neither. Not no more."

"Where's Morg?"

Patch said nothing. But they saw the band of buffalo turn back in toward the main herd slightly, and as the smoke cleared, they saw Looking Loon riding hard toward the place where they had last seen Morgan.

"Load it back up fast," said Patch, pouring powder down the barrel of his rifle.

"I got to get to Morgan," said Lem.

"You better have something to shoot, then. We got us trouble, son."

Lem heard it then, the high-pitched yelps, the *ki-yi-yi-yi* of many voices. The hairs on the back of his neck stiffened and he brought his powder horn to his mouth, bit the stopper and pulled it free of the spout. His hand trembled as he shook powder into his rifle barrel. He had no idea how much powder he had poured, but he let the horn dangle and fingered a ball and patch from his possibles pouch. Out of the corner of his eye, he saw Sisco ramming his own ball down with his wiping stick. Time seemed to slog by as he hurried the loading.

Patch rode off, toward the place where Looking Loon had gone, leaving Lem to finish seating the patch and ball.

The cries of the Pawnee hunters rose and fell in the thunderous roar of thousands of hoofbeats. Lem heard no gunshots, figured the Indians must be hunting with bows. He could see only buffalo as he rode toward the place he had last seen his son.

"Morgan," he called and knew that his voice was lost in the din of the passing herd. He dodged a lone cow, its hump bleeding from a single arrow that jutted from its hide, waggling like a feathered semaphore.

He rode through patches of blowing dust, smelling of buffalo and trampled grasses, plowed earth and mangled flowers. He saw the big bull, lying dead on its side, its blue tongue lolling from its mouth, dark blood streaks drying on its shaggy coat, its great head cocked at an angle, eyes shiny glass, smoked up from death.

A dozen arrows bristled from the bull's hump and neck, all with different markings, in various colors, on their shafts. Strips of rosy flesh hung in tatters from one of its black horns.

Lem stared at the hulk, measured it in his mind, weighed it. His facial muscles pinched in a look of amazement. His mouth went slack. He saw no sign of Morgan, felt a slight wash of relief that his son did not lie dead underneath the enormous bison.

"Over here," called Sisco.

Lem saw the cow he had shot. It had veered off its course and gone several yards behind the bull. Next to it, on the ground, he saw Morgan. With a heart that felt as if it was sinking through his chest, he rode up on Patch, who was kneeling next to Morgan.

"The boy's all right," said Sisco. "Got him a knot on his head the size of a quail's egg."

Lem dismounted. He and Patch helped Morgan to his feet. Morgan staggered as soon as the two men released his arms. Lem reached out to break his fall, but Morgan pushed his father's arms away.

"I'm just fine, Pa."

"You look kinda peeked to me," said Lem.

"You able to ride?" asked Patch.

Morgan nodded. He ran a patch down his barrel with the wiping stick, began to reload his rifle.

"Let me get some vittles off'n that bull and we'd better skeedaddle. When them Pawnee women come up to skin out the kills, they'll raise a holler. We'll have so many Skidi braves on our butts, we'll think we was hit by a swarm of Georgia hornets."

"Boots run off, Pa," Morgan said, after Patch ran over to the dead bull.

"I know," said Lem. "You ride with me and we'll find your horse."

Morgan climbed up behind his father.

"He took off thataway," said Morgan, pointing.

The horse had not gone far. Boots stood alone, reins dangling, as if waiting for its master. Lem rode up alongside

Boots, and Morgan jumped into the saddle. He leaned forward and grabbed up the reins.

Buffalo streamed past like a great surging river, their thundering hooves beating strong in Morgan's ears. He gaped at them in awe, feeling the immense power they generated, admiring their speed and grace. They did not seem driven, but surged forward of their own volition, kings of the prairie, lords of the earth itself.

He wanted to chase after them, ride among them, try and capture the feeling of running before the wind, racing in their midst like one of them. He had the strange feeling that he could become like them, could feel their hearts beating inside his own, feel their muscles and sinew as part of his own body. He felt lightheaded and giddy just looking at this tide of beasts flowing over the prairie like unchained lightning. It was their giant pulse that hammered at his temples. It was their raw energy coursing through his veins; it was their savage blood flooding his heart like wildfire, pumping through his flesh like volcanic lava.

"Morg, come quick," called Lem.

Morgan shook his head free of his wild thoughts, saw his father down on the ground next to Patch. They were both looking at the dead bull's chest. He rode over, dismounted.

"Son, looks like you brought this bull down," said Patch, pointing to the chest wound. "Them balls in its sides didn't do no more'n scratch his curly hide."

Morgan stared at the hole. Patch stuck his finger through it, grinned.

"Mighty fine shot, Morg," said his father.

"Let's get us some boudoins and cut out his heart and liver," said Sisco. "Then we best hightail it for other parts."

"Ain't we gonna get any of his meat?" asked Lem.

"Not if we want to keep our hair."

Morgan and Lem exchanged glances. There was no mistaking the look of warning on Sisco's face.

The Hawkes helped Patch turn the buffalo over on its side. As they watched, the old trapper cut through the animal's belly. He slashed into the dead flesh with brute force, ripped downward toward's the bull's tail. Working quickly, he pulled twenty or thirty feet of lower gut out of the bloody maw, cut it near the anus.

"Strip out that shit, Morgan," said Patch, "press it all out best you can whilst I get the heart and liver. Might even take a cutlet or two from under its spine."

Patch handed Morgan the slimy intestines. They slithered through his fingers, fell to the ground. Reluctantly, he picked up the serpentine mass.

"Do it over yonder," said Lem, pinching his nose.

Morgan carried the intestines a few yards away, began to work the fecal matter out the cut end.

Patch cut the heart free of its sac, severed the sinew around the liver. He then forced the body cavity wider and reached in, began cutting filets, sawing them, slashing them loose. He took one of the kidneys, then fell back, bloody and exhausted.

"Best we pack all this up and get to ridin'," he gasped. "Tell your son he can finish working the boudoins on the way."

Lem nodded, dazed by all that he had seen. The buffalo still streamed by, but he no longer heard the yips of the Pawnee.

"Here, son," said Sisco. "You take this heart. Be good eatin' when we can make us a fire."

Morgan took the bull's heart. It was heavy in his hands, slick with blood, grainy with fat. He stuffed it inside his shirt. It felt slimy against his skin. Patch handed Lem the kidneys, stuffed the filets in a saddlebag.

As the three men were mounting up, they heard a sound, then saw Looking Loon racing toward them, his horse's tail and mane flying. Behind him, three young Pawnee braves chased him hard, yipping and yelling at the tops of their voices. Morgan raised his rifle.

"Best not shoot yet," said Patch. "Could be they're just funnin'. Pawnee blood runs hot when they're a-chasin' buffler."

"But they might kill Loonie," said Morgan.

"Yep, they might."

Looking Loon ran a straight course for them, then changed direction. Two of the braves followed as if they were pulled along behind him on strings. The third veered slightly to intercept the Delaware if he continued riding in the same direction.

"They're goin' to catch him," said Lem.

"If you shoot, shoot at the Pawnee horses," said Patch.

"Why?" asked Morgan.

"Might not help. They hold their horses in high favor. But, if we kilt them young bucks, we'd have Pawnee on our backs clear to the Rocky Mounts."

Looking Loon hauled hard on his reins, turned his horse once again. He charged the lone brave riding to cut him off. This surprised the other two Pawnee, and they scrambled to change direction. The Delaware jabbed the butt of his rifle at the lone Pawnee and struck him in the chest, knocking him from the back of his pony. The brave somersaulted backward and landed on his feet. He shook his bow at Loonie, who wheeled his horse in a tight circle.

"Let's shoot them two horses out from under those bucks," said Patch, bringing his rifle to his shoulder.

Morgan had already taken aim on one of the braves. He lowered his sights, led the horse and squeezed the trigger.

The ball struck the pony behind its right foreleg, smashing through ribs, tearing up arteries, shattering veins. The animal's forelegs crumpled. The brave flew over the pony's head, landed in a crumpled heap a few yards from the stricken mount.

Patch shot the other brave's pony in the neck. It staggered a few yards, then fell over, pinning the Pawnee's leg underneath. Morgan heard a bone snap. The Pawnee's face was expressionless and Morgan wondered at that. The pony was kicking all four legs, trying to regain its footing.

Morgan was already reloading his rifle when Looking Loon caught up with them. The Indian looked at Morgan, grinned. He made the sign of a man wearing a belt. Morgan dropped his head, remembering. The buffalo bull's intestines were wrapped around his waist like a sash, forgotten in the excitement. The bull's heart bulged inside his shirt, staining the fabric with its blood.

"Let's light a shuck," said Patch, spitting a fresh ball and spit-soaked cloth patch down his barrel. He rammed the wiping stick down as he prepared to ride away. Looking Loon spoke to Patch in sign. Morgan could make out some of it. The Delaware was talking about mounted men hunting, and he was indicating the Pawnee were close.

"We're ready," said Lem impatiently.

Patch pulled his mount to the north.

But their way was blocked. The herd had split and buffalo were streaming in all directions, scattering like quail before an unseen threat. Patch halted, and Looking Loon began talking to him in sign. Morgan watched as buffalo streaked past them, veering sharply when they saw the four riders in their path.

"What do we do now?" Lem asked Patch.

"Looking Loon says that Pawnee split up this herd. Injuns'll be ridin' all through both main bunches, chasin' after strays."

"So?"

"So, it looks like we're caught in the middle."

"I don't see no Pawnee," said Lem stubbornly.

"Pa, look," said Morgan.

"You boys hold steady now," warned Patch.

Lem twisted in the saddle, saw what Morgan had seen.

Five Pawnee braves rode toward them from different directions. They met up about three hundred yards away and fanned out. They carried bows at the ready, arrows nocked.

Looking Loon made several signs to Patch. Sisco nodded.

"Yep," said Patch aloud. "That'll be the big chief hisself, Little Antelope. And, that's his onliest son with him, that lean one wearin' three eagle feathers in his hair. He be called Turtle."

"You know them?" asked Morgan.

"Sorta."

"They don't look too friendly to me," said Morgan.

"They ain't friendly at all," said Patch. "Just hold back your water, boys. Don't do nothin' lessen I say to."

Little Antelope rode up to the dead and gutted bull, halted his horse. The other braves with him stopped at that place, too. The Pawnee chief looked down at the bull. He leaned over and broke off the arrow that was sprouting from its hump. He looked at it, then showed it to the other braves with him. They each grunted.

"That was his arrer in the buffler," said Patch, his voice pitched low.

"He can't claim it," said Morgan, sharply.

"Keep quiet," whispered Lem.

Little Antelope rode around the bull while the other Pawnees sat their horses, none of them moving. They all stared at the four interlopers. Morgan saw that their faces were smooth, their features sharply defined. They wore only breechclouts and moccasins, carried knives and iron war hatchets, arrows in quivers slung over their backs. Each had an arrow nocked to his bowstring.

Little Antelope began speaking, not to anyone in particular, but loudly, almost shouting. Morgan tensed, although he could not understand a word. He looked at Patch out of the corner of his eye. Patch sat his horse calmly, did not even twitch.

Finally, the Pawnee chief rode toward them, stopped a few paces away. He pulled his arrow free from the string, laid his bow and the loose arrow across his bare legs. He continued speaking, but now used his hands in sign. He pointed to the giant buffalo carcass several times. Then, he was silent. He glared at the four intruders, as if waiting for an explanation.

"He said that this was a mighty bull," said Patch. "He said the bull has strong medicine. That means it's somethin' right special, I reckon. He said he was a-chasin' it, that he shot an arrer into it and the sting was no more than a gnat's bite. He wonders who killed the bull with a thunder-stick." Patch patted his rifle softly. "He wants to know who brought the bull down."

"How come?" asked Morgan, his mouth dry as the dust he tasted on his tongue.

"Dunno," said Patch.

"You tell him," said Morgan. He drew air in his lungs, thrust his chest out. "You tell him I done it."

"He might not like it none," said Patch.

"Tell him we all done it," said Lem. Morgan shot his father a sharp look.

"I'll tell him what's so," said Patch. He began to speak in sign. He pointed to young Morgan, then at the bull. He told how Morgan was on the ground and how the bull charged him. He said that the bull tried to kill Morgan, but the boy held his ground and shot the great beast at close range. So close, his hands said, the boy could feel the bull's hot breath on his face.

The Pawnees grunted and made humming sounds in their throats.

Little Antelope spoke again. His hands interpreted his words.

"He says that you have strong medicine, Morgan. He wonders what you have inside your shirt."

Morgan withdrew the bull's bloody heart, held it aloft.

The Indians muttered in approval.

"You take a bite of that heart and then offer it to Little Antelope," said Patch. "That will show him you were the one what kilt that bull. Injuns set a heap of store in respect."

"It's raw meat," said Morgan.

"It might help us keep our hair," Patch advised.

"Go on, Morg," said Lem. "Take a little bite, chew it good and swaller it."

Morgan braced himself, took a bite from the tip of the heart. He chewed the tough meat, held out the heart toward Little Antelope. The chief rode up, took the heart, bit into the middle of it. He wrenched loose a chunk of meat, seemed to swallow it whole.

Little Antelope handed the heart back to Morgan, touched a fist to his chest. He rode up close, reached out, put his hand on Morgan's rifle. Then, he looked at the medicine horn hanging at Morgan's side. He picked it up, looked closely at the markings.

"You have strong medicine," the Pawnee signed while Patch interpreted. "You are young, but you are strong. You hunt where the Pawnee hunts. Go away and do not hunt here anymore. We will take the meat of this great bull and it will make us strong. You eat the heart and you will be strong. Go."

"I reckon we better go," said Patch. He signed to Little Antelope that they were leaving. Little Antelope wheeled his horse and returned to the dead bull. He called loudly and women and children waddled up, carrying knives and hatchets. The Pawnees rode away, showing off their horsemanship, before attacking the herd. Morgan watched Turtle ride alongside a large cow and shoot an arrow into it. The cow staggered and finally dropped. Morgan shook his head in wonderment.

The four men caught up the pack animals and headed north, away from the path of the buffalo herd. Morgan saw the animals get smaller and smaller until they just blurred together and then became a thin line on the horizon that finally disappeared.

14

They rode a great distance over gradually changing terrain and camped that night in strange country.

The prairie was now broken and scarred as if by a gigantic plow. They seemed to be, Morgan thought, on the edge of a dead world. There were no trees and the grass was sparse. They seemed to have lost the river somewhere in their travels.

In the distance, Morgan saw great heaps of rolling land, and every so often, like beacons on a desolate landscape, small peaks that seemed like bumps on the land, hints of the great mountains beyond.

Patch selected a campsite on high ground. There, they could see for miles in every direction.

"What happened to the river?" Morgan asked.

"We'll pick it up again, tomorry," said Sisco. "Safer here for the time bein'."

That night, they feasted on buffalo filets and boudoins, the rest of the bull's heart and liver, and the kidneys.

Sisco made a white pudding from the boudoins, what the French called *poudinge blanc*. He added the filets and kidneys to the stew. He put in flour, salt and pepper, stirred in water enough to cook it through. They all ate portions of the heart raw at Sisco's urging, both in celebration of the kill and as part of some ancient ritual Sisco told them about.

"Injuns put great store in eating the hearts of animals they kill—'specially if the animal is big and pow'rful and strong and brave. They say it gives 'em good medicine."

"This is a feast," said Morgan.

"You can still taste the shit in them boudins," said Lem.

"That's what gives 'em their flavor." Patch laughed. "Buffalo shit's good for lots of things."

"Like what?" asked Morgan, chewing the crackle-crisp boudins.

"When their droppin's is dry, you can use 'em to make fires. Boudins is prime vittles to a mountain man."

After that, Morgan ate more than his share. Looking Loon looked pained when the last scrap was gone.

"That Injun dearly loves the boudins," said Patch, by way of explanation.

"You ask me," said Morgan dryly, "he'll eat anything."

Lem and Sisco laughed. Morgan thought about his dog, Friar Tuck, and wished, once again, that Looking Loon would choke on a piece of meat.

The next morning, they stayed in camp, mending clothes, sewing broken harnesses, trimming hooves on mules and horses. When Patch said it was time to go, they mounted up and rode westward, coming upon the Missouri River in mid-afternoon.

"Not far to go now," said Patch.

"Where to?" asked Lem.

"You want to see old Silas Morgan?"

"I reckon I would."

"We might just find the Crow, then. That's likely where he'll be found."

"Are them Crows friendly?"

"Sometimes. Hard to say."

Lem said nothing, but Morgan noticed his father was especially edgy the next few days.

The land kept changing and it seemed to be rising in a slow slope, so gradual it might have been a trick of the eyes. One day, Morgan saw the broken country, the flatness all rumpled and gouged by gullies and washes and the hills jagging up, and beyond, so far away he had to strain his eyes to see, a long blue mass that he thought must be the mountains.

They saw more buffalo, and elk, deer and antelope, often grazing on the same plain in fairly close proximity. Morgan was curious about the antelope.

"Tastes like goat's meat," said Patch. "But, if that's all you got, you can eat 'em."

He remembered Dick Hauser telling him the same thing at Spanish Jack's in St. Louis. But he still hadn't tasted antelope meat and he wanted to find out for himself if the meat did taste like goat.

Morgan chased after several antelope, but they were too fast for his horse. Patch watched him with amusement.

"You ain't never gonna get no goat thataway," he said.

"Well, how then?" asked Morgan.

"You got to trick 'em. They're curious critters. You can sneak up on 'em, to within a couple a hunnert yards, and lie down on your back, wiggle your legs in the air. They's some who ties a cloth to their rifles and waggle it like a flag. The goats'll come up close. Injuns, they wear antelope skins and steal up close enough to shoot 'em with arrers. But, you chase 'em like you're a-doin' and they'll run circles around you, laughin' all the time."

Morgan gave up trying to shoot an antelope, but he vowed that someday he would try one of Patch's tricks.

And, one day, the mountains were there, a dark mass on the morning horizon. The sight caught Morgan by surprise.

"Are them the mountains?" he asked Patch.

"Sure as rain."

"They're far off."

"They be far, chile."

"When will we get there?"

"Why, 'fore you know it," said Patch.

And so it was. One day, they could see the mountains clearly, and Morgan would ever after remember the thrill of seeing their snowcapped peaks, their sawtooth ridges. They seemed born of the blue sky itself, huge muscular giants basking in the golden sunlight, distant, mysterious, alluring. Even his father grew excited as they drew closer to the Rocky Mountains.

"That's where we'll make our fortune, son."

"You think so, Pa?"

Lem grinned so wide his face fairly shone.

———.———

Jocko DeSam did not like Josie Montez. The man was full of hate. He was not a trapper. He had been useful for the smuggling, but now he was like a stray dog that wouldn't go away. Worse, DeSam couldn't even kick him. For Josie was a dog that would bite, not tuck its tail and skulk off.

And, Montez was full of questions. He constantly asked questions about Lemuel Hawke and his son, Morgan.

"Where do you think this Hawke will go?" he asked every day, as DeSam paddled in the bow of the canoe. Montez paddled, too, in the stern, but not when he was talking, thinking out loud.

For days, DeSam had not known how to answer the Spaniard. Then, he remembered that day when he had first met the Hawkes, back in Nashville. Lem had talked about his friend who trapped in the mountains, a man DeSam knew, or at least had seen. Nobody really knew old Silas Morgan. He lived with the Blue Bead People, the Crow, up on the Yellowstone.

The mountains were close now. DeSam could almost smell the heady scent of the evergreens, taste the crystal waters of the streams. But he had this Spanish millstone around his neck, this jabbering jay who talked incessantly of killing a man he had seen but once, did not know.

"Tonight," he spat back at Montez, "we will talk, no? I have the idea."

"You telling me to shut my mouth, Jocko?"

"You talk too damn much, Josie."

Montez laughed. It was like a knife scraping over stone.

They dug their paddles in as the river took a wide sweep and then narrowed. The water ran swift in the narrows and corded muscles, swollen veins, stood out on the men's necks. Their arms were strong from paddling against the current day after day, and they bucked the dugout through the narrows into tamer water, where the swirling pools were almost hypnotic as they scurried by and disappeared.

"What is this big idea you have, Jocko?" asked Montez when he had his breathing back to a steady rate.

"I am thinking about it, Montez."

"A good idea?"

"Maybe, eh? You want this Hawke feller pretty good."

"I want him pretty bad, *amigo*."

DeSam winced at the Spanish word for "friend." He did business with Josie Montez, but he did not like him. A man had very few friends in this country. And, often, he did not pick them. Friends happened, like storms or golden mornings. One did not choose. But one could choose one's enemies, or those he did not want as friends. Montez was a dangerous man. There were many stories about him and his knife down in New Orleans. Some of the stories had been told by his brother, Spanish Jack. Others were carried up to St. Louis and out to the mountain camps by men who had survived Montez's knife or pistols.

"Well, maybe you will get your chance, Josie. You will have to hunt him, though."

"I am hunting him now," said Montez.

"This may be the easy part, *non?* You hunt a man you cannot see, a man who is maybe far away."

"He can't run forever," said Montez, grunting as he knifed the water with his paddle. Ahead, another dugout labored upstream, its men obscured by a cloud of deerflies or river gnats as big as houseflies.

"In those big mountains," said DeSam, "a man can hide forever." He was thinking about Silas, who lived with those damned Absaroke, the Crow. Married to a squaw, he was more Indian than white now. Jocko had known several such men, and their women never took up the white ways. Old Silas seldom came to the settlements anymore, and then only to buy gewgaws for his woman, whiskey, traps and supplies. He never stayed long, did not frequent the tippling houses in St. Louis. Never talked about his life in the mountains.

DeSam had seen him, once, hunting with the Crow, a half dozen of them. It was hard to tell them apart. Silas was just as lean, his skin just as red, darker even than some Crow, and without his beard, one would take him for a Crow. He even spoke the tongue, for DeSam had heard him conversing with his companions in Absaroke. He knew the sign, too.

He wondered if he should tell Montez about Silas Morgan, where he might find him. A smile flickered on DeSam's lips. Maybe the Crow would not like this Spaniard any better than he did. He could picture Montez's scalp dangling from a Crow lance. The thought gave him pleasure.

The sun fell fast in the sky, sank behind the mountains. DeSam put in where several of his brigade had already landed and were setting up camp for the night. He was tired, but elated. Maybe he would get Montez off his back soon. They were not far from the Yellowstone. A few more days and maybe Montez would go looking for Lemuel Hawke and whatever happened would be God's will.

The dugout growled against the sandy shore. DeSam scrambled over the prow, waited for Montez to climb out. Together, they pulled the craft up onto the shore, emptied it of their rifles, pouches and goods, and turned it over on its side.

"Now, you will tell me your idea, Jocko?" Montez fixed the Frenchman with hard brown eyes.

DeSam looked at the cloud-curdled sky, the setting sun just beginning to tinge the cloud-bellies a salmon-pink. The breeze on the river stiffened, and he knew there would be a chill in that July night. Two more dugouts rounded the bend, headed toward shore. The men in them looked exhausted, their shoulders drooping, their paddles spanking the water listlessly instead of carving in deeply.

"I will tell you what you can do," said DeSam wearily. "Come, we find a place to talk."

Some of the Frenchmen already on shore waved to DeSam, called out obscenities to him. He grinned and waved back. Their faces, even under their thick beards, were bronzed by the sun. Halos of flies and gnats surrounded their heads. They had started a cookfire and made it smoky to fend off the insects that swarmed off the river in search of fresh blood.

DeSam found a place out of earshot of the other men in his brigade. A small creek wound through a copse of cottonwood and alder thickets, streaming down through gently rolling land, the long grassy hills that buffalo had grazed for centuries.

DeSam sat beneath a tree, the sores on his butt long since scabbed over until they were like leather patches on his skin. Montez squatted a few feet away, braced against another tree. Below, they heard the voices of the new arrivals mingling with those on shore, a blend of French and English words of greetings and insults.

"This Hawke," said DeSam, "he has a friend in the mountains. He talks about this man all the time. He will probably look for him and find him."

"Who is this friend?"

"His name is Silas Morgan. Hawke named his son after him."

"Where does this Silas live?" asked Montez.

"He lives with the Absaroke, the Crow. If you find this man, you will surely find Hawke, I think."

DeSam described Silas Morgan the way he remembered him. He said that he was a few years older than Hawke and that he was more savage than civilized.

"Where do these Crow live?" asked Montez.

"The band he is with, I think, hunt along the Yellowstone, sometimes up on the Musselshell. But, I have seen them on the Judith, as well. They are wanderers, like all these tribes, hunters who follow the buffalo. They hunt the buffalo now and then will trap the mountains for furs when the snows come and the beaver coats they shine and become thick."

"You will go with me, help me to find this Silas, Jocko?"

"No, I do not want anything to do with the Crow."

"They are friendly, are they not? This Silas lives with them."

"They are a good people. The women are very beautiful and the men are handsome. But I trade with the Blackfeet and they do not like the Crow. The Crow do not like white men much. Some do, some don't."

"How will I find these rivers?" asked Montez.

"I will draw you a map and you must leave the Missouri at the Musselshell and go south to the Yellowstone. They may be hunting on the Big Horn, which would be to the east. If they are not on those rivers, then you must double back and look for the Crow on some of the creeks. There are many creeks and they camp on all of them."

"I will be alone," Montez mused.

"No, there are those who trap those mountains where the rivers are born. You will find men who know where the Crow are. The Major will trap those same streams. He'll put trappers all through that country, you bet."

"And where will you go, Jocko?"

"I do not like to say." But he planned to trap the Milk or the Marias.

"You will trade with the Blackfeet?"

"I will trade the whiskey for furs," admitted DeSam.

"When do we reach this Musselshell?"

"In a week or two. I would bet a day's trapping that you will follow Lem up that river. Old Patch, he traps the Absarokes and he trades with the Crow."

"Bueno," said Montez. "I will find Lem Hawke and kill him before the snow flies."

"Good fortune, then," said DeSam in French.

"Suerte," said Montez. But he meant it for himself, for he

would need all the luck he could get to find Lem Hawke and put a blade to his throat.

———·———

Angus MacDougal and his keelboats struck the Platte River and went as far as they could go before the water became so shallow they dared not risk further voyaging. He sent the last keelboat back downriver, set off overland on horses, with the mules in a pack train, following the North Platte. They were running out of summer and he was losing time. The Laramie range loomed to the south, reminding them of how small they were, how insignificant was their place in such a grand country.

The men no longer sang the boatmen's songs, but rode westward with determination, if not enjoyment. Angus loved every moment of it, for he saw beyond, saw the riches, the wealth the men could only dream about. They worked for him, for the Company, and they would never have more than enough money to squander in a day or a week after the season.

Two men had drowned that morning, stepping off a sand bank into a deep hole. The water was low, but swift, and they were swept away before anyone could save them. It was too bad, but the party had to forsake finding their bodies. There was a sullenness among the others following the accident, but Angus knew they would soon forget. Both were older men with not much experience. He had signed them on reluctantly, but they had that maddened gleam in their eyes and he thought they might make it through a winter.

At least they were not Scotsmen, he mused. One was a German named Ludwig something or other. The other had an English name—Wilson, or Miller, he could not remember. Like so many others who came out West, they would leave no trace. Their families would probably never know they had died. For certain they could not know until he had gotten back to St. Louis next year and filed his report with the company. He would write about the incident in his journal that night after supper, when he was in his shelter with his candle and his books.

Perhaps, Angus thought, he would play the pipes tonight, a dirge for the two who had died. It might not help the men's mood, but it would help his own. He needed to hear the skirling in his ears, feel the moan of the pipes in his blood. He needed that reminder of home and old friends among the uncivilized rabble trekking along a trail trampled by buffalo, following Fletcher Bancroft, in the lead.

Angus swabbed sweat off his forehead with a large handkerchief and cocked an eye at the setting sun. The clouds to the west were turning peach, rows of them flocked together like tattered batting. The river was streaked with gold and copper, veins of pale silver eeling through dark ripples, glazed at the edges by purple borders where the banks threw wavering shadows.

They must make camp soon, he thought, for the sun fell quickly behind those mountains, leaving cold ashes in the sky, the lingering dust of the day hanging like gossamer shrouds over the distant horizon.

Fletcher Bancroft shifted in his saddle, looked back at Angus, as if reading his mind. Angus nodded, stuck his handkerchief back in his pouch. There was no breeze and it was hot, dry as last year's mud dauber's nest.

A man named Tom Sheets turned and looked back, too. He had known one of the men who drowned, had tried to find a rope to throw to them. Once the two went under, though, they never came back up. Angus didn't ignore Sheets; he just looked right through him, as if he wasn't there. Tom had wanted to find the bodies, bury them. A singular waste of time in MacDougal's mind.

Sheets turned, said something to Ralph Parsons, who was riding alongside him. Ralph was Ernie's brother. Parsons nodded. Ahead, where the land made a wide bowl, Fletch turned right, following a shallow ridge. He stopped at its pinnacle and dismounted. The men following him surrounded that central point and picketed their horses, unloaded their gear, leaving scattered piles far enough apart so that they could set up their shelters for the night.

Fletcher began barking orders. A half dozen men brought up the pack train, rode some distance past the camp and started setting up a rope corral. Trask and Parsons waited until Angus caught up with them.

"Major," said Sheets, blocking his way with his horse, "we ought to lay up a day and get some rest."

"He's right, Major," said Parsons. "We must've come fifty miles today."

"More like thirty," said the Major. "A good stretch of the legs."

"Forty," said Sheets. "At least."

"We got a late start because of those two men frolicking in the river," said MacDougal. "That cost us five miles. We've got less than an hour of sunlight left. I could have gotten back that five miles and you both would have cursed me when you couldn't find your shitrags in the dark. We're running late on flat ground, so stop your bellyaching."

"My butt feels like a chunk of rock," said Sheets.

"Soak your butt in the North Platte," said Angus coldly.

"Major, we're all plumb tuckered," said Parsons. "The men been prickly as nettles all goddamned day. You ain't heard 'em, like we have, grumblin' and gripin'."

"And did this do them all some good?" asked the Major. "Did it shorten the miles? Did it soothe your feet, Sheets?"

"Well, now there you go, Major, a-twistin' everything up into knots," said Sheets. "What the hell difference does a goddamned day make?"

Angus had put down such minor rebellions before. He enjoyed it, actually. It strengthened his position as a leader. He could feel the thunder rising in his chest, the thunder that every great orator possessed. A shame to waste it on two whining men, but they had been the ones to speak up, not the others, who were already making camp. Perhaps it was just as well that he had only these two to contend with at the moment.

He felt like shooting them both, treating them like mutineers on the high seas. The Major was a man who settled scores quickly, if he could. He was reminded, once again, of Jacques Decembre's defection—that damned Jocko DeSam, who fancied himself a booshway. It was downright insulting. He and that riffraff, the Hawkes, would regret not working in his brigade. One way or another, Angus would have their hides. And if Sheets and Parsons didn't back down quick, he'd skin them, too.

"Gentlemen," MacDougal said coolly, "I sense that you possess little appreciation for the task ahead of us. We've a great deal of ground to cover and you'll want the best beaver streams for yourselves. Keep your grouses to yourselves or you'll get the poorest grounds to trap, I assure you."

Sheets opened his mouth, started to say something. Parsons reached out and grabbed his arm to stop him from making things worse. Nobody ever won an argument with the Major.

MacDougal stared Sheets down, until Tom averted his eyes and hung his head. Parsons saw the look on the Major's face and he turned his horse dejectedly.

"The bastard," muttered Sheets as he rode away. He could feel the Major's eyes burning into his back.

"I guess we ain't as tired as we thought," said Parsons.

"I got me a good mind to—"

But Sheets never finished his sentence. The Major galloped past them, looking as fresh as when they had started out that morning.

"Tomorry," said Parsons, "he'll log sixty miles in his book, you'll see."

That evening, the brigade ate badger, geese, turkey and the river furnished their larder with catfish caught on bone hooks baited with earthworms or spoiled jerky.

Tom Sheets cussed under his breath all evening long and didn't stop until he crawled into his blankets, but nobody paid him any mind. They knew he was just trying to get over the death of a friend he had made.

After the fires were put out, the Major played the pipes for a half an hour in the darkness and the men listened in silence. Some of them sobbed softly, crushed by the terrible loneliness they felt in that vast, desolate land, conscious that they were dependent on the Major for their livelihood.

And that was just how Angus MacDougal wanted them to feel—every man jack of them.

15

Morgan Hawke gazed at the distant horizon so long his father thought he must be in a trance.

"I reckon them are the mountains yonder," said Morgan. "Or just more hills like we been seein' and ridin' through."

"I reckon we're gettin' close," said Lem. "Don't appear to be too big. Probably no bigger'n the Cumberlands or the Smokies."

"Them ain't the Rockies," said Patch, overhearing father and son. "Just more hills, like you say, Morgan." Looking Loon ranged far ahead of them, glad to be free of leading the pack mules, which he had done all morning. They had journeyed south after coming upon a huge bend in the Missouri, a wide place that looked like a delta or a lake. Patch led them south on a river he said ran out of the mountains.

"Broad, ain't it?" said Lem.

"This be the Musselshell," said Patch. "We'll run up it, see if we can't find us a Crow what knows where your friend Silas be."

"I wonder how Silas is doing?" Lem mused aloud. Everyone but Lemuel called him "old" Silas. Even Hawke's ex-wife Roberta had called him that, too. He wondered why. Silas wasn't much older than he. But, he looked old. Always had, ever since Lem had known him. Maybe Silas was old, now that he thought of it. Forty-five or so. Couldn't be fifty yet, could he? Maybe. Morg hadn't been born when old Silas left Virginny to trap beaver and such. And now Morg was all but full growed, so Silas had to be a graybeard. Hell, the man could be sixty by now, the way time was a-rushin' by.

Morgan rattled the rope, jerked the mules into motion. Boots stepped out, snatching a tuft of twelve-inch grass from the prairie. Deer broke from cover, rising up from beds in the middle of a wide patch of grass. Their tails flashed golden in the sun and they disappeared, leaving narrow swaths in their wake.

The deer were different from the eastern whitetails. They had large ears and seemed bigger, with gray hides, gray as winter wolves in full coat.

"They call 'em mule deer," Patch told him. "'Cause of those big ears, I reckon. Chunky as hogs, ain't they? Mighty fine eatin'."

They had seen buffalo and antelope every day for the past several weeks, and mule deer way off, standing like sentinals next to timber, or scattering from a waterhole that appeared like a mirage in one of the long shallow valleys in the rolling countryside. Once in a while, they'd see elk, far off, in small herds. The buffalo were scattered, as if they had been hunted. Patch did not want to hunt them.

"This be Crow land," he said. "And the Sioux, they hunt here; Cheyenne, too. Sometimes the Blackfeet come down to fight the Crow. This be dangerous country for whiteskins, and some red 'uns, too."

There were huge prairie dog cities everywhere. Morgan and Lem were fascinated by their numbers, their shrill, high-pitched whistles of warning.

And, still, there were no mountains, only endless hills where small, scattered herds of buffalo grazed or antelope ran. Yet, there were days when he was sure he could see mountains in the distance. At times, Morgan wondered if they were not just an illusion, a trick of the light. Most often they turned out to be low dark clouds atop distant hills.

"When will we get to the mountains?" Morgan kept asking Patch.

"One day you'll see 'em," was all Patch said. "They'll be touchin' the sky and have snow on their peaks prettier'n anything you ever saw."

To Morgan, they seemed to be crawling across the prairie. The land was broken along the Musselshell, scarred and welted like the back of a man flayed with a brutal whip. They passed several places where Indians had camped. Morgan looked at the sites with fascination. He could almost see the Indians in his mind. It was thrilling to ride over the places where they had lived.

One day, Patch waved them back into a deep gully. Before they descended into the hiding place, Morgan and his father saw the Indians. They were far off and yelling exultantly. They were driving horses with mottled coats, twenty or so.

"Flatheads," Patch explained. "''Pears they been after the Crow and got 'em some ponies."

"Did they see us?" Lem asked.

"I reckon not. Them bucks are full o' themselves, braggin' and such that they kilt some Crow and got 'em some horses and scalps."

"Why don't the Crow go after them?" asked Morgan.

Patch shrugged. "Could be the Crow was hurt bad," he said. "Or maybe the Flatheads took all their horses. Injuns is funny. They don't look on fightin' like we do. It's a sport. They make a big to-do about fightin', lots of singin' and dancin', and when they do battle, they play it like a game, actin' brave and strikin' coup with sticks and warclubs. Don't make much sense—'cept to another Injun."

"Injuns is mighty strange," observed Morgan. Patch almost laughed. He could tell from the look in Morgan's eyes that the boy was fascinated by the redmen.

"That they be," agreed Patch.

They waited a long time before Looking Loon signed to them that the Flathead had gone their way and were no longer a threat. But Morgan kept looking for Indians as they drew closer to the mountains.

Looking Loon rode into camp one evening with a mule deer draped over his horse's withers. The deer had not been gutted out. Usually, the Delaware made his kill, removed the legs and head, skinned it, butchered the animal and brought the meat back all neatly rolled up in its hide.

Blow flies swarmed over the venison, thick as fur on a beaver. These insects had been their constant companions for weeks, attacking the meat from the time they gutted it to when they cooked it and while they ate it.

The Delaware began speaking to Patch in sign, his hands moving so rapidly Morgan had difficulty in following him. But he knew that Loonie was talking about Indians and that he was excited. Morgan couldn't tell by Loonie's signs if the Indians were hostile, but at the end of his silent recital, Looking Loon grinned.

"Looks like Loonie done found him a bunch of Crow," said Patch. "He shot two deer, gave 'em the other one as a gift. He told 'em we were here. He thinks they've got a camp somewheres near, up the Musselshell."

"Are these the Crow what Silas took up with?" asked Lem.

"Loonie doesn't know the difference 'twixt one tribe or another, but he says one of the Crow is a brave we've run onto before. Name of Moon Face. I reckon he's one of the Little Robe clan and that he be one of them with Silas last spring. We done some tradin'."

"What do we do now?" asked Morgan.

"Sit tight, I reckon. Be the polite thing to do. This is Crow country and we got to ask 'em can we come through, do some trappin'."

"How soon will the Crow be here?" asked Lem.

"Injuns got to do a lot of talkin' and studyin' on a thing before they make up their minds. Kinda like some of them Germans I knowed back in Pennsylvania. Don't do to hurryin' 'em none."

"Then we got no worries," said Lem.

"I couldn't exactly say," said Patch. "I'd see my pan was primed and keep a weather eye cocked. Don't make no sudden moves, but be ready, case they want to try us on for size."

"Did Loonie say anything about Silas?" asked Lem.

"He told 'em we were looking for Gray Hawk—that's what the Crow calls your friend."

"And, what did the Crow say?"

"They didn't say yeah or nay."

"Maybe Silas will come with them," ventured Morgan.

Patch shrugged. But the old trapper kept his rifle close and they all checked their pans for dry powder. Morgan touched his flint to see if it was secure in its leather sleeve, tightened the bolt down a notch. Lem rubbed the sweat off his palms, stayed close to a stand of poplar for cover.

Looking Loon laid the dead mule deer on the ground. He made no move to dress it out. Instead, he sat down and laid his rifle across his lap. He seemed, Morgan thought, to sit there in a trance.

Patch set out some tobacco, trade beads and a half dozen iron tomahawks. He laid them on a Hudson Bay blanket, neat and orderly, as if he had done such many times before.

"You might want to lay out some goods yourselfs," Patch said to Morgan and Lem. "Injuns dearly love presents."

They waited for almost an hour before there was any sign of the Crow.

Looking Loon was the first to hear the Indians approaching. His hands told Patch the Crow were nearby.

"Here they come," said the trapper. "Just be quiet and don't get excited. "Let me do the talkin'.""

A half dozen Crow rode boldly into camp. They carried both rifles and bows, but they were not painted. Morgan thought they looked arrogant and mean. He licked dry lips and let out a shallow breath of stale air from his lungs.

The lead Crow looked at the deer on the ground. He was a burly man with dark reddish skin, a handsome face, large straight nose, coal-black hair. He wore a breastplate of small bones, attached together with sinew in straight, horizontal lines. Beads dangled from the feathers that bordered the ornament. He wore a breechclout and beaded moccasins. His rifle was studded with brass tacks. It was a short-barreled flintlock. A single eagle feather dangled from its frontpiece.

"I am Lame Bull," he said in his native tongue. He signed his name to Patch. "You are One-Eye."

Patch nodded, signed that he was a friend. He offered Lame Bull and the others his gifts. He pointed to Lem and Morgan's blankets.

"Take," Patch said in English.

The Crow dismounted, strutted around the camp.

"This deer should be gutted and hung up," he said in Crow, as he poked it with his rifle. Then, he spoke rapidly in both sign and Absaroke. "Why are you here? Where are you going? Why do you ride through Crow land? What are you looking for?"

Patch patiently answered all of his questions, speaking in English for the Hawkes' benefit, making sign to Lame Bull.

"We go to the mountains to trap the beaver for the white man's shining buttons," said Patch. "Moon Face there knows One-Eye. These two white faces are father and son. They look for their friend, Gray Hawk. They are from his mother's country and they have a come a long way to see their good friend. Take these gifts and tell Gray Hawk we are here."

The Crow all seemed to disdain the gifts at first. Moon Face came up to Morgan Hawke and poked a finger in his chest, felt the muscles of his arms.

Morgan bristled.

"You just hold steady, Morgan," said Patch. "He don't mean no harm. Just his way of gettin' to know you."

Two Crow examined Lem. None of them seemed interested in Looking Loon. The Delaware still sat there, his rifle across his legs, staring into nothingness.

The other Crow looked at the mules and examined the horses, opening their mouths. They poked at the panniers, as if trying to see what goods were inside the packs. Morgan found that he could smell the Crow. They had a peculiar odor, a smell of smoke and grease that was very strong.

"This one has no tongue," said Lame Bull, pointing to Looking Loon. "He is not Crow."

"He is a human being from another tribe," Patch said aloud, making the signs. "He is not white."

Lame Bull laughed at that. "My eyes can see he is not white," he signed. "His skin is as dark as mine, but he is very ugly."

"Yes, he is ugly," signed Patch, "and he has no tongue. The Great Spirit has given him a brave heart in its place."

Lame Bull and the others laughed again. Then, the Crow began to snatch up the gifts, examining the tobacco and beads, talking among themselves. Moon Face fought over some tobacco and ended up with only a handful.

Finally, to Morgan's relief, Lame Bull made a sign that he could understand.

"Bring that deer with you and come with us," he told Patch.

"Well, boys, we're a-goin' to the Crow camp," said the trapper.

"How far?" asked Morgan suddenly. The Crow all looked at him. It grew very quiet.

"This one has a tongue," signed Lame Bull. "Does he also have a brave heart?"

"He kilt the biggest buffler I ever seed when it was chargin' him. The buffler was bristlin' with Pawnee arrers. He warn't more'n ten feet away when the boy brought the bull down with a single shot."

"He was on his horse," said Lame Bull disdainfully.

"He was standin' like he is now. He didn't run."

Morgan read the sign perfectly. His chest swelled slightly.

"You don't need to brag on me, none," he told Patch.

"Injuns like braggin'," he replied. "They like it a lot."

Lame Bull called the other braves to him. He spoke in Absaroke for several moments. He did not make sign. Morgan saw that the others were listening intently. Finally, Moon Face and Lame Bull turned toward Patch.

"We will return to our people," said Lame Bull. "We will talk to them and we will smoke. We will take this deer because it belongs to us."

Patch's eyes narrowed, but he did not translate. Morgan understood the sign anyway.

"We go," said Moon Face, his hand sign very curt. With that, two Indians lifted the deer, slung it over Moon Face's pony. Lame Bull spoke to them. The Crow mounted up and rode out of sight without uttering another sound.

Looking Loon stood up. His hands began to talk rapidly to Patch. Morgan could not follow all of it, but he knew that the Delaware was saying that they should leave before the sun went to sleep. Looking Loon traced a path that would take them wide of the river but loop back toward the mountains.

Patch did not reply to Looking Loon.

Morgan surprised all of them by speaking to Looking Loon in sign. None was more surprised than his father, but he beamed with pride as he saw the look of approval on Patch's face.

"Why do we run and hide like rabbits?" he asked.

Looking Loon made the sign of a bird and jabbed at his head with a finger, made the circular motion, pulled at his topknot.

"The Crow will scalp us."

"How do your eyes see this?" asked Morgan.

"My heart sees this."

Morgan snorted.

"I wouldn't argy with him none," said Patch. "Loonie gets a feelin' in his gut now and again. He thinks them Crow are up to no good."

"What about you?" asked Lem.

Patch shrugged. "It don't look too good to me."

"You want to run off?" Lem asked.

"Might be the best thing to do. Did you see Moon Face lookin' at our packs? That nigger might not want to trade for somethin' he can get free."

"I was hopin' we might see Silas," said Lem.

"Hell, they might have kilt him," Patch exclaimed. "I never trusted the Crow much. There's some as set store by 'em, but I just don't trust 'em. Me and Loonie are pullin' out."

"Pa," said Morgan, "maybe we'd better go with Patch and Loonie."

"I reckon we better go with 'em," said Lem. He ran fingers through his full beard. He had let it grow ever since they had seen Josie Montez. Morgan wondered if he had done it to hide his identity. If so, it sure had changed his looks. Morgan's face was clean as a hen's egg, although he had sprouted a few silken hairs on his chin that he had quickly plucked. He had a little hair on his chest, but it, too, was fine and blond, hardly noticeable.

"Let's get to goin', then," said Patch. "Them red niggers could be back anytime."

"Damn," muttered Lem. "I sure was hopin' to see Silas out here."

In less than ten minutes, they had broken camp and were riding a wide loop away from the Musselshell. The sun set quickly, plunging the small party into darkness. Patch kept them all bunched together as they rode blindly on, putting distance between them and the river. Finally, hours later, when the thin sliver of moon had risen, Patch called a halt.

"Don't unpack nothin'," he whispered. "Hobble the horses and mules. Me'n Loonie'll take the first watch. You boys get some sleep. I'll wake you in a couple of hours."

"It's sure dark," said Morgan, looking at the black sky, the tiny fingernail of moon.

"That's what they call a trapper's moon, son," said Patch. "Best time to hunt, catch beaver and such."

"It gives me the williwaws," said Lem softly.

"Me, too," said Morgan. "You can't hardly see nothin'."

"Take it as a good sign," said Patch. "We don't want to be seen now, do we? Same as the wild critters what feed at night. Yep, that's sure enough a trapper's moon."

"I just hope it bodes well for us," said Lem nervously.

He and Morgan laid out their bedrolls, kept their rifles close by as they made ready for sleep.

Morgan stared up into the Stygian sky, stared at the small thin moon. "Must be another month comin' to an end, Pa," he breathed.

There was no answer.

His father was already asleep.

Finally, Morgan slept, too. Weighed down by eyelids heavy as stone, he sank into a deep slumber.

Two hours later, he was yanked out of sleep. Not by Patch or Looking Loon, but by two Crow braves who jerked him from his bedroll, locked his arms behind him. He knew they were Crow because he could smell them.

Morgan heard his father grunt, then saw him roughly handled by three more Crow.

"You come, you come," said one of the Crow in a thickly accented voice.

"You speak English?" asked Lem.

"Come," said the Crow again.

Morgan heard a commotion. More Crow approached. He could dimly see that they had Patch and Looking Loon under restraint.

"Boys, they found us," said Patch. "We're a-goin' to the Crow camp with these fellers."

"No talk," said the English-speaking Crow.

Morgan felt a sinking feeling as his hands were tied. The Crow put their prisoners on their horses. Morgan knew their hands, too, were tied. There were at least a dozen Crow, he figured as they rode off.

The moon, like a sliver of errant quicksilver, disappeared behind scudding, high-flying clouds.

16

The sky lightened slowly under thick gray clouds. Morgan rocked in the saddle, fighting off sleep. His father shook him awake every so often when he began to lean over the pommel.

"You'll fall and break your neck you don't stay awake," chided Lem.

They had been riding for hours in total darkness. The captives had no sense of where they were, having lost their bearings as soon as the Crow had taken them away from their makeshift camp. None had spoken, nor did they talk among themselves.

Shortly after dawn, the Crow halted at a small stream, deep in woodlands. Many bared their buttocks and defecated on low ground several dozen yards away. Others urinated, spraying the grass with yellow streams. One Crow untied their captives' hands, motioned for them to pee or shit. After Morgan saw

Patch and Loonie relieving themselves, he did the same. He stared at the Crow, wondering which one had spoken English to them.

He did not see Lame Bull, Moon Face, or any of the other Crow they had met the night before.

"Are these Crow?" Morgan asked Patch, when they were back together, their hands retied, guarded by the watchful Crow.

"Sure as it gets daylight in the mornin'," Patch replied.

"Do you know any of them?"

"I reckoned them we saw yesterday warn't Little Robes. From talk I just heard, they were Filth-eaters. These here be Little Robes, or as some call 'em, Treacherous. Or maybe they be mixed. They all got names like that, or Sore Lips, Greasy-Inside-Their-Mouths."

"You understand their tongue?" Lem asked.

"Some. A little. These be talkin' about that medicine horn of your'n, Morgan. Lookee yonder."

Morgan stared in the direction Patch was pointing.

Three Crow were handling Morgan's possibles pouch, his powder horns. One was examining his rifle, holding it to his shoulder. He felt his stomach jolt with a queasy roll of muscles. It felt as if he had died and was watching Indians paw over his belongings.

One of the Crow was holding up Morgan's medicine horn, speaking to the other two. Others wandered over, looked at the markings on the powder horn. Several spoke excitedly and the one holding the horn traced his forefinger over the symbols engraved in the buffalo horn.

"Are they fixin' to kill us?" Morgan asked.

"They ain't wearin' paint and ain't carryin' spears. 'Pears to be a hunting party. I heard Lame Bull's name mentioned a time or two in passing. I can't figure this bunch out."

"I don't like bein' trussed up like a turkey," said Lem, "a-waitin' for one of them savages to slit our gullets."

"I reckon they could have kilt us long before now," said Patch. "No, they're a-takin' us someplace. Could be worse waitin' for us if they take us to be enemies."

"What do you mean?" asked Morgan.

"Oh, they's lots of things they can do. Best you not know any of it."

"Bastards," muttered Lem.

Patch said nothing. The Crow stopped looking at Morgan's personal belongings and the one holding the powder horn barked orders. The prisoners were handled roughly as Crow put them on their horses. Morgan, however, was treated much better. Two Crow helped him onto his horse and one of them untied his hands.

Morgan looked over at Patch. Patch shrugged.

The leader motioned for Morgan to ride with him in the lead. Reluctantly, Morgan did as he was told. He looked back at his father, tried to look apologetic.

The muscular Crow leader, like most of his followers, had long hair that fell past his waist, smooth skin, dark as highly polished leather. His eyes were dark as agates and shone with the morning light. He seemed not much older than Morgan himself. His moccasins were decorated with dyed porcupine quills, flattened and folded into patterns that formed ancient symbols; his fringed buckskin shirt was beaded and quilled in bright colors. He wore a single eagle feather dangling from his black hair, just below the left ear. He sat his horse very straight and proud.

"I am called Whistling Elk," the Crow said, suddenly, taking Morgan by surprise. "White man name."

"You speak English."

"Gray Hawk teach Whistling Elk."

"Where are you taking us?" asked Morgan.

"Go camp. Many tipi. Many Crow."

"Is Gray Hawk there?"

"Gray Hawk say come. Lame Bull come get."

"Why are we prisoners?" Morgan made sign to show hands being tied with rope.

"No run away," said the Crow. He looked sharply at Morgan to see if his words were believed.

"A man don't take another man prisoner for such a reason."

Whistling Elk shook his head as if he didn't understand Morgan. "Damn fuckin' good," he said.

"Silas teach you that?"

"Silas damn fuckin' good."

Before Morgan could reply, there was a commotion among the Indians. Their captors made bird calls which were answered from somewhere up ahead. The tweetering sounded back and forth until another band of Crow rode out of the woods to meet them.

"Why, there's Lame Bull," said Morgan. "And Moon Face. Godamighty."

Lame Bull did not acknowledge Morgan, just grunted and spoke briefly to Whistling Elk in Crow. He did not sign with his hands, so Morgan did not know what he said.

Lame Bull's band fell in with the Whistling Elk braves and they rode together until they reached the Musselshell again. Whistling Elk spoke no more to Morgan, but seemed to be looking for something that lay ahead.

Morgan heard a horse galloping behind him, turned to see his father riding up from the rear. His hands were no longer tied.

"Lame Bull untied us," Lem said as he slowed his horse to a walk beside Morgan.

"Whistling Elk there said they didn't want us to run away," Morgan said.

"That his name?"

"He's the one who speaks some English. I think Silas taught him."

"That'd be like him. Silas probably speaks Crow, too."

"Where do you reckon they're takin' us, Pa?"

"Patch thinks we're going to a big camp on the Musselshell. He said it can't be much farther. These Injuns ain't carryin' no food and not much water. I'm plumb parched."

"Me, too," said Morgan.

Whistling Elk turned to the Hawkes.

"No talk," he said.

In moments, they rode onto a wide plain where horses grazed, tended by boys. They heard distant shouts and soon a group of young men galloped toward them. Beyond, where the river curved into a half loop, Morgan saw the tops of tipis, their hides stark against the distant mountains, bone white under the gray of the sky.

The young braves rode back and forth, showing off. Morgan marveled at the way they stayed on bareback ponies while performing all kinds of riding feats. One young man rode his pony backward, another crawled underneath his mount, holding onto its neck with encircling arms. Some ponies wore hair or rope bridles, others had none. A Crow stood up on his pony's rump and waved to them, grinning. Others traded horses as they rode side by side.

"Pretty fair riding," said Lem.

"I never saw anything like it," admitted Morgan.

Whistling Elk seemed impervious to the dazzling display of horsemanship, but some of the others in his band began to show off, too. Patch and Looking Loon caught up with Lem and Morgan.

Soon, they saw crowds of women and children streaming from the village. They appeared first as brightly colored objects, then slowly took shape. Ahead of them, on a painted Indian pony, rode a man with a bearded face.

"Pa, look," said Morgan, pointing.

"I see him. Looks like Silas, sure enough." Lem grinned, slapped his thigh.

"Is it?" Morgan asked. "Really?"

"Who else?"

As the man drew closer, he began to wave. Lem and Morgan waved back.

"Gray Hawk," said Whistling Elk, in English. "Damn fuckin' good."

Silas Morgan seemed in no big hurry. Morgan agonized at how long it took him to reach their column. By then, they were surrounded by hooting and hollering Crow braves, all vying for attention from the Hawkes, Patch and the Delaware.

"Hoo haw," said Silas, as he rode up. Morgan had no trouble recognizing him, even though he was barechested and wore only a breechclout, a necklace, a quilled belt with a knife jutting from it, moccasins. "If you ain't a sight for sore eyes, Lemuel Hawke. And, thar be your boy, Morgan, my namesake sure enough. Hoooooeeee!"

"Silas, you ain't changed a bit," said Lem.

Silas rode close to Lem, leaned over and slapped him on the back, his carrious teeth visible through his thick beard.

"And, there's old Patch and his nigger, Loonie. How do, Patch?"

"Silas, you look fit," said Patch.

"I got it sweet, Patch. This old coon's got honey in the horn. Morg, I see Whistling Elk's got your medicine horn. You give it to him?"

"No, he took it," Morgan said, scowling. "They tied us up and brung us here."

"Well," said Silas, "the Crow been a mite skittery lately what with so many white men comin' in to their country. They got their hands full with other Injun tribes stealin' their horses and women and kids. Scouts been comin' in all month tellin' tales."

"What tales?" asked Lem.

"Keelboats on the Missouri, the Platte. Trappers and traders, a passel of 'em, headin' toward the Seedskedee and the Popo Agie."

Lem didn't understand a word Silas had said.

"That would be the Major and his bunch," explained Patch.

"I figgered. Angus taught me a lot, but he's a skunk all right. Jocko still trappin' with him?"

"Not no more," said Lem. "The Major tried to kill us all."

"Well, now, we got to make some talk when we get you all settled," said Silas. "I'll see you get your goods back right quick. You got to watch them Filth-eaters."

As they topped a rise, Morgan gasped. There were tipis dotting the plain, rows and rows of them like strange conical houses. Horse herds grazed in bunches and dogs roamed everywhere. It was a chilling and a thrilling sight.

Even Patch was impressed.

"Heap of 'em," he said.

"Won't stay long. Big pow-wow. Lot of smoke and talk. Been goin' on better'n a week."

"War talk?" asked Patch.

"Some, I reckon. We had a good winter, lots of prime furs. But, there's talk of whiskey tradin', cheatin' white eyes and booshway promises broke. Somethin's goin' on."

"I reckon," said Patch laconically.

Lem and Morgan gazed everywhere, drinking it all in, the

wonder of it, the maze of tipis, their poles scratching the cloudy sky, their lodge flaps open, buffalo skulls and totems painted on tipi hides. Women and children followed along, all talking and screeching, pointing and laughing. Morgan felt like he was in a parade. Boys tugged at Whistling Elk's legs, asking him all kinds of questions, but he shooed them away like gnats and never told them what they wanted to know.

"Looks like a one big mess, don't it, Lem?" asked Silas. "But all them tipis is in particular order. I spread my blankets with the Little Robe tribe over yonder." He pointed to a cluster of tipis. Morgan noticed that each camp was a separate circle. "Me and Lame Bull will talk to Whistling Elk, see can we get your rifles and possibles back. Just keep ridin' on toward that far circle of lodges. I reckon those are your mules and pack horses."

Lem nodded.

"It won't be no trouble, will it?" Hawke asked.

"I don't reckon," said Silas, but he didn't smile. "See you boys directly."

Silas rode off toward Lame Bull. Lem headed for the Little Robe lodges, followed by Morgan, Patch and Looking Loon. They were not followed, which seemed odd to Morgan. But as he looked again at the huge camp, he knew there would be little chance of escaping. Even if he had his rifle, he would be swarmed over by Crows the minute he tried to ride away.

"Pa, are we prisoners?" he asked abruptly.

"Why, no, I don't reckon. Are we, Patch?"

"I wouldn't make a run for it. Like Silas said, these niggers are mighty skittery. I don't blame 'em none."

"Huh?" asked Morgan. "We didn't do nothin' to 'em."

Patch halted several yards from the large circle of Little Robe tipis. Lem and Morgan stopped their horses, knowing the trapper had something to say. Looking Loon reined up, too.

Sisco moved his eyepatch to one side, rubbed his dead eye. Morgan thought it was a hideous sight.

"I been expectin' this, or somethin' like this," said Patch, speaking softly. "I been watchin' the doin's in St. Louis, listenin' to all the talk. They's big money in furs and there are them as don't care how they get the beaver. Ever since Manuel Lisa come here to trade, way back before Lewis and Clark come up the Missouri, they's been politics ahind ever' move, ever' brigade."

"Politics?" Lem asked.

Patch nodded, waggled a bony finger in the air.

"Rich folks back East been puttin' money into brigades, expeditions and such. Some say the government is behind some of it, or all of it. Not many white trappers out here back then, but they started comin' after Lewis and Clark come home and started braggin' on the country, how rich it was."

"Well, that's why we're here," said Lem. "That's why you come out here. And Silas."

"True enough, true enough," assented Patch. "I hired on with some of those brigades and I seen cutthroats hire on and seen men kilt for furs and coin. Lisa and his bunch fought with the Rees and beat back the Mandans and bluffed their way through the Assinboines. I seen him back down chief after chief with his talk and showing them his firepower. He traded with the Crow down on the Yellowstone and they was glad to get his goods. But things have been changin' the past few years."

"The Crows still want to trade, don't they?" asked Lem. "Silas has been livin' and tradin' with 'em."

"Silas come out here afore I did," said Patch. "He can read sign better'n most men I know. A long time ago, he saw all the fur companies formin' up and he didn't want no part of it. So, he become a red nigger and he's probably saltin' it away. I never could cotton to these red coons, and so I stayed with the companies until I seen what the Major was a-doin' and how greed had got into Jocko's blood. Ain't but a question of time afore this is all ruint and the redskins come after us—the Crow, the Blackfoot, the Sioux, ever' damn one of 'em."

"You think that's what's happening here?" Lem asked, trying to swallow a knot in his throat. "You think the Crow are fixin' to fight all the white men coming out here?"

Patch looked around him as if checking to make sure no Indian could hear him. His eye narrowed and the patch seemed to bulge with that dead eye trying to see right through it.

"Lem, I been thinkin' that for five years now. But, I never seed so many Crow in one place before. They's somethin' stirrin' out here, somethin' mighty peculiar and mighty dangerous. It's like you get a feelin' real deep down and you can't shake it nohow. These Crow are itchin' for a fight, some of 'em, and maybe they'll smoke the pipe and cool down, but I ain't about to bet hard coin on it."

"You mean we might not get to trap and make our fortune?" Morgan asked.

"Well, I ain't perdictin' nothin', son. It's just feels like somethin's tightenin' down and I don't hardly know what it is."

"Be a damned shame," said Lem. "Just gettin' close and havin' everythin' blow up in our faces."

"Now, don't get to jumpin' the gun on what I say," said Patch. "We maybe can talk with Silas and see if he feels the same thing."

"I'm glad we didn't go with the Major," said Morgan.

Lem looked at his son in astonishment. Patch cracked a dry smile and winked with his one good eye.

"Son, you're beginnin' to learn politics," said Sisco.

"And Jocko," said Morgan, "he ain't no better."

Patch nodded sagely. "Jocko DeSam learnt all he knows

from Angus MacDougal," he said. "Don't you forget that none."

Morgan sobered, looked back toward the main camp, trying to pick out Silas. Patch had made him very nervous and apprehensive. He expected to see every Crow in camp come riding down on them with knives and hatchets, screaming for their blood. He shook off the thought as he saw the children playing the hoop and stick game, chasing after each other in what looked like tag. Older boys tended the horses. It seemed very peaceful there. Maybe Patch was an old fussbudget. Maybe everything was going to be all right.

When he looked back toward the Little Robe circle, he saw two women walking toward them. They were followed, from a distance, by several older men, women and children. But the two women drew Morgan's interest. They moved slowly and seemed shy. One was older than the other. They were whispering to each other and the younger one was giggling.

"Looky yonder," Morgan said, without pointing. "Two squaws are comin' out here."

Lem, Patch and Loon followed Morgan's gaze.

They all stared, fascinated, at the two women. They had obviously spent a lot of time preening themselves. They wore elkskin dresses, tanned to a golden yellow, bright bead necklaces and painted shell earrings. Each woman had very long black hair; small eagle feathers dangled gracefully from beaded thongs woven through their tresses.

The older woman raised a hand in greeting. She was looking straight at Patch. The younger one hid her face.

"You know 'em?" Lem asked.

"I knowed that one. That's Blue Shell, old Silas' woman."

"Well, who's the other one?" blurted Morgan.

"Never seed her before," said Patch.

"Morg," warned Lem. "You ain't int'rested in no Injun squaw."

The young woman looked up as she and Blue Shell Woman drew closer. She seemed to be looking straight at Morgan, who was staring owl-eyed at the most beautiful girl he had ever seen. She was so small and graceful, and her face was radiant with light.

He failed to see the dark scowl on his father's face.

17

José Montez looked at the three men he had hired away from
Jocko DeSam. One was a Mexican who spoke little English.
His name was Felix Santiago and he had trapped with Manuel
Lisa, was a veteran of many Indian battles. One was named
Harold Bickham, thirty-five years old, who knew the moun-
tains as well as any. The last was a French-Indian halfbreed
named Pierre Doucette. His mother was of the Cree tribe, but
he had lived with the Cheyenne, deadly enemies of the Crow.

They had four pack mules with them. Montez had bought
one from a man who had two, paying too much, but knowing
that he was the richer for it. He knew they might have to trade
with savages or bribe them for information. Perhaps, as Jocko
had told him, having trade goods, whiskey, beads, weapons,
would come to mean the difference between life and death in
this wild, untamed land.

He had paid the men in gold coin and promised more if they

led him to Lemuel Hawke. The three hirelings had one thing in common: all were greedy and all had blood on their hands. In that, they were not much different than himself.

Indeed, over the weeks past, he had come to hold many of the men on the river in high regard—not for their qualities of character, but for their bravery and determination. He realized that they were hard men in their own way, some foolish, some stupid, but willing to undergo extreme hardship in order to attain riches. He and his brother had been like that, willing to take risks, great risks, in order to live like men and not like the sewer rats, the dogs and stray cats of Spain.

Montez also realized that he had gradually become more and more like the men he formerly scorned. He had regarded them as drifters enslaved to the booshway, men without backbones or men without *cojones*. Aimless men, without purpose. Yet, he realized now that while these companions had picked a hard journey, they remained fiercely independent while loyal to the booshway, DeSam. And so, he had become like them, at least for this journey, this quest for revenge.

He had seen his reflection in the river that morning and it was like seeing the face of a stranger. He had grown a full beard, and now he felt as if he was wearing a disguise.

The man he saw in the morning-still waters of the Musselshell resembled a mountain man, although he had no desire to wade in cold water and set traps for beaver and marten. It seemed curious, that was all, that he had unconsciously taken on the trappings of a mountain man even though he had never been to the Rockies before.

Perhaps that was as it should be, Montez thought. He would descend to the level of his quarry, if that was necessary, and when it was over, he would shave off his beard and become himself again. Still, the shock of seeing that bearded stranger peering back at him made him wonder if he had not lost his mind. He vowed not to forget the reason he had come this far, that his brother was still dead and Lemuel Hawke must pay·in kind, with his own life.

Montez smiled in satisfaction as his hired trackers looked over another of the Hawkes and their companions' camps, reading the sign left behind by four men.

"They keep the watches," said Doucette. He was a short, muscular man with knife scars on his chest and one ear that had been chewed into a shapeless mass of flesh. He wore greasy buckskins, thick-soled Cree moccasins and carried a large knife he had made from a wagon spring. Its handle was made of tough antelope antler, wound tight with glued buffalo hide thongs that gave his hand a solid grip. "The Delaware, he always sleeps by himself, away from the others."

"How close are we?" asked Montez.

Hal Bickham, stooped over the bent grasses, looked up at Montez. "Two days." Bickham was lean, slat-chested, stood five foot nine inches in his boot moccasins. His buckskins had been patched until his shirt looked like a leather quilt. He had pale, vacuous blue eyes, deep-sunk in a cadaverous face. His nose had been broken more than once, and there was a thin scar on his forehead that indicated he had once come close to being scalped. His forelock was bone white, in sharp contrast to his rusty hair.

"Three," said Santiago. *"Tres días,"* he said in Spanish. Bickham scowled at the Mexican. Santiago was from Santa Fe, an outcast, a wanderer. He had the high cheekbones of the Yaqui, the vermillion smear of Indian blood reddening his dark skin.

"Three, maybe," said Bickham. He looked again at the crushed grasses. "They been movin' fast, but I look for them to slow down some. They ain't kilt no fresh meat in two days."

"That is right," said Santiago, looking at the bones and gristle around a shallow hole that showed signs of fire-blackening. "They did not make meat for two days."

Montez knew that he had to rely on these men. He could not read sign, could not track a man in such a wild place. He was more at home in the squalid back alleys of Barcelona where he and his brother grew up, or on the docks of New Orleans, the dark, bayou-scented streets, where his boots made no sound on cobblestones made slick and wet by the swampy nightsweat and his breath was only a part of the gulf fog. But he knew he had picked the right men—he had watched them for days, and had seen that they trusted each other. And, now, he would have to trust them for as long as he needed them.

"There is little game," said Pierre. "The *Indiens*, eh? They have hunted much along this river. They drive the sumbitch game away."

Montez knew that to be true. They had seen only small animals all morning, antelope in the distance. There had been no deer or elk tracks, none fresh and no sign of buffalo. The sky was clouded up and he was afraid it would rain before nightfall. That would make the tracking harder, he knew.

"I want to cut those three days by one or two," said the Spaniard.

"You do not know this sumbitch country," said Doucette. "She makes a man go fast or go slow. She makes him blind and tricks him, eh?—ever' damn way she can. Is it not so, *mes amis?*"

"You got that plumb center," said Bickham. "'Bout all you got out here is time, Josie. Days don't make no difference. Ain't nobody waitin' for you to get anyplace. Ain't nobody goin' to get away, you stay on their track. If you ain't expected, it don't make no difference when you get there."

"What if it rains?" asked Montez. "There would be no tracks." They had encountered so many sudden rains on their journey, Montez almost expected it as a daily occurrence.

"Then," said Doucette, with a sly grin, "you have to track them in here." He tapped his index finger against his forehead.

The men chuckled at that, even Josie Montez. He knew what Pierre meant. The good hunter always had to think like his prey, had to learn the habits of the hunted. He had already learned, from traveling with Jocko DeSam, that progress was made at the whim of the weather, the river, of nature itself. Impatience was a killer in such country. It was not a trait he nurtured, but he knew that he had better start practicing patience if he wanted to find Lemuel Hawke and cut his throat.

Montez looked at the sky again, wondering if it would rain and delay the tracking. Finally, he resolved the questions in his mind.

"We will go on, then," he said. "Do you have any idea where those men are headed?"

Santiago shrugged, looked into the distance. Trees lined the Musselshell as it wound like a serpent through hilly, broken country. In the distance, behind clouds, the mountain ranges began. There were no boundaries, only those claimed by various tribes, and they moved around like the beasts in Eden, going where the game was, fighting with other tribes and stealing from them.

Bickham looked at his feet, at a loss for anything to say.

"They are headed where the river takes them," said Doucette, and that was sufficient answer for Montez. For all of his life, he had done virtually the same thing. He and his brother, the one they called Spanish Jack in St. Louis, had grown up in the slums of Barcelona. Their father, Ernesto Montez, had been a petty thief, their mother a washerwoman.

The family lived in poverty, but Ernesto always seemed to have pesetas enough to buy the wine. After he got drunk, he would beat his wife, Maria, until her screams went silent and she was senseless. When the boys grew old enough to protest, Ernesto beat them, too, not just with his fists, but with broom handles, wash paddles and iron burglar tools.

Josie and Jack, known then as Pepe and Juan, learned their father's trade by the time Jack was seven, Josie was eight. They learned to pick pockets at the bullfights, how to steal chicken and bread from merchants, how to steal purses in rich Roman Catholic churches.

When Josie was fifteen, he ran away from home. One day he found Jack sleeping under a bridge and learned that he had run away from home, too. He also learned that Ernesto had killed their mother, bludgeoned her to death with a bar he used to pry open windows in wealthy homes when the owners were absent.

Both boys lived on the streets, sleeping in country woods, stealing food and money, more than enough to fill their bellies and put fat on their ribs. They were husky and mean young men, wise in the ways of the streets and the back alleys, when they were shanghaied on a ship going to New Orleans. They jumped ship in New Orleans and found that thievery was just as profitable there as it had been in Barcelona. They saved their money, learned to steal not just enough for subsistence but enough to make a profit.

They learned the ways of the New World from an old pirate called Blinky. He had retired from the high seas and banded together a group of urchins whom he taught the finer points of larceny.

"Don't steal food from an untended wagon," Blinky told them. "Steal the wagon, the horse, and all the goods. Then you are in business. You can steal from a wharf and load the goods in your wagon. You can sell these goods at market just like any other enterprising merchant."

Blinky was murdered one night as he slept. Jack learned that two of the ex-mariner's men had done it, believing the old pirate had a sack of gold in his diggings. Jack killed them both, stabbing one in a fair fight, strangling the other with his bare hands in a blind rage.

Those first killings had opened up other paths to him. He became well known as a man who would do anything for money and none of it had to be legal. Some of his clients were wealthy men, others were criminals like himself.

So, he and Jack had followed many a river in their lives. Jack was gone, now, but Josie would avenge his death as Jack had avenged Blinky's. He had other rivers to follow before he gave up his ghost.

But he wondered where the river would lead them. His scalp prickled as he thought of the stories he'd listened to around the brigade campfires—tales of savage Indian attacks, scalping, torture. He wanted to kill Lemuel Hawke, his kid Morgan, if necessary, and be done with it. The men he had hired were free to go their own way after they found the Hawkes for him. Beyond that, he couldn't reason. All he knew was that he could get back to St. Louis on his own. He could follow the sun and the rivers back to civilization. Let these cursed half-wild trappers have this worthless, godforsaken land.

————·————

Morgan's eyes widened, his mouth opened, went slack. He felt a jellied quivering in his knees.

The girl hung back behind Blue Shell, peering at Morgan from behind her friend's shoulder.

"Patch," said Blue Shell. "You come back."

"Yes, Blue Shell. I come to trap the beaver." Lem looked at

the trapper, scratched the back of his head. He had never seen Patch act so polite.

"Gray Hawk say you bring white friend."

"This be Lemuel and his son, Morgan. They are friends of Gray Hawk."

"Morgan? Gray Hawk name Morgan."

Patch nodded. "This could be complicated," he said to Lem. "Any suggestions?"

"I named Morgan after Silas."

"And now the Crow call him Gray Hawk. So, you got Morgan Hawke and Silas Morgan Gray Hawk."

"Let Silas explain it," said Lem.

Blue Shell wore a puzzled expression on her face.

"Gray Hawk will tell Blue Shell about the white man's name," said Patch.

"Ask her who her little friend is," said Morgan.

"That might not be proper," said Patch.

"Morgan," said Lem, "you just remember that's a Injun gal. You keep your pecker in your pants."

"Oh, Pa, that ain't what I was a-thinkin'."

"I know damned well what you was a-thinkin'."

Morgan didn't want an argument with his father now, not in front of the Indian girl. She was still peering at him from over Blue Shell's shoulder, shy as a mouse.

The two women were joined by others, children, old men and women, all silently staring at the three white men and the Indian from an unknown tribe. Gradually, they began to speak among themselves and Morgan wondered what they were saying. He continued to look at the young girl with Blue Shell, taken by her beauty, fascinated by her long, raven-black tresses that reached well beyond her knees. She had glistening fawn eyes and smooth dark skin. She seemed, to Morgan, like something forbidden, like Eve, naked in the garden of Eden.

A few moments later, Silas and Lame Bull, along with two other braves, walked up, leading their pack mules and carrying their rifles and possibles pouches.

"Any trouble?" asked Patch.

"Some. You did the right thing, giving Lame Bull, and the others, those gifts. Them coons what tied you up wanted it all, 'pears like, but old Whistling Elk wanted to talk it over with his chief first. Otherwise you might not have no hair and be wolf meat."

Lem paled. Morgan shifted his attention from the girl to Silas as the mountain man handed him his rifle, pouch, the medicine horn and his priming horn.

"See you still got it," said Silas.

"I won't never part with it, Silas."

"That's another reason you still got your hair. That horn is powerful medicine, like I tolt you when I give it to you."

"I know," said Morgan.

"Tell Lame Bull we thank him," said Patch.

Silas spoke to Lame Bull and the other two braves, Little Fox and Crooked Face.

Lame Bull spoke briefly to Silas.

"He is going to tell his family to put up a lodge for you. He wants to be your friend. He has told us about Morgan shooting a charging buffler with one shot. The bull gets bigger ever' time he tells the story. He told Hunts the Sky, chief of the Little Robes, that the bull was as big as the medicine lodge and was breathin' on your face when you dropped it."

Morgan laughed.

"It was damned nigh that big," said Patch.

"And, it was a-blowin' steam on his face," said Lem, proudly.

"Come on to my digs whilst the Crow make ready to feast you," said Silas, suddenly serious. He looked over his shoulder toward the main camp. "There still may be some bad blood with Whistling Elk's bunch. We can figger out how to make peace with them whilst we chew the fat, catch up on past times."

Silas slapped Morgan and Lem on their backs. The crowd turned as if on a signal and streamed back to their lodges. The sky seemed to lighten and soon there was a break in the clouds. Shafts of light struck the tipis, made them shine like giant white beacons.

Morgan could tell that the Crow had been hunting buffalo. Everywhere he looked, he saw big chunks of meat drying on willow racks, the tongues black and fat, the big black pots steaming, smelling of cooked meat. There were deer and elk, fresh-killed, hanging from pole tripods, gutted out, their heads lolling. Women were skinning some of the deer, others were tanning hides. There seemed to be plenty of food in camp, and the people seemed happy. All of it was a wonder to Morgan, seeing so many Indians all at once, seeing how they lived. They seemed, oddly enough, like ordinary people except for their skin coloring, their dress and their lodges. The encampment was the strangest city he had ever seen, yet it felt just like a white man's city, except there were no stores, no taverns, no permanent dwellings.

"I see you met Blue Shell," said Silas as they followed the others back to the Little Robe lodge circle. "Fine woman, fine woman."

"Who's that girl with her?" asked Morgan.

"What gal is that?" asked Silas, winking.

"Aw, you know, Silas."

"I told him not to pay her no mind," said Lem. "We don't want no trouble like we had in St. Louis."

"Her name is Yellow Bead," said Silas. "She ain't never took up with a buck. Her pa was kilt by Blackfoot. She lives with her mother, Basket Woman. We all kind of help out with food and such."

"How old is she?" asked Morgan.

"Well, I don't rightly know," said Silas. "Thirteen, fourteen summers, the way Injuns count, I reckon."

There was a buffalo skull, blanched white by the sun, the hide eaten away by worms, sitting on a large rock outside Silas' lodge. The skull was painted with red, yellow and black lines, and decorated with mysterious symbols. Silas went past it, stood by the flap.

"Go on in and set," he said. "Walk to the left and around the fire. The Crow are mighty keen on ceremony. You got to do everythin' right or they think you got a bad heart."

Morgan went in first. He was anxious to see Yellow Bead again. His heart was pounding as he ducked down and entered the tipi. He blinked his eyes, trying to adjust to the dim light. He waddled to the left, following the circular perimeter of the lodge.

Blue Shell and Yellow Bead were stirring something in two pots hanging on cooking irons over the fire ring. The aroma of boiling meat and herbs made Morgan's stomach churn with hunger. The smoke from the fire went straight up through the smoke hole. The women seemed not to notice him. He waddled all the way around and sat down. His pa followed close behind him, then came Patch, Looking Loon and, finally, Silas himself.

The tipi seemed spacious to Morgan. There were buffalo robes for beds, lots of deer and elk hides and bales of beaver, marten and lynx furs stacked up along one side. Silas' flintlock rifle, his possibles bag, powder horns, tomahawks and extra knives in beautiful quilled scabbards lay on a platform of buffalo hides. There were cooking utensils, bowls, spoons and ladles all neatly arranged close to the fire.

Lem looked around, too, then sat crosslegged like the others.

"We got no chairs as such," said Silas. "Just lay your rifles and pouches back along the wall and make yourselves comfortable. The women'll have some vittles for us right quick."

Morgan heard Blue Shell say something to Yellow Bead. Yellow Bead had her head bent so that he could not see her face. She picked up some bowls and horn spoons, handed them to Silas, first, then to Looking Loon, Patch, Lem, and finally, to Morgan. She put another bowl in the empty space next to Morgan.

"Oho," said Silas, "looky there."

"What?" asked Morgan.

"Looks like Yellow Bead's taken a liking to you, Morgan. That's her bowl she set there by your side."

Lem tried to conceal his sudden frown, but Morgan caught it.

"Well, it don't make no nevermind to me," said Morgan quickly. He wanted no outburst from his pa. Inside, his nerves were jangling, his stomach quivering, and it wasn't from a hungering for food. Blue Shell said something in Crow to Silas. Then, she looked at Morgan and smiled.

"Yep, Morgan," said Silas, "it looks like you done made a friend. Blue Shell says that Yellow Bead is plumb stuck on you."

"Well, Morgan ain't takin' up with no Injun gal," said Lem.

"Lem," Silas said softly, "you can't keep on lumpin' all womens in the same pile as Roberta. One bad woman don't make 'em all bad."

"I ain't never met a good 'un yet," said Lem stubbornly.

"Pa, don't," said Morgan. "I ain't takin' up with Yellow Bead. I just think she's mighty purty, that's all."

Lem said nothing, but he fed on bitter memories of his wife, Roberta, Morgan's mother, who abandoned them and took up with another man. He still hated her. He hated all women, in fact, and he meant to see that Morgan learned how bad they were so's he wouldn't get hurt by 'em.

Blue Shell lifted one of the pots off the cooking irons and carried it to a flat stone wrapped in deerhide, a kind of small table in front of Silas. She set the pot down and handed her husband the ladle, one that Silas had bought in St. Louis.

"Let's eat," said Silas, dipping the ladle into the pot.

Yellow Bead and Blue Shell waited until all the men had taken food, then served themselves. Blue Shell sat by herself, but Yellow Bead sat next to Morgan.

"Buffler meat," said Silas as they all began eating. "Best vittles a man ever tasted."

Morgan barely heard him above the beating of his heart. Yellow Bead sat so close to him, he could smell the fragrance of flowers in her hair, the earthy smell of her body under the white dress she wore. When he shifted position, he put his hand down and touched a pile of her hair puddled on the packed earth next to him. It was soft to his touch.

Yellow Bead looked shyly up at him and his heart froze in his chest.

He caught Looking Loon staring at him. There was a twinkle in the Delaware's eye.

18

Lem didn't believe Morgan's excuse that he wanted to look after the horses. He suspected that his son wanted to do some sparking with Yellow Bead, who with Blue Shell had gone down to the river to do the washing.

"Silas," he said, after Morgan had gone away, "let's go somewheres by ourselfs and have a smoke and a talk."

"Fetch your pipe."

Patch said he was going to see Hunts the Sky, chief of the Little Robes. He said he wanted to give him some tobacco and gifts, renew their friendship. Looking Loon stayed in the tipi to sleep.

The two walked to a patch of timber, found a place where they could rest in the shade. The sun had burned through the clouds. There would be no rain that day.

Lem gave Silas some tobacco for his pipe, filled his own.

"Much obliged," said Silas. "Tobaccer's been scarce this summer."

"I'll leave you ten pounds when we set out," said Lem.

Lem used his magnifying glass to light his pipe. Silas struck fire from flint and steel into his bowl, blew on the sparks until they caught. The tobacco was good and dry, gave off a strong aroma.

"What's on your mind, Lemuel?" Silas blew a spume of smoke into the air.

"I want you to show me the way to the mountains. Me and Morg want to pull out in the morning. We aim to trap beaver hard as we can."

"What's your hurry, Lem? You just got here. They'll be feastin' tonight, and likely all the clans will want you to visit 'em. Ain't time to trap yet."

"We want to get settled," Hawke said lamely.

"Haw. Well, this old coon's goin' to trap them mountains this winter hisself. This camp won't be here in a week. The Crow got their buffler and will spend the rest of the summer in the cool high country. Some of the bucks will trap so they can do some tradin' in the spring. Just hold your horses, Lem."

"We really want to get movin', me and Morg."

Silas sucked deeply on his pipe, rolled the smoke around in his mouth. He let it out slowly, then looked off through the trees. Snatches of laughter and ribbons of Crow voices floated on the afternoon air. The sun made dappled shadows in the copse of trees. Water splashed down at the river from swimmers playing along the shore. There was a peace in the air that belied the turmoil inside the man who sat across from him leaning against a birch tree.

"Lem, you and Morgan don't want to be goin' off by yourselfs. I did it once't and paid dearly for it. Them mountains ain't no place for greenhorns such as you and your boy.

They're mighty partic'lar as to who comes into 'em and who comes out alive."

"You did it."

"Nope. I went with a brigade the first time. I went into the mountains on my own the next year and damned near died. These Crow saved my life, brought me out."

"What happened?"

"I shot me a elk with a rack big enough to hold a dozen coats and hats. Thought he was dead. They was snowdrifts higher'n a man's head and it were wet snow, stuck to you like feathers to tar. Welp, that elk upped and ran one of them long tines through my gut. Burnt like fire and I had to stuff my innards back in my belly. It were the snow what kept me from dyin' right off. I got back to my camp, no more'n a deadfall pine I rigged up for a shelter. I sewed my belly back up, but I was a-bleedin' inside. I packed my belly with snow so's I couldn't feel the burnin' no more. But I got the deleriums and the fever and some passin' Crow heard me, thought I was makin' big medicine."

Silas paused and Lem leaned forward to hear the rest of the story.

"What did they do?" asked Hawke.

"They rigged a travvy and carried me down the mountains. It were the Little Robes and Yellow Bead's pa made medicine over me. Her ma tended me with herbs and river clay until I no longer got the twitches ever' time I took breath."

"That was a accident," said Lem. "You ought to have known better."

"I was plumb hungry and crazy and cold. My old bean wasn't workin' right that day. I should have come up on the bull another way and had my fusil cocked. Point is, the mountains don't 'llow many mistakes. I was lucky. If them Crow hadn't come along, this old coon would have been wolf meat."

"Well, me and Morg are goin'. In the mornin', for certain sure. We'll get to the mountains on our own."

"You talked this over with Morgan? You might want to stick with Sisco. Him and that Delaware knows the country mighty well."

"Morg wants to get to trappin' pretty bad."

"You ever trapped beaver?" Silas asked, his voice low-pitched, deceptively smooth.

"Now, you know we ain't, Silas. But I been thinkin' on it, studyin' in my head what you tolt me about catching beaver and such. I reckon we'll do just fine."

"Well, you could trade for your furs and take 'em back to St. Louis and get a fair price. Save you a heap of worrisomes."

"We aim to trade and trap, too. Ain't that the way it's done?"

"That's so," said Silas. "If you go off on your own, you might trap some place that's already been staked out. You might have to fight for the skins you take."

"Other trappers?"

"And Injuns. They'll be a bunch a-trappin' them streams. 'Less'n you got a map, know which is which, you could get lost or worse, get kilt."

"I thought there was plenty of room up in the mountains."

"They is, but it gets more crowded ever' season. The Crow say they's a big brigade a-comin' up the Platte, Angus MacDougal's bunch, and more on the Big Horn and up on the Milk and the Judith. Crow don't like it none. I heard tell Jocko DeSam's goin' to trade with the Blackfeet up north. Runners come in the other day, sayin' four men from his bunch are comin' up the Musselshell, headed our way."

Silas looked at Lem closely.

"Four men?"

"Mighty peculiar, ain't it? You got any friends comin' after you?" Silas' eyes narrowed and his teeth clamped his pipe tightly. He did not draw on it, but waited for an answer.

"Did—was one of 'em a Spaniard?"

Silas took his pipe from his mouth. It was made of pink pipestone, a gift from Blue Shell's father, Turns Back the Enemy.

"The Crows what seen 'em knew three of the men. They been here before. They didn't know the other man, just that he was dark-skinned and had hair on his face."

Lem let out a shallow sigh. "Maybe it ain't him, then," he said.

"Who?" asked Silas.

"Spanish Jack's brother. Josie Montez."

"He's a bad one. What makes you think it ain't him?"

"I seen Josie once't. He was with MacDougal and Jocko. He din't have no beard."

"Man can grow a beard in a week," said Silas. "If Josie's a-huntin' you, maybe you and Morgan better wait and see if he's one of them four men. Be a heap safer here where you got friends. Runners said they was about three days ride from camp."

"I ain't afraid of him," said Lem.

Silas knocked the dottle out of his pipe, banging the bowl gently against an ash tree.

"You want to leave tomorry, I'll point you toward the mountains. You'll have no river to guide you once you leave the Musselshell, but you ain't got far to go."

"We'll be a-leavin'," said Lem.

"Sorry to see you go," said Silas. "Might not see you again."

"You're just tryin' to scare me, Silas."

"Hell, I hope I do."

He got up and Lem knew the conversation was over. He

hated to disappoint his old friend, but he still had memories of Spanish Jack burning up in that tavern in St. Louis, all over a slut that Morgan had peckered, who was just playin' his boy for a fool. He didn't want anything like that to happen again.

———·———

Morgan walked down to the river. Boys swam and splashed near the shore in the shallows. Downstream, he saw several women washing clothes, chattering and laughing among themselves. He scanned them for a glimpse of Yellow Bead and Blue Shell. Finally, he saw the two maidens, knee-deep in the river, spanking water at each other like schoolgirls.

He wandered toward them, trying to appear as though he were just walking along, not going anywhere in particular. Some of the girls down by the river saw him there and began to giggle. Their joyous titters struck red-tipped ears. Some of the young boys followed after him, teasing him with words he didn't understand.

He turned to shoo the boys away. They ran from him like antic birds, pretending to be mortally afraid as they scattered to escape his flailing arms.

Blue Shell saw Morgan coming. She waved him away. He kept on walking. Yellow Bead turned, saw him, then quickly turned away. Blue Shell stalked out of the river.

"Go away," she said in English.

"I'm just walkin'," said Morgan. "Mindin' my own business."

"You go," she said sternly.

"Can I talk to Yellow Bead? I can speak in sign." Morgan gestured to show her he could speak and understand the hand language.

Blue Shell shook her head. She signed back to him.

"Yellow Bead no talk. You go talk Gray Hawk."

Morgan started to protest, but now a crowd of women, old and young, were gathering around, all talking at once. The boys did not come near, but stayed well away, conversing among themselves.

Puzzled, Morgan retreated.

"All right, all right," he said. "I'm a-goin'."

"You go quick," said Blue Shell, pushing the air with her hands.

Morgan felt like a whipped cur as he walked back to the camp alone. He looked back once, but Yellow Bead had her back to him. He knew he had probably violated some Indian custom. Maybe that's what Blue Shell was trying to tell him when she ordered him to speak to Silas.

Silas met him as he came back into camp.

"Turned you back, did they?"

Morgan nodded.

"All I wanted to do was talk to her," he said sadly.

"I figgered that might happen. You never know with Injuns. Likely, Yellow Bead is taken with you and wants a formal courtin'."

"How do I do that?"

"The bucks I seen a-courtin' usually just stay within sight of the maiden and play a willow flute or act strange."

"Act strange?"

"Well, you know, they stand on their heads, or walk backward, anything to get a maid's attention."

"That's all?"

"No, they ask if they can walk with a certain gal or get permission to talk to her. They give a gal's father presents, maybe give the mother some little gewgaw. It's kinda complicated."

"Is that how you courted Blue Shell?"

Silas walked toward a far edge of camp where they could be alone.

"Not rightly. I just up and asked her pa if I could have her. I gave him three horses for her, a knife, a rifle, three blankets and two hatchets."

Morgan scratched his nose. He didn't have that many horses, no rifle he could give up. He could give up a knife or two, some hatchets from the goods he had brought to trade.

"But, you said her pa was dead."

Silas told Morgan that Yellow Bead's father had been a Crow medicine man named Black Wolf. According to Silas, he was highly respected and his death was a great loss to the Little Robe people.

"Her ma's name is Basket Woman. I don't know if she could give the girl away."

"I don't want no wife," said Morgan. "I just wanted to spark her a little."

"Ain't no such thing. You take her to your blankets, she's your woman."

"Well, maybe I ain't so keen to court her, then."

"Best thing to do is just be patient. Ain't nothin' draws a woman more'n a man who shows no interest in her."

"You mean just pay her no mind?"

"You do that, son, she just might come a-runnin'."

Morgan thought about it.

"How do I make a willow flute?" he asked after a few moments.

Silas laughed.

"You go cut you a young willer about a half-inch acrost and I'll show you."

——·——

That night there was celebration in the camp. Morgan, his father, Patch and Looking Loon went together to meet Hunts the Sky, the chief of the Little Robes. They feasted in the big medicine lodge, with its depiction of the Good Spirit on one side, the Evil Spirit on the other. Morgan counted thirty lodgepoles. There must have been at least forty men inside at one time. The men came and went until he lost count. But he saw Whistling Elk come in and eat, along with others of his clan. Everyone seemed to be in a gay mood. The Crow dressed in their finest raiment. Their wives and daughters served buffalo tongue, liver, hump, beaver tail, wild onions and some kind of pudding. Lem, Morgan, Patch and Looking Loon gorged themselves.

The Crow told stories and acted them out: hunting tales and accounts of battles with their enemies. Patch told them all about Morgan's killing of the huge buffalo. Silas pushed Morgan to his feet, made him tell the story.

"How?"

"Just playact it out, like you seen them braves do it."

Morgan mimed riding up after the buffalo. He bent over and put his hands up to show the buffalo. He used the sign language he had learned and made up some. He knew that the Crow were all watching him intently, but he got into the spirit of the storytelling. He mimicked being bucked off his horse, of falling. He rose with an imaginary rifle in his hands. He showed the giant buffalo charging him and then he brought the rifle to his shoulder. He took aim and fired, making the sound of a rifle booming. He switched back to the bull, showed him charging and snorting, then falling and skidding to a stop at Morgan's feet. He stood with one foot in the air as if standing on the beast's huge hump and the Crow inside the medicine lodge went wild with approval. Lem, Patch and Silas all cheered, and the Crow began yelling and yipping until Morgan's neck bristled with stiffened hairs.

Indians embraced him, clapped him on the back.

Then, Patch got up and told about the Pawnee arrows in the bull and how the Pawnee had let them go after hearing how Morgan had brought down the bull with a single shot at close range. The Crow went wild all over again.

Morgan spent the rest of the evening in a daze. Patch had given Hunts the Sky some whiskey and Silas had some himself. He and Lem drank a lot of it, and Patch made Morgan drink some as well. Looking Loon got very drunk and staggered off, found a spot next to Silas' lodge and fell asleep.

Morgan wandered out of the medicine lodge for some fresh air. His head was fuzzy inside. He felt as if he had grown a foot during the evening. He kept saying Crow words over and over even if he did not know their meaning. He felt part of these people, a brother to them. He was happy and smiling idiotically. He looked up at the stars and they seemed closer than they ever had before.

He had no idea where he was. The white cones of tipis rose up in the night all around him. He was lost in a forest of tipis. They all looked alike. Most of them glowed with light, some were dark, as if abandoned. He tried to get his bearings, but every time he changed direction, he found himself heading back toward the medicine lodge. He had to walk around a maze of skins staked out flat on the ground and those strung on poles, stretched to dry in the sun.

By the third time he had done this, Morgan knew he was being followed. He could not see who it was. Everytime he turned around quickly, whoever had been making noise behind him had disappeared. Finally, he set off in an entirely different direction. Then, he walked past the tipis and knew he had gone too far. Again he heard a noise behind him and turned around quickly.

There was no one there.

He walked back toward one of the tipis at the edge of the woods. He heard someone whisper: "Morgan."

The voice was faintly accented, thin, musical.

"Who's there?" he asked.

Yellow Bead stepped out from the shadow of a lodge.

"Yell Oh Bead," she said slowly. Then, she said something in the Crow tongue. But her hands beckoned to him.

"Yellow Bead," he said, suddenly even giddier than he was before. He felt light-headed, addled. He closed his eyes a moment, then snapped them open. She motioned for him to follow her.

"Morgan," she said. It sounded more like "Mo-Gan." His blood raced hotly as she took his hand, led him past tipi after tipi, avoiding the staked hides, staying to the shadows.

Finally, Yellow Bead stopped before a lone lodge. It was not joined to a circle but stood apart.

"You. Mo-Gan," she said, pointing to his chest.

"Yes. I'm Morgan," he said.

"Come, Mo-Gan."

To his surprise, she led him inside. It was dark and he could see nothing. He heard Yellow Bead giggle. It was a tinkling kind of laugh, so brief he wondered if he had imagined it.

She led him to the left. He touched the soft walls of the tipi, but was still blind, disoriented. She stopped, pulled him down. He felt the thick pile of a buffalo blanket. He sat on it, tried to see her face in the darkness. He looked skyward, through the smoke hole, and saw the faint glimmerings of stars, the only light inside the lodge.

Suddenly, he no longer felt Yellow Bead's hands on him. He

reached out for her, but his fingers groped only empty air. Then, he heard the faint soft crackle of deerskin, heard something plop to the ground. He heard other sounds, but could not make them out. He was afraid to speak, but his imagination flared like wildfire. He felt an unexpected stirring in his loins, a tug of desire beginning to stiffen him.

A few seconds later, he felt her sit beside him. She breathed into his ear.

"Mo-Gan," she whispered.

He turned, reached out for her. As his eyes grew accustomed to the light, he could make out her dim shape, a tiny silhouette lit only by starshine.

He put his arms around her, drew her close to him.

Yellow Bead was naked.

Her hands reached under his buckskin shirt and he felt her pulling it upward.

He released her and pulled his shirt off. Her hands tugged at his trousers. He kicked them off. She removed his moccasins and then shoved him backward onto the buffalo blanket.

Then, Yellow Bead crawled next to him, wrapped herself in his arms.

She touched his manhood with delicate fingers and he was ready.

Montez walked slowly back toward the camp, his mind racing, a plan of survival forming in his mind.

———·———

Yellow Bead pulled Morgan atop her. Her hands caressed him. She made little mewing sounds, spoke whispered words that he didn't understand. She found him with her hands, touched the hardness of him. He leaned down, kissed her face, found her lips. She returned his kiss with an eagerness that surprised him, made him flame inside, made his senses boil with a raging desire.

"Yellow Bead, Yellow Bead," Morgan said huskily as she guided him between her legs.

"Mo-Gan make baby Yalo Bead," she said.

"Yes, yes," he moaned as he entered her, sank into silk that was oiled slick and smooth, silk that was warm and soft, that clasped him tightly and pulled him deeper inside her.

She cried out softly when he drove in past her maidenhead, broke through the leathery barrier and sank deep. His lips brushed the fresh hot tears on her face, yet she did not beg him to stop, nor push him away.

"Heap good," she said.

"Yes. Heap good."

She moaned as he continued to plumb her depths. He wished he could see her face, look into her eyes. She kept saying things to him in her broken English and in her own tongue. He said things to her, things that he meant, but the heat rose strong in him, and in a frenzy, he raced to the finish, exploding inside her as rocket bombs burst in his brain. He felt his seed drain out of him and fill her womb. She clasped him tightly and held onto him, her body quivering in the throes of ecstacy.

She was still trembling when he slid off her, lay beside her, sated.

"I'm all bucked out," he breathed, before he realized she probably couldn't understand him.

"Mo-Gan good man," she said, and he felt her hand glide across his chest, tickling the fine hairs that grew there.

"Yellow Bead, you got to learn more English than that."

She said something in Crow.

"Never mind," he said. He swelled up with the pleasure of lying beside her, knowing he had taken her cherry, that she had been a virgin. He felt strong and tall and breathed with a deep satisfaction. It was wonderful to be alive, to be with this Indian girl. She made him feel wanted, needed. She had come to him. He had not had to court her or ask permission. It was so easy, he wanted to pinch himself to see if it all had been real.

He made love to her several times that night. Finally, he slept. When he awoke, Yellow Bead was gone. But his rifle was inside the tipi, and so was his possibles pouch. His medicine horn, his little priming horn were there, too. There were buffalo blankets all about and a new pair of moccasins, finely quilled, and leggings with both beads and quills decorating them. Atop the moccasins shone a single yellow bead.

Morgan sat up and smiled.

Morning light filled the tipi. Wisps of river fog blew past the smoke hole. He smelled food cooking and his stomach churned with hunger.

He dressed slowly, hoping Yellow Bead would return. He did not wear the new moccasins, but hid all the new things under a blanket. He wondered where his pa was. This was obviously the tipi that had been erected for him, his pa, Patch and Loonie, but none of them had slept in it. He rubbed sleep out of his eyes and opened the tent flap, crawled through it.

It was still early, and not all of the camp had arisen. He saw smoke streaming through the smoke holes of a few tipis, and some women were cooking outside their lodges. The river fog was burning off slowly as the sun sneaked over the horizon, splashing golden light through the trees that bordered the encampment.

There were two other lodges close by that seemed to have been newly erected. He wandered over to one of them, peered inside. He saw two sleeping figures: Patch and his father. He went to the other tipi and opened the flap. He was startled to see Looking Loon inside with a Crow woman. Both were naked. Looking Loon grinned at him. Morgan backed out, stood up.

He walked to the circle of Little Robe lodges, found the one where Silas lived. The tent flap was closed, secured with small sticks of wood.

"Silas," he called softly, not wishing to arouse the camp.

There was no answer. Morgan moved closer to the entrance.

"Silas, you in there?"

He heard rustlings, then a series of grunts and gutteral noises, followed by a softer voice.

"Morgan, that you?"

"You still asleep?"

"Ye gods, yes. Wait a minute. Christ, my head."

More rustlings. Then, a few moments later, the tent flap opened. A small brown hand beckoned for him to enter.

Blue Shell squatted by the fire ring, poking at the coals. Silas was sitting up, wearing only buckskin trousers. He was barefooted, his thin thatch of hair tangled from sleep. He rubbed a hand down his face.

"What are you doin' up so early?" asked Silas, one eye still closed, the other glaring balefully at Morgan.

"I dunno," said Morgan. "They put me up my own tipi."

"I know. That was Yellow Bead's doin'. Her and Blue Shell got some other women to help 'em."

"You seen Yellow Bead, Silas?"

"I ain't seen her. She's probably asleep or gettin' wood this time o' day."

Blue Shell said something to Silas in Crow. He didn't answer.

"She come to your lodge, did she?"

Morgan nodded.

"Well, that's a good sign. Kind of reminds me of Blue Shell."

"But she's gone this mornin'," said Morgan.

"She's got obligations. She'll be back."

"Does my pa know?"

"Know what?" Silas backed away from a tendril of smoke that scratched at his eyes. Blue Shell fanned the tiny flames until the wood caught. The smoke steadied and rose straight up through the smoke hole.

"About me'n Yellow Bead bein' together last night."

"I reckon not. He was pretty pie-eyed when I last saw him. Him and Patch was hittin' the whiskey pretty hard."

Morgan breathed a sigh of relief.

"Silas, you won't tell him, will you?"

"Hell, boy, I ain't no gossip. What you and Yellow Bead do in the blankets is your own business. Tell you one thing, though."

"What's that?"

"Your pa is dead set on headin' out to the mountains today. He's as ornery as a bottomland stump."

"How come he wants to go so quick? We just got here."

Silas stretched, slipped on a pair of moccasins.

"I got to pee," he said, standing up. "Come on. Blue Shell will cook us some breakfast." He spoke to his woman in Crow. Blue Shell nodded submissively. Morgan followed Silas outside. He had to pee, too.

They walked into the fringe of woods, picked out separate trees. Silas talked as he sprayed the flora.

"I tried to talk your pa out of goin' up to the mountains, just him and you, but he done had his mind set. The Crow made some smoke and talk last night afore the feast, anyways, and they decided to break up the camp. They'll scatter like leaves."

"Where will *you* go?" asked Morgan.

"Some of the Little Robes will go on up to the mountains. Me'n Blue Shell will likely go up with 'em."

"When?"

"Day or two. A week. Hard to tell about Injuns. Some will go off today, some tomorry. Some'll stay on another month, like as not."

Morgan finished his business. A moment later, Silas finished up, too.

"Where will Yellow Bead go?"

Silas cocked his head as if to tell Morgan how foolish his question was.

"Why, I reckon she'll tag along with you, if you want her, Morgan."

Morgan felt a surge of blood through his heart. Then, he felt a twinge of disappointment.

"Pa would never allow it," he said.

"Morgan, ain't none of my business, but you're full-growed and haired over some. Your pa, well, he's set in his ways. He's plumb sour on the womens 'cause of what happened with your ma. But, he ain't a-goin' to live your life for you. You want you a squaw, you take you a squaw. Yellow Bead's better'n most. She'd keep your blankets warm in winter, cook your food, clean your clothes, dress your meat. You want her, take her."

Morgan wondered if he dared. He and Silas stood there, neither moving, while he pondered what the old trapper had said. He knew in his heart that Silas was right. He also knew that his pa would kick up a whale of a fuss if he was to take Yellow Bead with them into the mountains.

"I want her, Silas, but my pa, he comes first."

"As it should be," said Silas, "but you got to think of yourself, too. You go on off and leave that Injun gal behind, you'd be mopin' and frettin' the whole time. 'Sides that, she's comin' ripe, and if you don't take her, some buck might play his flute outside her lodge and walk right off with her."

Silas started to go back to the lodge. Morgan stepped alongside him, considering the possibilities if he didn't take Yellow Bead with him now, when he had the chance.

"Would you help me, Silas?"

"Help you?"

"I mean help me talk to Pa."

Silas stopped walking, looked Morgan straight in the eye.

"Son, I think this is somethin' you got to do all by yourself. If you're goin' to be a man, you got to face up to things like a man."

Morgan nodded in agreement, for he had known all along that it wasn't Silas' place to take his part. It was something Morgan had to do himself, man to man. It was just that his father was so touchy about women.

He remembered his father barging into that bedroom up over Spanish Jack's, when he, Morgan, was with Willa, Jack's daughter. He remembered the look in his father's eyes, the rage he showed when he saw his son and Willa naked as jaybirds. And then, the fight, the fire and Spanish Jack dead. He had hated his father, then, and they had almost split up for good.

If he took up with Yellow Bead, his father might do something bad again. He was liable to get mad at everybody: Silas, Yellow Bead, Blue Shell, the whole passel of Crow. He didn't want that to happen. He had seen the rage on his father's face at Spanish Jack's in St. Louis, watched the tavern burn to the ground after the fight had broken out. A lamp had been turned over, and although his father had tried to save Spanish

Jack, the fire had driven them out before the man could be rescued.

Silas asked Morgan into his lodge for breakfast.

"I—I want to talk to Pa," he said.

"You get hungry, the pot's always full," said Silas.

"Thank you kindly, Silas. But I got to be goin'."

But Morgan didn't go to his father's lodge. Instead, he wandered around the camp, trying to get his jumbled thoughts in order. At one circle of lodges, he saw a Crow brave running from tipi to tipi. Then, he saw another, and another, doing the same thing. Morgan stood near the circle, watching.

Boys ran to the horse herd and began cutting horses out of the herd, leading them back to the great circle. Other youngsters began catching dogs, dragging them to their respective lodges. Children tied harnesses and sticks to the dogs, began loading bundles on the hastily rigged travois. The women started untying the thongs that bound the tipi hides to the ground. Then, at a signal, the skins began dropping, sliding off the lodgepoles.

The women divided the poles into two bunches, fastened the small ends on the shoulders of horses. Then, they tied short poles across the two bunches at right angles, just behind the horses' rumps. Girls and women spread out the lodgeskins and put their cooking utensils and household belongings in the center. Some rolled the skins up, others folded them. They put these bundles on their respective travois and tied them all with ropes or leather thongs.

Morgan stood fascinated, watching one entire circle of lodges come down, leaving a great emptiness of land and sky where once there had been a community. The women loaded packs on their backs, as did some of the children, and they piled atop the loaded travois. The smaller children drove the dogs, with their fifteen-foot travois poles, in behind as the warriors rode ahead on the best horses, preening and strutting before the whole camp. Other braves rode along the flanks, and some brought up the rear as the caravan moved out. The whole operation had taken less than an hour. The column of Crow rode to the north, and Morgan watched them until they had disappeared from sight.

He felt an emptiness inside to see them go, as if he might never see them again. For a moment, he was struck with a sense of loss. He felt a hollowness in his belly that was not from hunger. What if Yellow Bead had gone with them? He did not know one clan from another. He turned quickly and rushed back to the Little Robe circle of lodges, sick in his heart that Yellow Bead might be gone.

Seeing several lodges still standing gave him some comfort, but he didn't know which one was Yellow Bead's. He began looking for her, trying to appear calm and unconcerned.

Crow braves waved to him as he passed each lodge, some spoke to him in sign. He acknowledged each one, admired their fine physiques, their long hair, their breechclouts and moccasins. Some of the men had hair so long, their tresses dragged the ground when they walked. A few men carried their hair under their arms, all rolled up. He saw some women dipping a deerskin into a brine of ashes and water, while others were scraping off hair from one previously dipped. He saw other women combing their men's long hair and wondered why the women did not wear hair as long—only some of the young girls had let theirs grow out.

One woman was smearing bear grease in her man's hair, making it shine like an otter's skin. Morgan could smell the grease and it made his empty stomach roil.

Some women were stretching hides on the ground, driving stakes through the edges. He saw two women putting a hide inside a hole in the ground where rotten wet wood was smoking furiously. They tied a canopy of hard buffalo hide over it to hold the smoke and heat inside.

Morgan felt reassured. These people were not making preparations to break camp. He went around the entire circle, stopping for a few moments to watch a mother and her daughters braid and stain porcupine quills with colored dyes.

Finally, he saw Yellow Bead near the last lodge in the Little Robe circle. She and her mother, Basket Woman, and two other women, were sewing parts of a man's buckskin shirt and pants together in front of their lodge. All of the women, except Yellow Bead, watched him closely as he approached. She was the only one he recognized, but he knew the others must be relatives. He tried to figure out which one was her mother. The two older women had short hair, but one of them was groomed, the other was not. The unkempt one's hair appeared to not only have been cut haphazardly, but pulled out in large chunks. This woman had very sad eyes.

Morgan didn't know whether to stop and talk or just keep on going. He decided he had better just walk on by and pretend that nothing had happened between him and Yellow Bead.

Yellow Bead did not look up as Morgan passed by, his heart thumping in his chest. He kept on walking, but knew the women and girls were all staring at his back. He was about to let out the breath he had been holding when he heard a giggle, then someone tugging at his shirttail.

He turned, and there was Yellow Bead, wearing a plain buckskin dress as white as snow, staring up at him.

"Come," she said in sign. Then, she rubbed her belly, made the sign for eating.

He started to shake his head, but she took his hand, led him back to her lodge. The women sat there, staring at him.

"This is my mother," she said in sign. "Basket Woman. This is my aunt, Calling Dove." Morgan did not understand that name or the relationship. Finally, she pointed to her little sister. "This is Gray Mouse. My sister." He understood the mouse and sister part, but not the sign for gray.

"Mighty pleased to meet you," Morgan said awkwardly.

Basket Woman grinned through broken black teeth. He knew she was Yellow Bead's mother, but she was hideous. He wondered how Yellow Bead, or even her sister, could be so beautiful. Their father must have been handsome, he decided.

He followed Yellow Bead inside her lodge. She made him sit, gave him a horn spoon and a bowl filled with meat and something that looked like grass and tubers. He ate while she watched him. She kept filling up his bowl until he waved her off. He patted his belly, signed that it was full.

Then, Yellow Bead lifted her skirt and lay back on a pallette of buffalo robes. She smiled at him invitingly. He stared at her like a man transfixed, struck dumb. He had never seen anything like it. She was so bold, so natural, she took his breath away. She held her skirt up until he took off his trousers and came to her.

Morgan wanted to muffle her voice when he began to make love to her. She screamed and screeched so loud, he knew the whole camp could probably hear her. He felt embarrassed that her mother, that other woman and her sister were just outside, listening to them.

But he couldn't stop and he knew, afterward, that he could not give up Yellow Bead, even for his father.

20

Montez guessed that he had been on watch for at least two hours. He was tired, but not sleepy. He had used that time to think, and he had thought long and hard. Tonight, he decided, would be a test. If nothing happened, then he could probably trust these men. But if there was any treachery, he would soon be ready for them.

He had heard the others talking about the money he was carrying. It was hard to conceal the wad of banknotes and coins he kept in his belt pouch, but he had done his best not to tempt them. What was hardest to swallow was that they thought him a tenderfoot, a pilgrim out of his element. That galled him more than their stupid greed, their clumsy cunning, or their ill-conceived treachery.

He had met such men before and they wore their secrets on their faces, uttered them in their clandestine whispers when they thought he was asleep or out of earshot. He had dealt with such men on many bloody occasions, and yet it was different this time. They were close at hand and there were no streets or alleys in which to stalk or hide. So, he would meet them on their own ground and teach them that he was not so dumb about the ways of men as they might think.

From the talk he had overheard that day, they planned to do away with him on such a night as this, possibly when he was asleep, during the dark of the moon.

Before he woke up Doucette for the next watch, Montez took his other pistol from his saddlebag. He carefully unwrapped it from the oilcloth. He worked in the dark, cleaning it, loading it, priming the pan. He reloaded his spare rifle, leaned that against a tree where it could not be seen. Finally, he placed his saddlebags, bundles of goods and other bulky objects inside his blankets. Now, as he finished up, in the faint light of stars, he saw that his bedroll resembled a man sleeping.

He shook Pierre Doucette awake, spoke to him softly.

"Time for your watch, *amigo.*"

"Eh? So soon?"

Montez laughed. When Doucette sat up, rubbing his eyes, Montez went to his bedroll, lay down beside it. He pretended to sleep as he watched Doucette stand up, rifle in hand, and start walking the perimeter of their camp. As soon as the breed had his back turned, Montez crawled toward the tree where he had left his spare rifle.

He moved very slowly, quietly. When he reached the tree, he sat behind it. From there, he could see the other two men sleeping soundly. Soon, he saw Doucette glide into view, walking soundlessly, stopping every so often to listen.

Doucette walked beyond Montez's position, stopped once again. The breed was very difficult to see when he was stationary. Montez blinked his eyes, trying to separate Doucette's shape from his surroundings. But as he looked around, every object took on a mystical quality. Every shape looked like an Indian or a deer or a buffalo. It was maddening to sit there, blinded by darkness, befuddled by tricks of the mind and shadows that changed shape with every flicker of stars. The Milky Way shimmered in the obsidian sky like scattered diamonds. The moon, waxing now, shed pewter light on the trees, limned the grasses with a leaden glaze.

Crickets droned in a million sawing voices and mosquitoes sang in his ears with a grating whine. Frogs harangued their kindred in the insect din, a bass chorus in counterpoint. In the dark sepulchre of the night, every noise seemed amplified. Montez strained his ears trying to hear any alien sound. He felt a mosquito land on his face, winced as it needled through his flesh, began to siphon his blood. He did not move.

An owl flapped by like some aimless shadowy pennant, startling him. He could hear its pinions beating the air like someone breathing close at hand. The bird disappeared ghost-like into the trees, but Montez's heart continued to pump at a rapid rate. The pulsebeat in his ears added another voice to the strange harmony of nocturnal orchestras.

The moments crawled by like sluggish inchworms, and far off, he heard the piping yip of a coyote, then an answering string of chromatic yodels from a different direction. Pierre Doucette was nowhere to be seen. Montez drew in a deep slow breath and turned slowly, wondering if the breed was sneaking up on him. There was nobody there, but his uneasiness grew as he tried to find Doucette with his eyes, tried to penetrate the darkness with his will.

Later, Montez heard the scream of a rabbit and knew the owl must have made the kill. The cry of the mortally wounded animal startled him, but still he did not move. There was no sign of the breed. He figured Doucette had not moved in over fifteen minutes, perhaps as long as a half an hour.

Montez fingered the trigger guard of his rifle. His palm was slick with sweat. The musk of the river clogged his nostrils, and he became aware of the soft sob of the waters lapping at the bank, the gutteral croak of frogs as the singing of the crickets died out suddenly.

Finally, he saw a shadow move. It was Doucette. Montez let out a pent-up breath. Then, he heard Doucette relieving himself. Montez heard the rustle of the man's buckskins, saw him lay his rifle across his arm and walk the circle as he had before.

Montez relaxed. His eyelids drooped, felt as if they were weighted with Galena lead. Weariness seeped through his muscles, dulled his brain. Had he been a fool? Was the wilderness making him into a savage? Had he been so long away from civilization that he was now behaving more like a wild animal than a human being? Montez shook his head to clear his brain. Now, he would look like an idiot if he went back to his bedroll. Doucette would see him, wonder if he wasn't the one to be mistrusted.

Montez yawned soundlessly. His eyes began to cloud with sleepiness. He was about ready to call it a night and go back to his bedroll when something made him hestitate. A sound, different from the threnodic hum of insects, the bass groans of bullfrogs, caught his attention, pricked his senses to a state of full alertness.

Montez blinked his eyes to clear the fog of sleep from them. He listened intently, trying to identify the sound should he hear it again.

Nothing.

Then, he heard the sound again, saw movement out of the corner of his eye. Doucette strode into camp from the far end, walked straight to the place where Hal Bickham was sleeping. His leggings brushed against the grasses. That was the sound

Montez had heard before. Doucette should have been well out of earshot of the camp so he could hear any approaching danger, so why was he creeping back like this? His watch was not over and had there been any danger he would have sung out to alert the camp.

Doucette stooped over, shook the sleeping man. Montez heard a faint, harsh whisper, then watched as Hal got up from his blankets and stood there. Something glistened silvery near his hand. A hatchet, Montez thought. He stared, unbelieving, as Doucette strode over to Felix Santiago's bedroll, nudged the sleeping man in the side with the toe of his moccasin.

Santiago crawled out of his blankets, arose. He, too, grasped a hatchet in his hand. Doucette pulled something from his belt. Montez could just make out that it was a long skinning knife. He had seen it many times in days past, seen how skillfully the halfbreed had used it to skin out a deer. He had admired the knife, in fact, and now he shuddered to see it in Doucette's hand, poised to strike.

The three men walked over to Montez's bedroll. Santiago and Bickham flanked the mound of blankets where Montez's head might have been. Doucette straddled it. Santiago and Bickham raised their hatchets over their heads, awaiting a signal. Doucette squatted over the hump under the blankets, raised his knife with both hands.

"Now," Doucette whispered.

Bickham and Santiago struck at the same time, smashing their hatchets downward into the mass of blankets. Doucette plunged the knife straight down, lunging behind the blade to give it force.

"What the h—?" Bickham exclaimed.

Montez raised his rifle, lined up the barrel on Felix Santiago's back. He held the trigger in while he cocked the hammer. He squeezed the trigger just as Santiago was lifting his weapon to strike another blow. There was a slight puff and a brief flash as the thin-grained English powder ignited in the pan. Blazing orange flame lit the three figures hunched over the pile of blankets and gear. White smoke belched from the barrel, billowed out into a blinding cloud.

Montez heard the ball thunk home, heard a groan as he laid his rifle down, reached for the other, leaning against the tree. He cocked the hammer back as he drew it to his shoulder. He sidled away from the tree, crabbed to another position.

He sighted on Hal Bickham as the man started to run toward the smoke, tomahawk raised. Montez fired point-blank at Bickham's chest. The smoke obscured his vision, but he heard the ball strike buckskins and flesh. Hal crashed to the ground, gushing blood from his chest.

Montez dropped the second rifle, grabbed both pistols, the pair of Spanish flintlocks, from his belt. He ran through the smoke, dissipating it into cobwebby wisps. Doucette rose from the ground, turned to face the charging Spaniard.

Montez fired both pistols at Doucette, first one, then the other, as he ran. He realized that Doucette had ducked just before he triggered the first pistol and that his second shot had gone wild.

"*Sacré . . . ,*" Doucette muttered, and lunged toward Montez.

Montez threw both pistols at Doucette, saw them fly harmlessly past him. He clawed for his own knife, drew it just as the halfbreed slashed the air with his blade, missing Montez's belly by a hair's scant breadth.

"*Cabrón,*" growled Montez and drove his knife towards Doucette's midsection. The breed sucked in his gut and sidestepped out of range.

Montez went into a crouch, began to stalk Doucette. Pierre was on his guard now and he, too, bent to a fighting crouch.

The two men circled each other warily. On the ground, Hal was wheezing through blood bubbling up in his throat. There was no sound from Santiago. He lay there with his spine shattered by a flattened lead ball, one of his lungs shot away, the other just barely inflating and deflating with his shallow breathing.

Doucette feinted, but Montez was not deceived. He feinted, in turn, then slashed Doucette's unprotected arm, felt the blade slice through the breed's sleeve, strike flesh and bone.

Doucette cried out in pain, reacted by charging straight at Montez. But Montez moved two steps to the side and brought his blade around, jabbed it at Doucette's midsection. Doucette saw it coming, tried to avoid the blow. He caved in his side and the blade only ripped a two-inch furrow. But the shock staggered the breed and he turned too slowly to avoid the catlike quickness of the Spaniard.

Montez caught Doucette's arm, spun him around. He grappled with him, drew him close. Then, he sank his blade into Doucette's leg once, twice, so quick that Doucette didn't feel the pain at first, but his leg started to buckle. Doucette brought his blade up to try and fend off the close attack, but it was too late.

Montez bent Doucette's arm backward until it snapped at the elbow.

Doucette screamed.

Montez dropped the rag of an arm, kneed Doucette in the groin, then drove his knife up into his belly as the breed bent over in agony. Doucette coughed with the pain of it. Montez jerked his knife free as Doucette was pitching forward. He grabbed the breed behind the neck, then plunged his knife hard between Doucette's shoulder blades, sinking it to the hilt. He twisted the knife and gouged out a chunk of meat the size of a walnut.

Doucette collapsed on the ground, bleeding from his wounds. There was the fetid stench of torn bowels in the air.

"Puerco," Montez said in Spanish. "Pig."

He stood there, panting, wiping his bloodied blade on his leggings. He switched the knife to his other hand and wiped his palm on his buckskin shirt, smearing it with Doucette's blood. His own blood raced in his veins. His temples throbbed. He felt good all over, adrenaline pumping through his bloodstream like wildfire. He listened to Bickham's wheezing, Santiago's shallow and fluttering breathing, the low groans from Doucette's throat.

"You goddamn bastards," Montez whispered, struggling to get back his breath. "You sonsofbitches."

Finally, Montez staggered away to retrieve his pistols, pick up his rifles. He made a small fire, cleaned and reloaded his weapons. He cleaned his knife lovingly, sharpened it on an Arkansas whetstone as the fire blazed, showered the darkness with golden sparks, sent a column of smoke skyward, lapped the bodies of the three trappers with dancing shadows.

All three men were dead by morning. Doucette managed to crawl a few yards, then collapsed. Santiago was the last to die. His breathing finally stopped. Montez stripped their bodies of clothing, took their moccasins and weapons. He packed everything up, cooked a hearty breakfast of venison, sour beans and flour dumpling balls. He made coffee and drank three cups. When the grounds cooled, he saved them in an empty tin. He washed the breakfast utensils in the river, put all of the animals on a lead rope and headed up the Musselshell. He carried three loaded pistols, a knife, two tomahawks and two loaded rifles.

He never looked back at the naked bodies bloating in the sun, but later, he saw the buzzards circling in the sky and smiled with a deep feeling of satisfaction. He had been right.

The men he had hired were treacherous. Had he not been alert, he would be the one lying back there, dead and forgotten.

———·———

Lemuel Hawke was in no shape to go anywhere. His head throbbed with a relentless pounding, seemed swollen five times its normal size. His tongue was as fuzzy as a hedgehog. Daggers pierced his eyes from somewhere inside his aching skull; he knew they were bleeding. His stomach was sour, full of noxious gases. His joints pulsed with arthritic pains. The light inside the lodge was blinding. He crawled under the buffalo blanket to shut it out, groaned.

Patch looked at the pitiful lump of man and grinned gap-toothed. Truth was, he did not feel so good, either, but he was more used to strong traders' whiskey than was Lem Hawke.

"Best thing to do is," Patch said, "take some of the pizen from the snake what bit you."

"Shut up, Patch," grumbled Lem, his voice muffled under the blanket.

Patch laughed. He shook the jug of whiskey so that Lem could hear it slosh, then gurgled some down his throat noisily. He smacked his lips loudly, belched, then let out a long, slow, "Aaaahhhhhhhhh."

"Patch, shut the hell up," griped Lem.

"Gives a man a whole new way of lookin' at the day," bragged Patch. "Puts lead in your pencil, good whiskey does. And they's plenty of Crow squaws to write to, by gum."

Lem groaned, burrowed deeper under the heavy blanket.

Patch pulled on a fresh buckskin shirt, wriggled his toes inside his moccasins. He took off his patch, rubbed the dead eye vigorously. He replaced the patch and adjusted it by feel.

"I done did my mornin' ablutions," said Patch, "and feel fit as ever. 'Twas a fine evenin', it was. Best vittles I ever et this side of the Smokies. Whiskey warn't too bad neither. I don't recollec' much after we got to the second bottle, but it were a fine evenin', sure enough."

"Don't mock me, Patch. I'm dyin'."

"You ain't dyin', Lem. You're prayin' to die, but you ain't a-goin' to. Not yet. It's a bright day and the Crow are at peace with the white men. They's pretty Crow squaws in abundance and I aim to find the one what was givin' me the eye last night."

"Fuck the Crow," said Lem.

"I aim to." Patch grinned, standing up, the whiskey jug gripped in his right hand.

Lem could stand no more of the man's taunting. He threw off the blanket and sat up, glaring at Patch.

"Can't you leave a dyin' man alone?" pleaded Lem.

"Oh, you was alive enough last night, Pilgrim. You was a-tellin' Hunts the Sky 'bout killing a whole tribe of Tuscarory Injuns, scalpin' 'em and savin' a whole passel of white pilgrims from certain slaughter. You was braggin' and boastin' and old Silas had to shut you up before you offended the chief and all his kin." Patch looked slyly at Lem. "'Member?"

"No, I don't remember any such."

"Oh, you were shinin', all right, Lemuel. Whooeee. You was talkin' sign and even getting some Crow words out of your jabberin' mouth. I was right impressed. So was Hunts the Sky and all the other Crow braves a-watchin' you."

"You're mockin' me again, Patch."

"No, I ain't. I believe you got the makin's of a true mountain man. Why, you stay up in them mountains like you was a-braggin' to do last night, you'll be a genuine, full-blowed hivernant, a grizzly b'ar, by Jesus, who can lick ten men before breakfast and ten more after."

Lem sobered.

"Did I say all that? About goin' up to the mountains?"

"Yep, you was a-goin' to do it all by yourself, you and that boy of your'n and be gone by daybreak."

"Shit fire," said Lem.

"Oh, yes," needled Patch. "You had it all figgered out. You didn't need no help. You was a-goin' to tame them Rocky Mounts all by your lonesome self, catch ever' damn beaver, marten, otter, ring-tailed cat and fur-bearin' critter what ever roamed the high places and lug 'em all back to St. Louis and become a rich Mason a-throwin' six-pence to the poor."

"Jesus," said Lem, holding his head with both hands as if to compress the swelling. "I must of made a damned fool of myself."

Patch walked over to him, one hand behind his back, squatted down in front of the suffering Lem.

Lem looked at Patch, waiting for him to say something.

Patch winked his good eye, grinned.

"No more'n any of the rest of us," he said softly. He brought his hand around, held out the jug of whiskey, offered it to Lem.

Lem shook his head.

"Be good for what ails ye. Take that fur off'n your tongue, the swellin' out of your skull, the bile out of your belly."

"That's what did it in the first place, Patch. I ain't a drinkin' man."

"Ho now, pilgrim. You done us all proud last night. Or was that your twin brother?"

"Damnit, Patch, don't keep a-mockin' me."

Patch set the jug down in front of Lem, rocked back on his haunches.

Lem looked at the whiskey jug, shook his head again. Patch sat down, crossed his legs.

"Naw, I can't," said Lem.

Patch said nothing. He just sat there, looking very wise, Lem thought.

Lem stared at the whiskey jug. Patch removed the cork, held it under Lem's nose.

"Smells right sweet, don't it?"

Lem felt the bile rise up in his throat. But it subsided as Patch held the cork close.

"Maybe a taste," said Lem. "Just to get you to shut your flap."

"Just a taste," said Patch. "Hair of the dog."

"Hair of the dog," monotoned Lem. He lifted the jug, smelled the fumes. His stomach didn't rise up and choke him to death. He brought the jug up to his mouth, tilted it. He let the whiskey flow into his mouth slowly, swallowed it. He drank another swallow and felt the whiskey burn down his throat, warm his stomach, settle it. He closed his eyes, let the whiskey take hold of his senses, calm the throbbing in his head, blunt the needles behind his eyeballs.

"Feel better?" Patch asked after a few moments.

Lem opened his eyes.

"Ah, yes, much better," he sighed.

Patch corked the jug.

"You ain't goin' to no mountains today, pilgrim," said Sisco. "Nor by yourself this season. Not you and the boy by yourselfs."

"No," said Lem, his tone heavy with resignation. "I ain't fit to travel."

Patch smiled.

"Bunch of Crow done pulled out already this mornin'. They'll all be gone in a week. Silas is a-goin' too, same place as we are, by gum. We can go with 'em, and that'll be shinin' times, Lemuel, shinin' times."

"Silas tell you that? He's goin' up to the mountains. Soon?"

"Day or two, likely. Before high summer makes these plains a blazin' oven. Be sweet and cool up there. Just don't get ants in your britches, pilgrim."

Lem sighed again. The whiskey had magically cleared his mind, blown away all the cobwebs. His tongue was no longer an alien object in his mouth.

"Shinin' times, huh, Patch?"

"Shinin' times, Lem," said the trapper.

Lem looked around the lodge.

"You seen Morgan?" he asked.

Patch avoided Lem's look.

"No, I ain't seen him," he lied.

"Wonder where he went," said Lem.

"Oh, he's probably made him some Crow friends already."

"Just so's he ain't with that little squaw," said Lem, trying to rise under his own power. Patch had to help him stand up.

"Don't you worry none, Lem," said Patch, but he knew there was trouble ahead once Hawke found out that Morgan was all googly-eyed over that young Crow squaw, Yellow Bead.

21

The Little Robe clan of the Absaroke struck their lodges two days later, headed up the Musselshell. By that evening, the entire Crow encampment was deserted except for one old woman, a member of the People of the Whistling Waters clan, who had gotten sick and was left behind to die. She had food to last her a week or so, two stomach skins of water, a knife, and a puppy tied to a stake. She could kill and eat the puppy if she became stronger. Her name was Starling and she had seen more than ninety summers.

Starling sat under the shade of the big ash tree, singing to the Great Spirit, chanting her prayers. Through watery eyes she saw a man riding up the river, leading a string of packhorses. She knew the man was not a Crow. She continued to sing, much louder, for she thought this man was Death coming to take her. She was ready for Him.

————·————

Josie's scalp prickled when he rode into the camp where the Crow had been. There were fresh horse droppings everywhere, the smells of recent habitation: rotting meat, decayed vegetables. He had been seeing tracks for the past hour and knew that he must be close to the Crow camp. He would not have ridden up like this, in the open, had he not seen that the Indians had all left hours before.

Now, he saw more signs that the Indians had left: worn-out buckskin garments, moccasins, broken eating utensils, hunting arrows, piles of bones, mounds of reeking human offal, the nose-scratching scent of ammonia lingering in the still air of afternoon.

The earth was gouged by travois poles, mangled by pony tracks, the grasses flattened by the tread of many moccasins. Now, he could see holes where the tipi stakes had been driven into the ground, the circles left by the lodges. The grasses there were whiter, crushed by a huge weight.

It was eerie riding through the deserted camp where so many Indians had been a short time ago. He had certainly not expected to encounter such a large camp. He felt a mixture of disappointment and relief.

Then, he heard the threnodic chant from somewhere beyond the edge of the plain. He shortened his reins, brought his horse to a halt. He sat there listening, wondering what the strange sound meant. He braced himself for an attack, nervously fingered the lock on the rifle that lay across the pommel.

The singing was meaningless to him. The voice was shrill at times, monotonal at others. Sometimes the voice faded away, then returned at another pitch. There seemed to be nothing threatening in the chant.

Josie angled toward the sound, careful to look all around,

ready for anything. He changed his course often as he rode closer to the singer. Finally, through the trees, he saw the old woman sitting there, staring into space. A small dog was tied nearby. The dog arose when Josie rode up, started yapping and running around, confined by its tether.

"Vieja," Josie said in Spanish, *"que pasa?"*

The old woman continued her endless chanting. Her skin was very old and wrinkled. She wore white buckskins with ribbons of porcupine quills sewn around the sleeve borders and the hem of her skirt. She had a large bundle next to her and a buffalo robe pallet close at hand.

"Where are your people?" he asked in English.

The woman stopped in the middle of her song and said something in Crow. She raised her hands to the sky, seemingly in supplication to the spirits.

"Stupid old woman," Josie muttered in Spanish.

Starling brought her hands down to her lap. She closed her eyes for a moment. Her lips quivered as if she was trying to speak. Then, her eyes opened wide and she stared straight at Josie Montez. She lifted both arms and beckoned to him, her palms flat and facing the sky. She spoke in Crow.

Something about her, about the way she looked at him, made Josie look over his shoulder, as if to find that she was looking at someone else. But there was nobody there, and when he looked back at her, she was still staring wide-eyed at him, her eyes black beads floating behind a watery film. The eyes were penetrating, fierce. They seemed to burn into him, burn straight into his soul.

Josie crossed himself out of a childhood habit that he thought he'd forgotten.

"Jesus, Santa Maria," he said involuntarily.

Starling croaked at him again. Then, she dropped her arms and pointed a single bony finger at Josie.

Josie backed his horse away, although he knew had nothing to fear from this old, dying woman. It was just that odd look on her face, the way she looked at him. And she was saying something he didn't understand. Putting a curse on him, perhaps, condemning him to Hell.

"A curse on you," he said in Spanish. *"Maldita fea."*

Josie turned his horse quickly, jerked the lead rope savagely. The deserted camp seemed full of ghosts. He thought he heard children's laughter and the wild cries of warriors, but it was only a trick of the wind in the trees, a sobbing in the willows. Still, he did not want to stay in this empty place any longer.

Josie rode around the edge of the abandoned camp, but saw no one else in the fringes of trees. He wondered why the tribe had left the old woman behind, but decided she was harmless. He felt foolish about backing down from her. She was probably half-blind, mistook him for one of her own people. Shaking off his thoughts, he rode westward, following the Musselshell and hundreds of tracks. Among them were those he sought: iron-shod hooves on large horses and the tracks of pack mules, deeper than those of the horses. He thought, perhaps, that he was learning something about tracking.

As soon as he had left, the woman began to singsong her prayers.

She had seen Death, she knew. She saw it in his wolf face, a face she had seen in her visions. Death was a timber wolf in a man's body. His shaggy face could belong to no other.

Starling believed that Death had passed her by.

But she hoped He would return soon.

———·———

Morgan had never felt more alive, never been happier. He had come to love Yellow Bead and her people in the past few days. Now, traveling with the Little Robes, he felt a part of them, a brother to the Crow. So far, he had managed to hide his affections for Yellow Bead from his father, but he knew his pa was sure to find out, sooner or later. Morgan was even learning a few Crow words and Yellow Bead had learned to say several things in English that were not obscene. She was a quick study, seemed eager to learn his tongue. And, best of all, she was ready for him whenever he wanted her.

The two lovers had worked out an elaborate plan to be together at odd times of the day. Morgan had met some of the young men who had heard the stories about his killing of the giant buffalo at close range, on foot, with a single shot of his thunder-stick. These young men, good hunters, already blooded in battles with other Indian tribes, were Bear Paw, Lizard and War Shield. When Yellow Bead wanted Morgan, they rode up on their ponies and told him, in sign, that they were going hunting. They asked him to go along. He always went, for that's when Yellow Bead sneaked away on her own pony and met him. They would ride off together and find a private spot. There, they would make love and talk. They would always catch up to the slow-moving caravan and go their separate ways. All of the Crow, and Silas, knew of this little trick, but they also knew that Lemuel had a bad heart for this Crow waif and so they did not tell him.

"He sure does hunt a lot," Lem said to Patch on the third day after they left camp. "I guess them Crow bucks like him."

"I reckon," said Patch dryly. He, too, knew of Morgan and Yellow Bead's meetings. He knew, too, that they shared their blankets at night, long after Lem had gone to sleep. War Shield or Lizard or Bear Paw would sneak up to Morgan's bedroll and gently awaken him. No words were spoken, but Morgan would get up, fully dressed, and go to Yellow Bead's shelter. He always came back before dawn, with Lem none the wiser.

On the fourth day after breaking camp, the Crow turned south, leaving the Musselshell behind. The Little Robes split up into two groups, then into a third, thinning their numbers.

Runners came and went each morning and night, bringing news of game and enemy tribes, other bands of Crow. It was mystifying to Lem.

"Where are they all a-goin'?" Lem asked Patch when another group started riding off together as if by a prearranged signal.

"They got their own places to go," said Patch. "This is their country. Some are a-goin' down on the Rosebud, some to the Tongue. They'll hunt and trap, same as us, and meet up somewheres this winter or maybe in the spring."

"Where are we headed?" asked Lem.

"Why, the Yallerstone, didn't Silas tell you?"

"Silas has been actin' like I got the pox," said Lem. "He's more Injun than white, you ask me."

"The country does that to a man," said Patch.

"Not to me," said Lem.

Hunts the Sky bade farewell one morning and rode off with a large number of his clan, holding his lance straight, the eagle feathers in his long, luxuriant hair bouncing on his shoulders. Yellow Bead's mother, her aunt and her sister were among this group. Lem saw them saying good-bye to Yellow Bead.

"Ain't she a-goin' with that bunch?" asked Lem, suddenly suspicious.

"I reckon not," said Patch laconically.

There were very few women with their group, now. Silas had Blue Shell with him. There were five or six others— Willow Woman, Laughs in the Wind, White Moon, Lark, Sleeping Heron and Lady Looking Glass—besides Yellow

Bead. There were no children. The women stayed together during the day, cooked the meals, tended to the men. Looking Loon had taken up with White Moon, Lem knew, but he had no idea with whom the other women belonged. They seemed to be camp property as far as he could tell.

They crossed numerous creeks, saw hundreds of antelope each day, always heading south to the Yellowstone. They passed a striking landmark that Silas told them was called Pompey's Pillar, a huge monolith rising off the plain. Soon after, they bathed in the bright waters of the Yellowstone. They spent two days swimming, fishing, feasting on their catches. Yellow Bead and Morgan found a secluded stretch of river where they spent pleasant hours in the sun, making love on the banks and in the water. Morgan was sad when Silas pulled up stakes and they continued their leisurely journey to the mountains. Then, one day, a ripple of excitement gripped the band when the mountains loomed up on the horizon. Morgan felt an intense excitement.

"Are those really mountains? What I seen before was only clouds and hills when we was first on the Musselshell."

"Them be the Absarokes," Silas told Morgan. "This here Yallerstone River runs right out of 'em."

"Is that where we're goin', Silas?"

"Sure is. Should be a fine season to trap."

"Will we all stay together?"

Silas knew what Morgan was thinking. Blue Shell had told him how strong the bond was between Yellow Bead and Morgan. She said that, in the eyes of the Crow, the two were as good as married. Lem hadn't fully caught on yet, but Silas knew it was only a matter of time until he did.

"Well, now that depends on what you mean by that."

"Are you taking Blue Shell up in the mountains with you?"

"I am."

"Then, I reckon I'll take Yellow Bead with me."

"Better tell your pa, first."

"I ain't tellin' him, Silas. The time ain't right."

"He ain't blind, you know."

"I know," said Morgan.

After a week, Morgan knew he couldn't keep on sneaking away from his father. It was getting more difficult to see Yellow Bead during the day. The three braves had left the day before, taking their traps and women. Now, there was only Silas, Blue Shell, Yellow Bead, Lem, Morgan, Patch, Looking Loon, and Blue Shell's family—her father, Turns Back the Enemy, her mother, Lark, her brother, Tracks at Dark and her sister, White Moon, who had taken up with Looking Loon.

Morgan told Yellow Bead that they could not go off into the woods anymore during the day, and that he'd better not see her at night, either. It was just too difficult trying to stay awake during the day when he had been up half the night. The worry was getting to him, too, but he didn't tell her that.

"Mo-Gan no love Yell-oh Bead no more?"

"I love you, Bead," he said in English. He signed the rest of it to her: "We got to wait until we make camp in the mountains."

"Yellow Bead's heart is on the ground," she said in Crow, and she rode off by herself. She stayed sullen and solitary the rest of the journey up the Yellowstone. Morgan brooded in silence until they began to see beaver dams in the streams, aspen stumps by the water's edge everywhere they looked. They rode still higher, through thick stands of spruce and pine and fir. The air grew thinner, the sky closer, bluer, with clouds so white they seemed the purest thing in nature. They saw lots of mule deer and elk feeding in vast green meadows.

The nights grew cold, but the days were warm. They were

following Silas now, and sometimes it seemed to Morgan that they would never get anywhere, that they would never arrive at a place where they could make a permanent camp, stay the winter.

Silas showed Morgan clawed trees where a grizzly bear had established his territory, and he found a pile of scat one day, the scent so strong it scared all the horses and mules. Yellow Bead stayed close to Blue Shell and her family, and it seemed to Morgan that she had forgotten him altogether.

"You been moping around like a whipped pup," Lem said to him one night. "What's gnawin' at you, anyways?"

"Nothin', Pa."

"It's that Injun gal, ain't it? I ain't seen you chasin' after her lately."

Morgan's heart felt like a lead weight in his chest.

He said nothing.

"Good riddance, I'd say," said his father. "Injun blood don't mix with white."

"That ain't so, Pa. She's the same as ever'body else."

"So, you been sparkin' her, huh?"

Patch, who had been dozing in the shade of a spruce, got up quietly and moved away.

"She's nice, Pa."

"You stay away from her and them other squaws, you hear?"

"Don't you tell me what to do, Pa. I'm full-growed."

"Pah!" spat Lem. "You're nothin' but a pup. Still wet behind the ears."

"I ain't, neither."

Their voices carried to the others, who were making up their beds for the night. The air was cool and the sun would be down in an hour. Ghostly jays flitted among the spruce and the women were hunting mountain partridge in a nearby meadow. Silas and Looking Loon looked over at father and son.

"Don't you sass me, Morgan."

"Just leave me alone," said Morgan.

"Just you leave that Injun slut alone."

Morgan felt the anger rise in him, but this was not the time to stand up to his father. The last thing he wanted was a fight. Besides, he was afraid he'd lose. He felt frustrated as he clenched his fists and fought against the rising anger in him. His pa was being so unfair. He stalked away, fists still clenched. When he reached the creek, he picked up a rock and hurled it into the waters as if he could expend his anger against his father with a single violent whip of his arm.

"This looks like a fair place to make a winter camp," Silas said, coming up behind Morgan.

Morgan felt as if his heart had jumped a foot inside his chest. "Huh?"

"Plenty of beaver hereabouts. This whole mountain is laced with cricks and ponds the beaver built. Plenty of fur to go around, I'm thinkin'. I've seen none better."

"You ain't just sayin' that?"

"Nope. Tomorry, I was fixin' to take you to a place all your own, set your pa on another with Patch and Loonie. If you can tend six sets a day, you'll come out with enough pelfries in the spring to buy you most anything you want in St. Louis."

"Sets?"

"Ways we set the traps, places where the beaver goes. I'll show you how to use the bait and set your traps so's they drown theirselves."

"I heard Patch a-talkin' about that. Is it hard?"

"Simplest thing a man can learn, son. Your Injun gal can be a big help to you."

"I think Yellow Bead's mad at me," said Morgan.

"She's peeved, but she ain't mad. She'll go with you, I reckon."

"My pa won't like it none."

"He'll get over it. I'll have a talk with him, maybe."

"Would you, Silas? I'd be mighty obliged."

"I'll think on it."

Morgan's heart soared. He felt warm inside. They had been seeing a lot of beaver and sign for the past couple of days. Silas had been out most of the day scouting around. Morgan looked across the meadow. He had seen and heard beaver splashing around in the little streams that fed into this one.

He looked back toward the camp. Silas was talking to his pa and Patch, probably telling him that they had come far enough. Here is where they'd live through the winter. Morgan felt good. He felt like singing.

——·——

The wolves came for the old Crow woman in the night. Starling had not eaten in eight suns and was very weak. She heard them coming, saw their dark shapes as they circled her, tongues lolling, tails dragging the ground. She tried to sit up, but couldn't move her muscles. They were stiff from disuse. She managed to rock back against the tree, watch the wolves as they came closer and closer.

One wolf was black like the coming night and he was bolder than the others. This was the one she thought might be the one she had seen before when he was in the form of a man. The more she looked at the wolf, the more sure she was that he was the man she had seen that first afternoon after her people had gone away.

She wondered when Death would change back into a man, when He would come for her.

She did not have long to wait.

She did not cry out when she felt the first bite on her leg. Then, she felt herself being dragged away from the tree. She heard the snarling, felt the teeth sink into her arm, then the pain stopped and she didn't feel anything but a warmth flowing through her veins.

——·——

Montez knew he was getting close. The tracks were very fresh and easy to follow. He had seen them going in and out of the marshy places, crossing and recrossing the small beaver streams dotted with dams that diverted the water in all directions.

He stopped and examined a pile of horse droppings. He broke open one of the nuggets, smelled it, felt it for moistness. It had dried some, but they could not be more than a day old.

Montez smiled, sucked in a deep breath. He had learned to track from the men he had killed. He had learned very well from them, as they had learned from others before them.

Lemuel Hawke did not have long to live.

22

Morgan pitched his tent some distance from where his father set up his camp for the night. He set out some items he had been working on in secret, covered them with a trade blanket. Blue Shell and White Moon made a lean-to from deerskins, then helped Lark put up shelters for their brother, Tracks at Dark and for Lark and Turns Back the Enemy. White Moon strung hides boxlike in the trees for herself and Looking Loon. Patch made his shelter several yards downstream on a rise of land where he could watch the beaver before the sun set.

"You and me could have slept in the same shelter," Lem told his son. "How come you pitched your tent way off like that?"

"I got my reasons," said Morgan.

"I'll damn well bet you do," said his father.

"Pa, I got to make do on my own. Sooner or later."

"Morgan, don't you make up no lies now. Just go on about your devilment."

Lem stomped off upstream. He was glad he had his pipe and tobacco with him. He needed to be alone, do some tall thinkin'. That boy would be the death of him. Morg hadn't learnt a damned thing in St. Louis. Warn't the love of money that was the root of all evil, but the love of women. Hell, Morg's own mother ran off with another man, abandoned her son when he was just a tad. And that Willa at Spanish Jack's. Playin' Morgan for a fool. Wasn't a damned woman in the world worth the powder to blow her to Hell. Injun or white.

He knew why Morgan wanted to camp off by himself. It was that little squaw, Yellow Bead. Well, let him, then. Maybe he'd finally learn that she was just another whore.

Lem filled his pipe, struck flint to light it. He heard the beavers splashing and watched as one waddled through the wet grasses. This was what they had come for, he thought. Silas said the fur would be prime in a month or so. They had a month to build a log shelter, get ready for winter. They'd have to hunt and put meat by, store up enough provisions to get through until spring.

He was glad he hadn't come to the mountains by himself. They were mighty big, and if it weren't for Silas, he'd be plumb lost. But he had learned a great deal. The rivers and the creeks were the highways for the trappers and Indians. You could guide yourself by the stars at night and the sun by day, but you had to stay to the rivers and learn where they flowed.

Silas had told him he would put him in a place to trap the winter, build a shelter. He hoped Morgan would throw in with him, not go off by himself. Hell, he might even let him live the winter with that Crow squaw.

Lem sucked on his pipe, let the warm smoke waft to his

nostrils. Yes, he might do that, just to keep the boy close at hand. Morgan wasn't as growed as he thought he was, and he was a worry to a father's mind, big as he was getting.

Meantime, Lem thought, there was nothing like a good smoke to calm a man down, let him do his thinking. He drew in a big puff and it tasted sweet on his tongue.

———·———

Morgan walked downstream to the place where Patch had just finished putting up his shelter.

"Tomorrow, Silas is going to set us all on places where we can get beaver," he said.

"Want to see 'em work before supper?" Patch asked.

"Sure," said Morgan.

"You got to be real quiet to sneak up on 'em."

"I know."

"We'll go around yonder and crawl through them tall grasses. You watch me. Don't move 'less'n I do. You'll likely get your britches wet."

"I'm ready," said Morgan eagerly.

"Ain't much light left, but we might catch us a sight of beaver. They's a big pond just beyond that clump of alder bushes. I been hearin' 'em."

Morgan followed after Patch, who walked into the grasses, then dropped to his belly. They crawled slowly, like snakes, through the grasses and around the thick bushes. Finally, Patch stopped, looked back at Morgan. He beckoned for the boy to crawl to him.

Morgan crawled up beside Patch. Patch pointed to the pond. It was beautiful in the twilight, daubed gold and peach and purple, shadowy banks reflecting aspen and evergreens, like a painting that was alive. He was surprised to see beaver felling timber or swimming across the pond with sticks in their mouths, leaving gentle wakes that wrinkled the colors in the water.

"Why don't we get us some of them beaver furs, Patch?" Morgan whispered.

"Fur ain't prime, yet," said the trapper, his voice soft and low. "Meat's good to eat by now, and ain't nothin' so fine as beaver tail."

"I could eat me some beaver," said Morgan. His speech had become so much like Patch's over the days.

"Maybe we'll get us a beaver or two, tomorry," said Patch.

Morgan opened his mouth to say something else, but he was stopped by the sound of a beaver striking the water with his flat tail. It sounded like a rifle shot in the stillness. A moment later, the beaver on the banks dove into the pond and all that were swimming there dove under the surface. They were all gone in an instant and the ripples on the pond faded away at the shore, leaving only a smooth pane of tinted glass, slowly darkening in the twilight.

———·———

Morgan signed to Yellow Bead that night at supper that he wanted to make talk with her afterward.

She nodded meekly, chewed thoughtfully on a piece of partridge breast. Blue Shell smiled knowingly. Silas cleared his throat and his woman's smile vanished.

Lem caught the exchange and said nothing. When Patch looked at him, Hawke only shrugged.

The moon slid over the tops of the evergreens. It was pale and thin against the faded blue sky of evening.

"Be a trapper's moon tomorry night," said Patch.

"That's so," said Silas. "Another month, them beaver'll be growin' hair like silk."

Lem stroked his beard. It had grown so long, it covered part of his chest. "Reckon, I'll have to take a blade to some of my own hair," he said, "elseways somebody's liable to trap me."

And so the banter went, as the new trappers talked with the old and the moon rose like a silver sickle high above the tallest trees.

Morgan set a twig afire, left the gathering carrying the faggot with him. He blew on it to keep the flame alive.

Morgan met Yellow Bead out of sight of the others, took her hand.

"Mo-Gan love Yelloh Bead?" she asked in her newly learned English.

"Yes, Morgan loves Yellow Bead."

He took her to the place where he had pitched his tent. It was getting almost too dark to see. He had set his camp back in the trees, surrounded by blue spruce and lodgepole pines. There was a large deadfall nearby. He had hung his possible pouch and powder horns on the stubs of broken branches.

Morgan got a candle from his pack, lit it with the burning twig. He set the candle on the deadfall. Its flickering light played shadows on Yellow Bead's face.

"Will you live here with me?" he asked, in broken Crow and sign. "Tonight?"

"Mo-Gan want Yellow Bead?"

"Yes," he said, drawing her close to him. He felt her trembling as he held her tightly. Her small breasts pressed against his chest and he could feel her warmth. In Crow, he said: "Morgan's heart is full for Yellow Bead. He wants Yellow Bead for his woman."

"Yellow Bead wants Mo-Gan," she said in Crow. "My heart is full for Mo-Gan. I will be your woman."

"I have something for you," he said in English.

Yellow Bead looked at him quizzically.

"Wait," he signed. He reached inside his tent, pulled aside the trade blanket. He grabbed the two items he had been making in secret. "Close your eyes," he said, making the sign with his hands.

Yellow Bead covered her eyes.

Morgan put a strand of beads around her neck. They were tied together with sinew. He pulled her hands away. She looked down at the necklace, shrieked with joy. Her hands were moving so fast he couldn't follow her and she was babbling in Crow.

"I had help with this," he said, producing a flute he had made. "Tracks at Dark helped me make it and taught me to play this little song."

Yellow Bead shook her head, signifying that she didn't understand. Morgan put the willow flute to his lips, began to play the courting song he had learned. His notes were wobbly, but he saw that Yellow Bead's eyes were shining in the candleglow. He finished the song. The last note seemed to linger on the air.

"I'll get better at it," he said.

She leaned over, threw her arms around Morgan's neck and began peppering his face with kisses. He grabbed her, returning her kisses tenfold.

"I've missed you, Yellow Bead," he said in English, then, in Crow, "My heart has been on the ground not to be with you. You make my heart soar."

"You make my heart soar," she said.

"I want you."

She formed her lips carefully as she pronounced each word in English.

"I want you, Mo-Gan."

"Come," he said in her native tongue. He took her hands and pulled her into his tent. She giggled and he knew it was going to be all right. A few seconds later, he crawled outside and blew out the candle. When he entered the tent, he closed the flap.

The others could hear their laughter, her cries, as they made love in the dark.

"It's what I figgered," said Lem, knocking the dottle out of his pipe. Black soot showered onto the glowing coals.

Silas looked at his friend across the dying embers of the cookfire.

"It don't bother you none?"

"It don't bother me much," said Lem.

"You told Morgan that?"

Lem shook his head. "I'll do it by and by," he said. He pulled on his long beard.

"Make sure you do. He's nervous as a coon in a bear's den."

"Tomorry, I'm going to take a knife and hack some of this bush away," said Lemuel, trying to change the subject. The old trapper didn't say anything. "Aw, Silas, good night, damnitall."

"Good night to you, Lemuel," said Silas, a tone of amusement in his voice.

He watched Lem make his way to his own shelter. He looked up, saw that the stars were out, the Milky Way a band of lights through the window in the trees. The creek danced with diamonds and he heard the distant call of an owl.

"Looks like ever'thing's goin' to be all right, Blue Shell," he said.

His woman came to him and he put an arm around her waist.

"He carries much in his heart," she said to him.

"He can't change the way things be," Silas mused. "Can't nobody change what's bound to happen."

Blue Shell laid her check on her man's shoulder.

"You are very wise," she whispered.

"I am, ain't I?" Silas said, and they both laughed softly as she gave him a loving squeeze. "Gray Hawk is one wise old coon, all right."

———·———

Josie counted the tracks very carefully over a distance of a thousand yards. Until he was sure.

They were not so many now. Mostly shod horses. That cut down the odds considerably. That morning, he had seen the horse droppings. They were still steaming when he had come up on them. Very fresh.

Late that afternoon, when he was climbing a steep stretch, staying to the woods, but knowing where the tracks lay, he heard voices. Faint, but not far away. They were speaking in English.

He stopped, rode back the way he had come. Then, he went deep into the woods, blazing the lodgepole pines every fifty yards or so with his tomahawk as he passed them.

He hobbled and tied his horses, kept the packs on. He hurried back on his trail on foot, carrying a rifle, packing two pistols and plenty of powder and ball. He wanted to look over the camp before it got dark.

The sun was just setting when he saw the glimmer of a campfire through the trees. Josie circled, careful not to make a sound.

He lay flat on his stomach, crawled through the trees, circling, moving slowly, trying to make no sound. When he got short of breath, he stopped, listened. He could hear the talk. They were all eating. He crawled still closer, his pulse throbbing in his throat, blood pounding in his ear.

He saw them, then, and his heart froze. He recognized the boy. Then, he saw Patch and the Delaware. He didn't know who the other old coot was. The Indians were sitting off by themselves, but he counted them. A man and a woman, then three more women and a young buck. There were less people than horses, but some of the horses and mules were carrying pack, he was sure.

He lay there a long time. He saw young Hawke go off with one of the Indian girls. Then, the other Indians walked away. Finally, he figured out which one was Lemuel Hawke. The one called Silas addressed him as "Lem." Josie didn't recognize him with his full beard.

I got you now, Josie thought. "Tomorrow, you will pay for my brother's death. Tomorrow you will die." He mouthed the words soundlessly. He watched as Lem said good night and walked down the creek to a shelter.

Josie knew he could not kill Hawke now. He would never find his way back to his own horses if he was running for his life. No, he would come back in the morning, lie in wait. He would shoot Lem the minute he saw him.

He waited another hour, then crawled away, heading for his camp by dead reckoning. He was as careful going out as he had been coming in. When he saw the first blaze, he relaxed and stood up. He was chilled from being on the ground, but his mind was burning with plans.

"Tomorrow," he said, and this time he could hear his own words. His horse whickered when he came up. He felt like cutting its throat.

———.———

Turns Back the Enemy heard the faint sound. He sat up, listened. He did not hear it again. He crawled from his shelter, crabbed to his son's tent. He went inside. Roughly, he shook his son awake.

Tracks at Dark muttered something.

"Wake yourself," said Turns Back the Enemy.

The boy sat up, blind in the darkness.

"Why do you awaken me, my father?"

"I heard a sound."

"A frog," said the sleepy boy. "An owl."

"No, a horse. Not one of our horses. Not a horse of the white eyes."

"A wild horse," said Tracks at Dark.

Turns Back the Enemy snorted, but he did not hear the nicker of the horse again.

"Maybe I am hearing things," he muttered.

"I want to sleep," said his son.

Turns Back the Enemy snorted. Tracks at Dark lay back down on his buffalo robe and pulled another one over him. It was getting chill and it would be a long time until the sun was born again.

Turns Back the Enemy returned to his own lodge.

"What do you do, my husband?" asked Lark.

"Nothing. Go back to sleep."

He lay next to her, listening. After a while, Lark began to snore softly.

———·———

Looking Loon heard the nicker of the horse, too. He was the closest and knew that it was not from a horse in their own camp. It sounded far away, back down the mountain. Unless one of the horses had gotten loose. He felt for White Moon. She was already asleep. There were times when he wished he could speak.

He listened, but did not hear the horse whinny again. Perhaps it was only his imagination. He wondered if he should check to see if any of their horses had gotten away. Perhaps one from another tribe was stealing their horses away, one by one.

It bothered him, a horse making a noise like that. He could

not sleep. He put on his buckskin trousers, grabbed his rifle and knife. He slipped into his moccasins. He knew it would be cold outside. He made little sound as he crawled from the lean-to, stood up. He found his way to the little meadow where the horses and mules were hobbled.

He waited there, in the shadows, listening for any sound that was not animal. The horses and the mules grazed in silence, dark shapes in the grasses. Finally, he went to the meadow, stealing up to each animal and making a count.

None of their stock was missing.

This was perplexing to Looking Loon. He could make no sense of it. He left the meadow, walked back to his lean-to. He stood there for a long time, listening in the darkness. He heard nothing, not a sound.

Finally, Looking Loon crawled back under the lean-to. White Moon was still asleep. The Delaware did not take his buckskins or moccasins off, and he kept his rifle close by his side. His ears strained to pick up the horse noise he had heard before. He dozed, but did not sleep.

He waited for the morning light, knowing something was wrong.

———·———

Lem dreamed that he was trapped in the mud inside his pigpen back in Virginia. The tax man, Brown, was climbing over the fence. Brown had a whip in his hand. The whip's handle was made of rolled-up tax receipts. Lem struggled to get free of the mud, but the pigs, snorting and squealing, kept trampling him back down. One of them had a snout in his face and was pushing him deeper into the mud. He could hear the loud snorts of the pigs as they wallowed in the slop. From somewhere, he heard Roberta calling to him, but he could not answer.

"Lem, you snorin' son of buck, wake up," said Patch in a loud whisper. Patch shook the sleeping man mercilessly for the tenth time.

Hawke heard the sounds of the dream fade away as he swam up through bewildering layers of darkness.

"You're a heap harder to wake than the dead," said Patch.

"Patch? What's a-goin' on?"

"I don't know. Loonie woke me up a few minutes ago, made me listen to what he had to say. It warn't easy in the dark, but that nigger's got somethin' in his craw, and I think you better hear what I got to say."

"Damn, Patch, it ain't even mornin' yet."

"It's mornin'. The sun's puny, but it's risin'. Get your duds on and let's get out where we can see our hands in front of our faces. Bring your fusil."

Lem had slept in his 'skins, but he pulled on his moccasins and slipped his possibles pouch over his shoulder. He grabbed his powder horns and pulled his rifle from its buckskin sheath, a gift from Hunts the Sky.

Patch and Looking Loon stood outside Lem's tent, holding their rifles at the ready.

Lem stood up, rubbing sleep from his eyes.

"Goin' huntin', Patch?"

"Maybe. Loonie here heard a horse down our backtrail last night. Just heard it nicker once't, but it warn't one of our'n."

Lem checked the powder in his pan. It looked damp. He slung his powder horns over his shoulder, cleaned the pan out with a patch from his possibles bag. He poured fresh powder into the pan and blew off the excess. He closed the frizzen, ran the wiping stick down the barrel to see if the ball was still seated snugly.

"So, what you gettin' at, Patch?"

"Might be somebody's been a-follerin' us," Patch said.

Lem looked down the mountain. It seemed peaceful enough. The sky was gradually turning light. There was a mist on the beaver ponds, hugging the grass like fresh smoke.

"Who?"

"Maybe Josie Montez."

Lem felt his throat constrict.

"Could be," he admitted.

"We thought we might take a walk down thataways, see what we see," said Patch. "You, me and Loonie."

Lem nodded. He started to step away, when he saw something out of the corner of his eye. It was just a shadow, a blur of something through the trees. He started to say something to Patch, but then he saw something else.

Josie Montez stood up, took aim at Lem's chest. Lem could feel the barrel come to rest on his chest. It was like being poked with a twenty-pound lead pig. He could feel the muzzle of the Spaniard's rifle pushing against his chest.

He felt as if he was trying to move underwater. Everything slowed down and he knew he was going to be too late. He saw the man in the woods brace himself and lean into the long rifle. He saw the sparks come out the barrel first, then he heard a soft crack and felt a smack in his breastbone. White smoke billowed out of the woods, obscuring his attacker.

Someone yelled in his ear, and a terrible pain surged through his chest and back. His arms went slack and his rifle floated from his hands, hands that were numb and lifeless. The woods spun and he felt his body shake violently on the way down as his legs went out from under him.

The pain spread through his shoulders and to his brain and then there was a moment of peace just before there was no more feeling. His breath went out of his lungs and he never got the chance to breathe any more in because everything went black except for the tiniest pinpoint of a light that was like a distant star winking only once before it turned to ash.

Patch fired at the smoke, then heard another crack and spun around in a half circle as a lead ball tore his shoulder to ribbons. Looking Loon was running toward Josie when Montez stepped out of the cloud of smoke, raised a pistol and fired at the Delaware at point-blank range.

Looking Loon clawed at his chest as the ball smashed through flesh and bone, rammed out his back, tearing loose a chunk of meat the size of a cannonball.

The Delaware died while he was still running toward Josie Montez.

Morgan heard the shots, snatched up his rifle and stuck his knife in his belt. He ran toward the sounds, saw Patch go down, then Looking Loon start running. There was white smoke everywhere, mixing with the fog rising off of the beaver marshes.

His father lay in a heap just beyond where Patch sat, holding onto his shattered shoulder, blood oozing from his wound. Morgan wheeled, saw Josie Montez jump aside as Looking Loon's body slid to a stop right in front of him.

Morgan brought his rifle to his shoulder just as Josie raised his other pistol and fired.

Morgan ducked, heard the ball sizzle past his ear like an angry hornet. He pulled the trigger, heard the flint strike steel. There was no puff of smoke, no explosion of powder in the barrel.

"You sonofabitch!" Morgan yelled, and ran straight for the Spaniard.

Montez drew his knife. Morgan threw his rifle straight at Josie. Josie swayed to one side, then lunged forward, knife held low, ready for a gutting jab.

Morgan grasped his own knife, never breaking stride.

Josie knew he had his man. He brought the knife up to impale the Hawke boy as he charged.

Morgan fooled him.

Yelling like an Indian, Morgan broadjumped from two yards away, came down on Josie's arm with both feet. Pain shot through Montez's arm. He held onto the knife, but his fingers wouldn't work right. He hit the ground, felt his arm snap at the wrist. The knife slid from his grasp.

Morgan tumbled over Montez, the momentum of his leap carrying him beyond. But he was on his feet like a cat. He whirled just as Josie was reaching for the knife with his good hand.

Josie's fingers touched the knife.

That's when Morgan buried his own knife deep in Josie's throat. The blade sliced through veins, the carotid artery, the pharynx and the larynx. Blood gushed from Josie's throat like a fountain.

Morgan pulled the knife free, ready to strike again, blinded by his own fury. Montez collapsed and there was a low gurgling in his throat as the blood strangled him. His legs quivered for several seconds, then he lay still.

Morgan lifted his bloody blade, feeling cheated. He felt a strong hand close around his wrist, stay him from stabbing the dead man again and again.

"He's dead, Morgan," said Silas. "You kilt that Spanish bastard, sure enough."

"Huh?" Morgan snapped out of his blood-blind stupor, looked at Silas.

"You can get his scalp, if you want it."

"Pa? Where's Pa?"

Silas took the knife from Morgan's hand, led him back to where his father's body lay.

"He's dead, ain't he?" Morgan said. Patch nodded. He sat there, holding his shoulder, grimacing with the pain.

Morgan sat down by his father, lifted him in his arms. His pa didn't hardly weigh anything at all. There was blood all over Lem's chest. He was still warm. His eyes were closed and Morgan knew he wasn't breathing.

"Pa, oh, Pa, I'm sorry."

Morgan smoothed out his father's beard, brushed the dirt out of his hair. He remembered all the times they had hunted together when he was growing up, the rifle his pa had made for him, the first time he rode a horse and shot a squirrel. He remembered all the times he and his pa had been together, and they seemed more precious to him now than they ever had at the time.

The tears came, then, and he tried to fight them back until his throat hurt and he couldn't see anymore, couldn't talk, couldn't tell his pa how much he loved him and always had loved him and always would.

"Good-bye, Pa," Morgan squeaked when he could talk.

He laid his father's body gently down and stood up on shaking legs. There was blood all over his bare chest and he realized he had no clothes on. He didn't know if the blood was his father's or Josie's. He didn't care.

Silas slipped an arm over Morgan's shoulder.

"Come on, son," said the old trapper. "Let's have a smoke and let the women wash your pa, get him ready for his journey."

Morgan wiped the tears from his eyes and drew in a deep breath.

Yellow Bead came up to him, took his hand.

"Mo-Gan," she said. "My heart is on the ground."

He reached out his arm, drew her close to him. There were no words to say how he felt, but he was glad she was there.

He was glad that Silas was there, too. And Patch was still alive.

Blue Shell signed to him in Crow, then began her trilling. Yellow Bead, Lark, and White Moon joined in, and they went to clean the dead and dress them for their journey to the stars.

"I think I'd like to have my pa's pipe when we have that smoke, Silas."

"Fittin'," said Silas. "Right fittin'. Want me to fetch it?"

"No, I'll get it. I need a few minutes to—to think about things."

Morgan slipped from under Silas' arm and walked back to where his father had died. The women had taken him away. The blood was already drying where he had lain. The mist in the marshes had wafted away and the sun made the grasses into emerald gardens. The aspen shook in the breeze and their leaves jiggled and threw off varying shades of light. Everything was green and golden and he heard a beaver tail smack the waters of the pond.

Morgan found his father's pipe and his little pouch of tobacco. He held these things in his hand and it was like holding the medicine horn for the first time. There was power in these objects, and he could feel his father's strength flow through him and into his heart.

He put the pipe between his teeth and felt his father's teeth marks with his tongue.

"Good medicine," he said aloud. Saying it gave him a good feeling.

He didn't realize until later that he had spoken the words in the tongue of Yellow Bead's people, the Crow.